RACHANI

HEIR OF AMBER AND FIRE

KINGDOM LEGACY BOOK ONE

Heir of Amber and Fire

Kingdom Legacy, Book One

Editing and proofreading by Tom Loveman

Cover art by Fiona Jayde Media

Also by Rachanee Lumayno

Kingdom Legacy
Heir of Amber and Fire
Heir of Memory and Shadow
Heir of Magic and Mischance

Chapter One

THERE WERE TIMES I really hated magic.

This was one of them. I was working on a new spell I had recently learned, one that was proving to be particularly challenging. I couldn't seem to get the hand motions exactly right. If I could eventually master that, then I wasn't able to hold my concentration long enough to marry the gestures to the spoken part of the spell. I had been working on this for the greater part of an hour, and my head was throbbing.

"Your Highness!"

Gracefully, I sketched a figure in the air —

"Princess Jennica! Where are you?"

And then I — Oh, never mind.

I stood up, brushing the leaves off my dress, and moved away from my little hiding spot in the palace gardens. I turned the corner, trying to make it appear like I was just strolling among the roses. As soon as she spotted me, Taryn, my lady-in-waiting, rushed over to me.

"Your Highness, there you are! I've been looking for you everywhere!" Taryn said breathlessly. She dropped into a belated curtsy that somehow conveyed respect and hurry up all at the same time. Her blond curls bobbed around her face as she straightened and took a good look at me. "What have you been doing, sleeping in the bushes?"

I smoothed my hands down my long, straight black hair. My hands found a twig, some leaves, and a little fuzzy prickly bur.

"No, I was practicing my magic." I aimed for dignity but ended up sounding faintly defiant. "Is there a problem, Taryn?"

She clicked her tongue at me, her green eyes dancing in mild disapproval. "Just as well you were practicing out here. You know how His Majesty feels about you learning magic."

"Don't remind me." King Hendon's hatred of magic and magicians was widely known. Earlier this week, Father had dismissed my magic tutor. That was the fifth one he had sent away, for no concrete reason other than a vague dislike of all things magic. I often wondered how he was able to tolerate ruling in Calia, a kingdom known for its magicians. Pretty much everyone in the land was born with some innate magical ability, although only those who could afford lessons were able to cultivate their talents. Of course, Hendon had inherited the kingship when he married my mother, Queen Melandria, and my grandfather had passed away. But still, for him to hate the very thing that set Calia apart from the rest of the Gifted Lands.... Well, there were many things about my father that, even after nineteen years of being his daughter, I have never understood. "Well, if you're not here to stop me from practicing, then why were you looking for me?"

"Your Highness, we need to get you ready for dinner right away," Taryn said. She stopped just short of grabbing my hand and tugging me, but we both knew she was thinking about it. Taryn wasn't the type to be easily flustered. Whatever sent her out here in a panic to find me must be pretty important.

"All right," I acquiesced. "I'm coming."

We left the gardens, hurrying through the ornamental rose garden and then past the fruit and vegetable patch used by the kitchen servants. Taryn chattered at me as we walked, catching me up on the latest news and gossip. Passing by the stables, we entered the courtyard. As we walked, various courtiers and servants saw us and dipped low, bowing or curtseying and murmuring variations on, "Greetings, Your Highness." I barely noticed. My attention was captivated by the sight of the palace, as it always was when I saw it.

My family had ruled Calia for at least ten generations; I believe we had founded the kingdom, although after all those generations the history gets a bit fuzzy. Somewhere in our family lineage we had a water mage, who loved water (obviously) and had designed the Calian palace accordingly. Cool grey stone shimmered in the sunlight, reflecting off the blue and green cobblestones which were laid out in an eye-catching pattern in the courtyard. It gave you the sensation of swimming. Two impressive stone fountains flanked the front doors of the palace, always flowing with pure, clear water. Although the overall effect was very calming, it didn't quite resonate with me. I could appreciate the palace's beauty, of course, but privately, I would have preferred something more... exciting.

And speaking of exciting... I pulled my attention back to my one-sided conversation with my lady-in-waiting. "Excuse me. What was that, Taryn?"

Taryn paused mid-ramble. "Sava ate too many blueberries, and now the kitchen staff is unsure there will be enough for the dessert Cook had planned, but I doubt Sava will be punished for it?"

"No. Before that."

"Oh! Sava's brother came home. Sort of. They found him sleeping on the street, in an alley in the town, just a few blocks from my brother Rufan's house."

We entered the palace, the guards standing at attention as we passed them. The Great Hall stood before us, its imposing wooden doors firmly closed. The room had been used by generations of Calian kings and queens for banquets, formal events, and — most importantly — weekly open forums where the people of Calia could bring their issues before their sovereigns for assistance and judgment. Nowadays, the Great Hall was usually silent; when my grandfather passed away, my father didn't keep up the weekly tradition of listening to his subjects' petitions, much to my mother's disappointment. The most we used the room for was the occasional, and uncomfortable, family dinner. On those rare occasions when I was in the Great Hall, I envisioned it as it might have been in my grandfather's time — full of people talking and laughing. Joy was something in scarce supply these days, at least in the Calian palace.

The great gilt-framed painting that held a place of honor right by the entrance to the Great Hall caught my attention. I slowed my pace slightly to take it in, as I liked to do whenever I passed by it. It depicted the most recent event in royal history. And for me, it was the most personal.

As a little girl, I would spend hours running up and down the torchlit corridors of the castle, which held our family history in various paintings. And while I loved looking at our family portraits — the water mage who built our palace, the princess who could command air, the king and queen who raised an earthquake against an invading army — it was the painting by the Great Hall that always captivated me. Chronicling the events from twenty years ago, it depicted my brave, handsome father, back when he was the knight, Sir Hendon. In the painting, he defiantly held a shield against the flames from a massive golden dragon, whose claws clutched a beautiful maiden and held her captive.

The entire kingdom of Calia — and beyond — knew the story of how my parents met.

The people loved their love story, and we celebrated Hendon's victory every year, along with their marriage and coronation anniversary. How an evil dragon had ravaged the kingdom of Calia, and taken my mother as a tithe. How my grandfather, the former king of Calia, had called upon the neighboring kingdoms, asking any brave princes or knights to rescue the Princess Melandria, in the hopes of winning her hand in marriage and, thus, the kingdom. How the noble knight Sir Hendon faced down the wicked beast, driven it away, and rescued the fair maiden. Sir Hendon and Princess Melandria's wedding had been the biggest event Calia had ever seen; their marriage and their love, legendary.

Well, I knew from personal experience, living in this household: Sometimes legends lie.

Taryn and I continued on, down the grey stone corridors, up a flight of stairs and down more hallways toward the private apartments of the royal family. My room was at one end of the hallway, with my mother's rooms at the other end. My father's much larger suite of rooms was around the corner from my mother's, further down the hallway. As befitted his status as king, his chambers took up nearly the entire wing.

My lady-in-waiting was still talking, recounting (again) the story about Sava's brother. Well, I *had* asked. I reeled in my attention (again) and tried to follow her story.

I vaguely remembered hearing about a situation with Sava, one of the kitchen maids. Her twin brother, who was apprenticing with the blacksmith, had gone missing about a week ago. Taryn had mentioned it while doing my hair one morning; it had been a bit of scandal, apparently, since the boy was known to be a conscientious worker. Unlike his flighty twin sister. No one knew what would have caused him to run off, and the family had been worried sick over his disappearance.

"Well, that's good that he's back," I said now. "But why wouldn't he just go home? Was he afraid of being punished?"

"That's the thing," Taryn said. "He's completely lost his mind. Won't talk for days, and then he'll start screaming out of the blue, and it's hard to get him to stop. He didn't recognize anyone in his family, not even his twin sister. And you know what a strong bond twins have."

Since I was an only child, I could only guess. But I did know that certain bonds between people were stronger than others, and that twins especially had strong magical ties to each other.

"That's a shame," I said. "Poor Sava, she must be heartbroken."

"It's odd," Taryn mused. "She's more jumpy than anything. She said she had nightmares every night while her brother was missing, and now she's afraid something might happen to her. Poor thing."

I agreed, but didn't really know how I could help. While I was skilled with magic, I didn't have the ability to take away a young girl's nightmares. "I guess... I could talk to Cook and definitely make sure she's not punished for the blueberries?"

Taryn laughed and pulled open the door to my chamber. Once inside, she all but pushed me in a chair to start dressing my hair. Her hands were a blur as she combed, teased, tucked, and pinned my heavy black hair into something she muttered was "acceptable." I watched her flitting about in the mirror as my hairstyle took shape. It was fancier than I expected.

"Taryn, what — "

"Here, Princess," Taryn interrupted me. She must have really been frantic to let such a breach of etiquette take place. She stepped back, indicating a dress that lay on the bed. "Your father requested you wear the red."

Now *I* was nervous. The dress in question was gorgeous, the most stunning gown in my collection. But the fact that my father wanted me to wear it was suspect. Whatever his reasons were for wanting me to look extremely elegant tonight, I knew I wouldn't like them.

"Taryn, it's just dinner with my family. There's no need to be so dressed up." I reached up toward my hair, intending to pull a pin or two out.

Taryn made a motion as if to grab my hand, but pulled her hand back and pushed it through her hair instead. Seeing her consternation, I slowly lowered my hand and left the hairstyle intact.

"Please, Your Highness." Taryn was all but outright pleading with me. "You need to wear the red dress. Please."

I looked at my lady-in-waiting sharply. "What's wrong, Taryn?"

Her voice barely above a whisper, Taryn said, "The king insisted you wear the red dress and come to dinner formal. In the Great Hall. Otherwise, he'll have me dismissed immediately, with no pay for the last month."

I was seeing red, but it wasn't just the dress. How dare he threaten Taryn like that? Taryn gave me an imploring look, knowing my thoughts. "Don't say anything to His Majesty," she begged. "Please, just wear the dress. And we need to hurry and get you into it. We're running late as it is."

Sighing, I turned and let her nimble fingers roam over the laces of my current attire, loosening my day dress and letting it slip to the floor in a heap. I silently stepped into the red dress, feeling the satin swish against my skin. Taryn had a matching pair of slippers ready, and then I was out the door, heading toward the Great Hall for what was supposed to be dinner.

Instead, it felt like my doom.

Chapter Two

I KNEW I WAS IN TROUBLE the minute I stepped into the room.

The first indication was when I approached the door to the Great Hall. The footman flung the door open dramatically and announced, "Her Royal Highness, the Crown Princess Jennica Allayne Kenetria Denyah of Calia." What a mouthful. My formal title included the names of my two grandmothers and one of our ancestors — Allayne the Clever, who had saved the kingdom of Calia with her quick thinking against the Djinn of Krean. It was customary for royal children to have at least one name honoring an ancient ancestor, with the thought that the qualities that made that ruler so revered would be passed on to the namesake. While I loved hearing the legends surrounding Allayne the Clever, I doubted I would ever be called upon to save the kingdom like she did.

And why introduce me like that, when the only others dining were my parents?

Except it wasn't just the three of us. There was another man present, who, along with my parents, stood when I entered. That was my second clue.

My father and mother were arrayed in their formal finery as well. In addition, my father, King Hendon of Calia, was positively dripping with the royal jewels. It was a constant source of amusement to the courtiers and the servants (or so Taryn told me) that the king liked to wear more jewelry than his wife, Queen Melandria. My mother only ever wore her simple gold wedding band; she hated fussing with other pieces of jewelry, and barely tolerated wearing her crown for official functions. In contrast, my father adored showing off his wealth and position. His fingers boasted a myriad of rings, and he often wore at least one, but usually several, gaudy adornments around his neck. Tonight I could see a deep red ruby at his throat, ostentatious even for him.

Once I reached the table, my father introduced me to the newcomer. "This is Prince Anders, of the kingdom of Rothschan. Prince Anders, may I present my daughter, Jennica."

Prince Anders bowed over my hand, placing a delicate kiss on it. "You're lovelier than I could have imagined, Princess," he said. "You look beautiful in that dress. Of course, red is my favorite color." The prince himself was resplendent in a deep red and gray tunic — the colors of Rothschan. Now my father's insistence on choosing my dinner dress made sense.

Rothschan, to the west, was where my father was from. He didn't talk much about his life before coming to Calia; all I knew was that his parents had died when he was young and he served for several years as a squire to a renowned knight who was stern, but fair. Shortly after my father was knighted, his master died in battle, and the newly knighted Sir Hendon left Rothschan to find his fortune.

"Thank you," I stammered, unsure of how I should react. I looked at my parents. My father had a smug look on his face. My mother, however, looked worried.

Sign number three.

"No need for such formality," my father declared. I gave him a dirty look, considering *I* was the one who had been forced into formality for this surprise meeting. My father handily ignored me and swept his arm across the table. "Shall we dine?"

We all sat. My father was in his usual spot at the head of the table. My mother was in her usual spot on the king's left. I, however, had been unseated. Prince Anders was at the king's right, which was my normal place at the table. It moved me down one seat and put the prince in between me and my father. The seating arrangement ensured that I would have to talk to the prince during the majority of the meal. I could still converse with my parents, but it would be potentially considered rude, since they weren't directly next to or across from me and I would have to talk over our guest's head to address them.

Clever, father. Very clever.

The first course appeared before us. I picked at the food on my plate, my appetite gone.

Putting my fork and knife down, I stared straight ahead, my eyes alighting on the swords hanging on the walls. Like the paintings, these also represented the rich history of Calia. Many of the swords had belonged to former kings and queens, with the Sword of the First King in a place of honor by the throne. It was mostly used for ceremonial purposes, although we hadn't had a knighting or anything like that in a few years.

Prince Anders ate a few bites of his dinner, then sat back and looked at me squarely with piercing blue eyes.

"So, Princess, tell me of yourself," Prince Anders said, pushing his blond hair back from his face.

"What would you like to know?" I asked, a bit shyly. He really was handsome, the kind of man Taryn and my other ladies-in-waiting would giggle about when they thought they were out of my earshot.

"Anything," he said. "How do you fill your days? My two younger sisters are accomplished at dancing and embroidery."

"I learn those things as well," I said. "But my favorite thing is magic study. My tutor says I'm quite proficient at it."

Prince Anders made a choking sound. I thought he was trying to stifle a laugh, and I relaxed, thinking I had found a kindred spirit. Over the table, my father glared at me and shook his head ever so slightly. I looked again at the prince. He wasn't laughing. In fact, his gentle face had turned stormy.

"As Rothschan is a land of military might, not magic, we do not trust something so illogical and esoteric," Prince Anders declared. "I understand Calians are born with this 'gift' — if it could even be thought of as such. Personally, I don't think anything so unnatural could be a good thing. It is abhorrent, and not an acceptable thing for a princess to learn."

I gasped at the insult. My father rushed in to smooth things over.

"I completely agree, Prince Anders," he said. "After twenty years in this kingdom, it's refreshing to hear such truth spoken. I've often despaired at being a good ruler when my heart disagrees with something the people consider inherent to their happiness. But you are right. It is a disgusting, unbecoming custom here in Calia. That is why Jennica will no longer be studying such things. I have already dismissed her magic tutor. I will have her magic books burned tonight."

I gasped again, this time at Father. Studying magic was the one thing, of all my lessons, that I actually enjoyed and excelled in. While my father wasn't indulgent of me, he had never interfered in most aspects of my upbringing.

Until now.

"But, Father, why — "

My father cut me off. "A girl — no, a *woman* — of nineteen hardly needs something as repulsive as magic. It's about time you represented your station well."

"But — "

"Don't fret," Prince Anders interrupted smoothly. "When you're my wife, you won't need such frivolities to amuse yourself."

"What?" I recoiled from the prince. "What are you talking about?"

"It's all set," my father informed me. "It will be a perfect political alliance."

"Rothschan looks forward to uniting with Calia," Prince Anders said, inclining his head toward my father.

My mother's eyes flashed between worried and sad.

"I can't believe this!" I cried. "No one told me any of this! When is this to happen?" I looked at my father, who had that smug look from earlier back on his face.

But instead of my father, it was the oily voice of Prince Anders that answered me.

"Soon, Princess. In one month's time, you shall be my bride."

Chapter Three

I SPENT A MISERABLE hour crying. I didn't think there were any tears left in my body. But all I had to think about was the prospect of marrying Prince Anders, and I'd start all over again. My eyes were puffy and my head was fuzzy, but I couldn't stop. My bed was a rumpled mess, a testament to the fact that I had tried to muffle the sounds of my crying.

After Prince Anders had announced our upcoming wedding, Father had taken one look at my face and dismissed me from dinner immediately. He couched it under the guise of, *My dear, you look unwell, perhaps you should lie down.* But I'm sure he was worried I would embarrass him, or worse, somehow threaten his pact with the prince. I was glad to get away, even though escaping from dinner didn't mean I was escaping my fate.

A tentative knock sounded at my chamber door.

"Come in," I said thickly, sitting up. I needed a handkerchief badly, but instead had mopped my eyes and face on my dress. My red dress. The dress that was, "of course," the prince's favorite color.

How could I have been so stupid? I walked right into that trap.

The door opened, and Taryn entered with a tray carrying a cup and a pitcher of water. She closed the door carefully behind her, then set the tray down and filled the cup with water. Handing it to me, she studied me carefully as I drank the whole thing without stopping.

"Thank you, Taryn," I sniffled. I put the glass on the bedside table.

Taryn sank down in a nearby chair, across from me still sprawled on the bed. Intensity radiated from her, in a way I had never seen from her before. She opened her mouth to speak, then changed her mind about whatever she had been about to say. "If I may, Your Highness..." she started.

"Please, speak frankly, Taryn. You know you can always be honest with me."

"How do you feel about marrying the prince?"

I fought the tears that threatened to come back. "I don't know what happened! Father and I have had our differences, but I never thought he would just marry me off without even discussing it with me first."

"But do you want to marry Prince Anders?"

"No," I said readily. "I don't know him, but the little I learned of him tonight seems horrible. A life without magic! I couldn't give it up."

Taryn nodded, as if what I was saying was the correct answer. She stood up and extended her hand to me. "Come, Your Highness."

"Where are we going?"

"We are going to see Queen Melandria."

"Now? It's getting late, I don't want to disturb Mother."

"You won't be. She told me to bring you to her tonight, as soon as you were ready." She grimaced at my tear-streaked face and messy dress. "I honestly wasn't sure how long that would be."

I sniffled, laughing through my tears, and got up from the bed. I walked over to my chamber door, but Taryn put her hand over mine on the handle before I could open the heavy wooden door. She quickly shook her head at me.

"Taryn, what — "

She held her hand up, stopping me from saying more. Easing the door open slowly, she poked her head out in the hallway. All was quiet. She slipped into the hallway, opening the door a little wider so I could follow. We crept the few feet to my mother's apartments, Taryn looking around furtively, me looking at her curiously. Taryn lightly tapped on the queen's door and then opened it, ushering me inside. My mother, who had been sitting by her fireplace, stood when I entered. Mother's eyes met Taryn's; the queen nodded, and Taryn dipped her head in response. She left, shutting the door quietly but firmly behind me.

I stood in the entryway, unsure of what to do or what was happening.

My eyes went back and forth, following my mother as she paced back and forth in front of the fireplace. The smell of ink lingered faintly in the air; looking at my mother's writing desk, I saw some handwritten pages strewn across the surface, allowing the ink to dry. An unlit candle lay on the table next to the paper.

Mother was fidgeting with a simple gold necklace from which a small moonstone pendant hung. In my entire life, I had never seen my mother — stately, reserved Queen Melandria — *fidget*.

The gem caught my eye and I stared, drawn in by some allure it held over me. My heart started beating faster and my breath came fast. I didn't know why, but I wanted that necklace. I *needed* it. If I couldn't possess it, I would surely die. My hand started to reach out toward it.

My mother gently put my hand back down at my side and fastened the necklace around my neck. My breathing eased. My hand flew up to the pendant.

Finally, I had to break the tense silence.

"Mother, what's going on?"

My mother's eyes slowly met mine. "Jennica, forgive me."

My blood ran cold. I rushed to her, grabbing her by the shoulders. "What do you mean? Forgive you for what? Are you about to do something desperate?"

Tears sparkled in her eyes, threatening to fall. She touched my cheek. "My darling, beautiful girl. There's something I should have done a long time ago."

"Mother, you're scaring me. What's going on?"

"Sit." My mother indicated the love seat by the fire. I sank down in the plush velvet. Mother sat next to me. She took one of my hands in hers, stroking it gently. She flipped it over, studying my palm. Whatever she was looking for didn't seem to be there, as she sighed heavily and flipped my hand back.

"Mother, what's going on?" I repeated.

There was a light, quick tap at the door, and then Taryn slipped back into the room. She had donned a traveling cloak in her absence. She was holding a plain dress, a long, dark cloak, and a pair of boots in her arms. Over her shoulder was a worn leather knapsack.

"I checked out the window in Princess Jennica's room. They're on their way, Your Majesty," she said to my mother.

Mother moved faster than I had ever seen her move before. She turned to the wall next to the fireplace, patting the stone about eye level. Suddenly, a door noiselessly opened next to the hearth. A dark tunnel yawned wide.

A secret passage? Nineteen years I had lived in this castle, and I never knew it had secret passageways!

"You'll have to go, now, before they get here," Mother said.

"Go? Where? Before who gets here?" My head snapped between Mother and Taryn, who stood by the entrance to the secret passage.

"Shh!" My mother gave me a fierce, quick hug. "No time for that! Taryn will lead you out of the palace."

"But — "

Mother scooped up the candle and the papers on her desk. Shoving them into my hands, she pushed me into the passage. "This letter is for you — I've explained everything. Keep it private. If you see any Calian soldiers on your way, avoid them. King Hendon is not to be trusted, Jennica. He's not even your father."

"What?!" Mother couldn't just throw something like that at me and expect me not to have any questions. "What do you mean, he's not my father?"

"It's in the letter, Jennica. Now go!"

"But where am I going?" I was stubbornly holding on to the stone framing the passage's entrance, wanting *some* sort of answer. Taryn had her arms around my waist, practically pulling me into the passage.

"To Orchwell, the kingdom a few days south of here," Mother said. "Find Kye of Orchwell, the famed dragon seeker. Have him bring you to Joichan, the dragon who held me captive."

Taryn succeeded in pulling me away from the door. Mother blew me a kiss as the door to the secret passage closed. The last thing I saw were her lovely gray eyes, sad and hopeful at the same time.

And the last thing I heard, before the darkness swallowed Taryn and me, was the sound of the door to my mother's chamber opening.

Chapter Four

I STAYED FROZEN IN place. For one thing, I couldn't see in the total darkness. For another, I was worried about my mother. Should I go back?

I felt for the door behind me, expecting to find a hidden latch or switch to open the door back into my mother's room. Instead, I felt Taryn's hand on my arm and heard her voice in my ear.

"Your Highness, we must continue. Come."

Without waiting for me to agree, her hand slid down to mine and she guided me deeper into the passageway. It unnerved me, to walk without seeing where I was going, but Taryn's cool hand led me forward.

I estimated we had walked for perhaps a quarter of an hour when Taryn stopped. I nearly plowed into her. Quietly, she asked, "Do you still have the candle your mother gave you?"

"How did you know she gave me a candle?" I asked, just as quietly. "You were ahead of me."

She laughed softly. "Princess, we've been planning this for some time. The queen has her own set of spies in the palace, and she learned that the king was going to move forward with this marriage alliance. She came up with her own plan to protect you. I'm aware of every part of it. Including the part where your mother gave you a candle, since I would have my hands full."

Even though Taryn couldn't see me in the dark, I shook my head, annoyed at my obtuseness. Of course Taryn was aware of everything. Her efficiency and lack of surprise were obvious giveaways. And even if they weren't, her intensity when she questioned me about my feelings toward Prince Anders should have tipped me off. While Taryn and I were close, more than most royalty would normally be with their servants, there were certain boundaries Taryn never crossed with me. Including personal probing questions.

I was about to give Taryn the candle when I realized I wasn't holding it any longer. My right hand was still clasped around Taryn's. My left hand was clenched around Mother's letter only. No candle.

"Taryn, I'm sorry," I whispered back. "I don't have it anymore. I must have dropped it."

Taryn's voice held a tinge of dismay. "We need light, Princess. I've been guiding us so far by following the wall with my free hand, but I know the passageway forks up ahead and I need to be able to see which is the correct one to take. One of the corridors will take us outside, but the other doubles back into the castle and into the Great Hall."

"We could turn around and look for it," I suggested.

"No," Taryn said. "We can't waste any more time. There's a very narrow window in which I can sneak you out before the guards change. We'll just have to keep going and hope I pick the right passage."

She started to move forward, but I stayed put. I felt a tug on my arm from Taryn. "Princess, please. We need to keep going."

"Wait," I said. Letting go of Taryn's grasp, I held my hand in front of me, palm up. "*Illumine.*"

A small, cold light appeared above my outstretched palm. I looked up at Taryn — whose face I could now see — and smiled. The ball of light didn't illuminate much, but the passageway was quite narrow. With my magical light, we would be able to see a few feet around us in any direction.

"You've come further in your studies than I thought," she said, with an appreciative, answering grin.

"Conjuring lights is basic spell casting," I said modestly, although I was pleased at the compliment.

"Still, considering you've only been studying magic for a year, I'm impressed," she said. Shifting the dress and shoes she carried, she adjusted the pack on her back. She held out her hand for my mother's letter. I wordlessly handed it over. She stuffed the papers in the pack and then turned to face the passageway again. "Come."

Feeling a little guilty, I asked, "Do... do you want me to carry anything?" The thought would never have occurred to me before tonight, but the situation we were in was anything but typical.

Taryn shook her head as she started walking. I hurried after her. "You'll be carrying this pack soon enough, Princess," she said wryly. "And for longer than you like."

After that we didn't talk much. My world narrowed down to focusing on Taryn's back and making sure I put one foot in front of the other, endlessly. I didn't want to think about what I was leaving behind, or what might be happening to Mother. I hoped she was safe.

When we came to where the passageway branched off, Taryn chose the left without hesitation. I understood why she would have been unsure without being able to see where she was going. The left branch was unobtrusive; it would have been easy to miss in the dark.

We didn't walk too far when Taryn stopped again at a blank stone wall. She felt along the wall, squinting in the dim light for something. Once she found what she was looking for, she nodded in satisfaction. She flipped a latch and, to my surprise, the wall popped open slightly. It was a hidden door, so skillfully made it blended into the castle facade.

Taryn turned to me. "We need to get you changed into something less conspicuous."

Nodding, I untethered the ball of light so it hung in the air just above our heads. Taryn helped me out of the heavy red gown and into the plain dress she had been carrying. I exchanged my fancy slippers for the sturdier, more practical leather boots. Taryn also undid my hair, pulling out the pins so it flowed freely down my back.

"I've packed a comb and ribbons for you, but it's not worth going through your pack to find them," Taryn said quietly. "But fortunately, it's dark enough out — and I have one more thing to disguise you." She bundled up my finery in her arms and put her hand on the unlatched door. "Your Highness, please extinguish your light."

I swallowed my instinctive question and instead held my hand out to the light, willing it to tether to my hand again. Once it reconnected, I placed my left hand, palm down, over my right. The light winked out.

In a low voice, Taryn said, "Wait here, Your Highness. I'll let you know when it's safe to proceed."

Barely breathing, afraid of making any sound, I whispered, "All right."

Taryn opened the stone door just enough so that she could slip her slender frame through it. The door closed behind her, but not completely. I could make out the tiniest sliver of fading light through its crack. As I waited impatiently, I clenched and released my fists repeatedly.

The door opened a little wider. Taryn's face filled the frame. She motioned for me to follow her.

I stepped clear of the stone door and Taryn, with a little effort, pushed it shut behind me. The door became a nondescript castle wall once again. My eyes slowly adjusted to the semi-dark outside the castle. The moon shone overhead, but the cloudy night obscured its light somewhat.

Taryn shifted her weight as she pulled the long cloak from the pile of clothes she carried. She handed me the pack and the cloak, whispering, "Wear the pack, and then put on the cloak. Pull the hood up."

I did as she instructed. Taryn bundled up the dress and shoes tighter and started across the grounds. I did my best to keep up with her pace, but with the laden pack on my back, and in such an awkward position, I found myself hunching over with an uneven stride.

We kept to the shadows, moving as silently as we could. Well, Taryn moved silently. I was sure the entire palace guard could hear me stomping across the grass and gravel. But, even with my less-than-princess grace, we miraculously made it to the edge of the palace grounds. Beyond would be the path to town and freedom.

Just when I thought we were free and clear, a voice to our right commanded, "Stop."

Chapter Five

I FROZE, MY HEART POUNDING. This was it. We were caught. Taryn would be sacked, or worse, thrown into the dungeon. I would be returned to the palace, locked in my room until the wedding. I would be married to that hateful Prince Anders and —

Taryn calmly turned to the guard who now blocked our way. "Evening, sir," she said politely.

"State your business," the guard said.

"We're ladies-in-waiting to Princess Jennica," Taryn said. "We're going into town to bring this — " she indicated the bundle in her arms " — to the seamstress Kellen to be fixed."

"Now? At this time of night?" the guard eyed us suspiciously.

Taryn sighed, putting just the right touch of long-suffering servant into her voice. "Unfortunately, yes. It's her intended's favorite dress, and he wants her to wear it again tomorrow night. So she told us to have it fixed immediately. But it's beyond my simple skill, which is why I have to go into town and bother poor Kellen for her services. Kellen will grumble, but at least the king will pay double the usual amount for her trouble."

"Royalty!" the guard said, clicking his tongue in sympathy.

"Don't I know it!" Taryn agreed. She and the guard chuckled in mutual understanding.

I didn't know what I was more curious about — Taryn's skill in charming the guard, or if all those in our employ gossiped about us in such unfavorable terms, and how often.

"Go on, then," the guard said, shooing us away. "Good luck with your errand."

"Thank you, sir," Taryn said. We hurried away.

When we were safely on the road to the town with no one around to hear us, I said, "Taryn, I am impressed! I had no idea you were so skilled at prevaricating."

"The best lies have a bit of truth in them," she said with a shrug.

"It does make me wonder... have you ever used that skill on me?"

Taryn laughed. "I don't think there's a good way for me to answer that," she chided me. "If I say no, you may still wonder if I'm telling the truth. If I say yes, then you'll lose sleep worrying which of my words it was."

She was right, but it didn't dampen my curiosity. "All right, then, if you won't tell me that... do all servants gossip about the royal family the way you and the guard did just now?"

Taryn didn't answer right away. I suppose it was a naive question. Of course servants would gossip about us, just as we royals gossiped about the people in our lives. But I had never thought about it much. Our servants were people, of course, but... they were just servants. I never thought of them having lives and thoughts and feelings of their own.

"Your Highness, it's always been a pleasure to serve you," Taryn finally answered. "And although I am your lady-in-waiting, I also consider you my friend, even though we've never addressed it directly. I would hope you consider me yours."

"Of course, Taryn! You've done more for me tonight than some of the nobles I've grown up with."

"Anything I've ever said about you to others has only been the highest praise. But, yes, people talk. And sometimes, it's the invisible people who know the most."

I mulled over her words as we continued our walk to town.

Chapter Six

WE MADE IT TO THE TOWN without any other trouble. The house of Taryn's older brother, Rufan, was mostly dark, with one lone candle shining in the window. When Taryn knocked quietly on the door, it opened immediately. We slipped inside and the door closed behind us. In the darkness, I heard a bar fall into place on the door, shutting us in completely.

The candle from the window moved, appearing in the hand of a tall, muscular man. It illuminated Rufan's drawn face. He put a finger to his lips and pointed upstairs, indicating we should all speak quietly.

"We thought you weren't coming," he told his sister. "When you didn't make it in time for dinner, we assumed you were caught up at the palace and weren't going to be able to visit tonight."

She reached up and gave him a quick hug. "I'm sorry," she said. "We had some delays trying to leave the palace."

"We?"

Taryn stepped to the side, revealing me behind her. Rufan gasped, then bowed low. Abashed, he said, "Forgive me, Your Highness, for not greeting you properly. Welcome to our humble home. We are honored by your presence. Let me wake up my wife, and we'll prepare — "

"It doesn't matter," I said, waving away his offer of hospitality. "These are strange circumstances."

"Circumstances, Your Highness?" Rufan looked from me to his sister uncertainly.

"Rufan, I'm so sorry to put you in this position, but we need a place to stay for the night," Taryn explained.

"The palace is not sufficient?"

"Let's just say, the less questions you ask, the better it will be," Taryn said.

Rufan looked troubled, but nodded slowly. "I trust you, sister. Were you followed?"

"I don't think so."

"Good." He gestured down the darkened hallway. "Come, then, and make yourself comfortable, Your Highness."

He held the candle higher and led us farther into the house, where he lit a small lamp and blew out the candle.

As we followed, I commented to Taryn, "I daresay, once I left the palace, I'm no longer a princess."

"You'll always be a princess," Taryn said, warmly. "But in a sense, you're right. It would be dangerous for you to be addressed or treated as such from here on out."

Yet another odd thing to get used to, but I would have to adapt. No time like the present.

"Then I guess I'm just Jennica now," I said, a bit sadly. "No more Your Highness or Princess."

"Begging your pardon, Your Highness," Taryn said. "But you might want to use a different name. Your given name is too recognizable, and it would be sure to get back to King Hendon if you used it."

"Good point, Taryn." I thought a minute. "What about Allayne? Since it's one of my middle names, I'll still answer to it."

Taryn nodded her approval. "It's a little old-fashioned, but much more commonly used than Jennica is."

Rufan chimed in, "A baby girl born two weeks ago here in town was actually named Allayne. Her parents had always admired the stories."

"Perfect, then. Allayne it is." I felt a twinge at having yet another part of my normal life stripped away. But at the same time, being able to choose my own name felt strangely exhilarating. Like Princess Jennica was one person, and Allayne was someone else. And Allayne could be anyone she wanted to be.

Rufan's small lamp spilled light across a wooden table in a modest kitchen, where the lone window had curtains drawn against the night. I was grateful for the imposed darkness of the kitchen; it would be harder to see any lights here in the back of the house.

"Are you hungry, Prin... Allayne?" Rufan asked me.

I hadn't eaten much at dinner, which felt like a lifetime ago. I was also parched after the adrenaline-filled flight from the castle. I was suddenly acutely aware of just how empty my stomach was.

"If it's no trouble," I told my host.

"Not at all," he said, carefully opening a cupboard. He reached in and grabbed something, quietly closed the cupboard, and then placed the items on the table in front of me. A sliver of cheese and a slice of bread.

"I'm sorry it's not much," Rufan said apologetically.

I was already tearing into the cheese. "No, this is wonderful," I said, trying not to talk with my mouth full.

Rufan poured some water from a pitcher into two glasses and handed one each to Taryn and me. For a few moments the little kitchen was filled with a small pool of light and the sounds of two people drinking and munching.

"How are Patrice and the girls?" Taryn asked Rufan after she had put her glass down.

"They're well," Rufan said. "Now that the girls are both school-age and gone for most of the day, Patrice has a lot more energy. Until the girls come home, of course."

Taryn smiled at that. To me, she said, "My nieces are sweet, but a handful. The youngest just started school this year and loves it. Feels like she's a big girl 'just like her older sister.' And the older one is level — what? Three? Four?"

"Level Four," Rufan confirmed.

"Oh, that's lovely," I said politely. "I look forward to meeting them."

Rufan and Taryn exchanged a look with each other. "Not to be rude, Your... Miss... Allayne. It's probably best if you don't. My girls are very excitable. If they met someone new, they'd be liable to gossip about it with their friends."

Instantly, I understood his hesitation. I was increasingly becoming aware of the danger I was in. As Taryn had mentioned, people — no matter their age or station — liked to talk. I would have to take extra care not to give myself away by accident, or my true identity would easily get back to King Hendon.

Rufan looked apprehensive. Lack of titles or not, I was still the princess and could enforce my will upon him.

"I understand," I told him. He visibly relaxed.

"My wife takes the girls to school early in the morning," he said. "After they leave, then it would be safe for you to leave your room."

"Look on the bright side, *Allayne*," Taryn said, winking at me as she emphasized my new name. "At least we get to sleep in tomorrow."

Chapter Seven

EVEN WITHOUT RUFAN'S warning to avoid running into his family, I was exhausted enough from the flight from the castle that I slept in quite easily the next day. When I opened my eyes, Taryn was already up and moving about.

"My sister-in-law and nieces have already left," she told me. "I'll head downstairs to find Rufan. Join us when you've gotten dressed."

"Dressed?" I repeated in dismay.

Taryn pointed at the bag. "There's an extra change of clothes in there, if you like, or you can just wear what you wore yesterday."

Those clothes were piled in a heap on a side table.

"But Taryn, I..." It seemed embarrassing to say that at nineteen, I required aid to dress myself. But it was the unfortunate truth.

She smiled at me sympathetically. "I know, Princess." She picked up my dress from the table and turned it front and back, showing off the simple pullover design. "When I packed your bag I took that into account. I actually gave you some of my clothes. It will be easier for you to put them on, and they won't attract as much attention as yours would have."

I laughed. It was my first real laugh in what felt like forever, and it felt good. "Taryn, I can't wear your clothes! I'm the wrong size!" Taryn was several inches taller than me.

She laughed with me. "You already did," she said, indicating last night's outfit. "Just belt up the dress if it's too long. When you have some extra time, you can hem up the dresses properly. I've included some needles and thread in the pack for you."

"Sew?" I said it with such incredulity it caused Taryn to laugh again, this time a bit sympathetically.

"I'm afraid so," Taryn said. "At least all those embroidery projects will finally come in handy."

I made a face, even while laughing with her. Needlepoint was one of my least favorite activities, as several sad tapestries in the palace could attest. At least all of my fruitless hours would now serve some practical purpose.

Taryn went downstairs, leaving me with the task of getting ready. I pulled the blue dress over my head and belted it up. Instead of fashionably hanging over the belt like it had last night, I somehow got the fabric tangled in the belt and created a pillowy second stomach for myself. Dreadful. My hair was even worse. Rummaging through the pack, I found the comb Taryn had mentioned and ran it through my tangled hair. I attempted to braid it, but that was dreadful too. I settled for pulling it up in a ribbon and added to my mental list: *Learn to hem a dress. Learn to braid my hair. Learn to belt my dress properly.*

Stuffing the comb back in the bag, I grabbed it and tidied the room as best I could. Since I didn't normally — make that, ever — tidy my room back home, I sort of arranged the pillows and pulled the blankets over the bed and hoped that looked good enough. I wanted to be a good guest and was very conscious of my failings.

I found Rufan and Taryn in the kitchen, looking over a map. There was a cheerful fire burning in the hearth, and in the middle of it was —

"My red dress! My shoes!" I cried, dropping the pack on the floor and rushing over to the fire. I reached out, as if to grab my clothing back from the fire, and then pulled back. My dress and shoes were beyond saving.

"It would be better if I didn't bring them back to the palace," Taryn said. Getting a good look at me, she smiled and shook her head. Standing, she came over to me where I was still staring in shock at my burning finery in Rufan's hearth.

She deftly adjusted my outfit so I looked more presentable. "Hopefully that guard won't remember us, but if he does, seeing me bring your dress back will just trigger his memory. And we don't want to do that."

Seeing the flames lick at the remnants of my beautiful dress really reminded me that I was leaving my old life behind. I saw the sense in what Taryn was saying, but it still made me sad.

"Prin... I mean, Allayne," Rufan said gently. "Why don't you eat breakfast and then take a look at this map with us? I think it will help you in your travels."

Numbly, I padded over to the table and sat down, putting the fire with my former dress at my back. Rufan put a plate of food in front of me as Taryn took her place at the table again. I grabbed the bread and a liberal amount of butter, until I caught Taryn's look of horror. Embarrassed, I tried to subtly scrape some of the butter off my knife so I was taking a smaller amount. Rufan was honoring me by putting butter on the table. I had forgotten that things like butter, which would have been considered a commonplace staple at the palace, would be expensive for non-nobility.

My gaffe went unnoticed by Rufan, who was studying the map intently.

"My sister has told me a bit about your search," he said. "Here is the kingdom of Calia." He pointed out our country in the northern part of the map. "Dragons typically live in the south, unless they're ice dragons, but those are rare."

"My mother told me to go south to find a dragon named Joichan," I said. "But that's rather vague, and a lot of ground to cover. She suggested I find Kye of Orchwell."

"That makes sense," Rufan said. "Orchwell is known as the Land of Seekers."

"Seekers?"

"Yes. Everyone in Orchwell, from the poorest beggar on the street to the nobles in their fancy houses, possesses an innate ability to find things. They specialize, of course; and sometimes what an Orchwellian is able to find is dictated by bloodline. For example, one of the oldest families in Orchwell is famous for its ability to find missing relatives. It's not always things or people either; sometimes they can detect the slightest flavor in a glass of wine, the imperfection in a weaving, or the faintest note in a piece of music. It all depends on their distinct talent."

"They must be very expensive to hire, if they're so specially inclined," I said dubiously.

"They can be," Rufan said. "Seekers usually get paid a small fee up front, with the rest of their payment given after the job is complete. If the queen recommended this Kye person, then perhaps they'd be willing to help you regardless of payment."

"And perhaps knowing that a queen is paying them at the end, they'd be willing to forgo the initial advance fee." I could only hope.

As I munched on the rest of my breakfast, Rufan showed me the road I should take to get to Orchwell and pointed out a few places I would find an inn or farmstead along the way. He estimated that it would probably take me about two days, possibly three, to get to Orchwell traveling on foot.

Now that my course was settled, I turned to Taryn. "What are you going to do back at the palace?" I asked. "How are you going to explain my absence?"

Taryn said cheerfully, "Since we have a month before your wedding, it might be prudent if the princess was busy preparing for it, don't you think?"

I caught her meaning. Wedding tradition for Calian nobles dictated that the bride prepare for the wedding thirty days before the event. Only a close female family member, or in my case as an only child of royalty, my lady-in-waiting, could attend the bride during her preparation month. I sometimes found noble traditions stuffy and pointless, but I blessed this unforeseen advantage.

"I'd be happy to spend my bridal month in solitude," I smiled. "But that doesn't give me much time to find the dragon. And what will you and Mother do when the wedding day arrives and I'm not there?"

"I'll discuss it with Queen Melandria. I'm sure she has a plan in mind." Although Taryn spoke confidently, I could see the worry in her eyes.

I would have happily stayed in Rufan's kitchen, clinging to the last remnants of familiarity. But I was also acutely aware of the day passing by, and of the danger I was sending Taryn back into.

I pushed back from the table and stood. "I suppose I should get going, then."

Taryn and Rufan both stood along with me.

"Let me get you some food to take with you," Rufan said. He picked up my forgotten bag, then moved to the larder and began pulling some items out.

I turned to Taryn and said quietly, "Perhaps, while I'm in 'solitude,' you could sneak my meals out here to your brother. I'd hate to see all that food go to waste."

Taryn smiled, watching as her brother generously filled my bag to his satisfaction. "That's a fine idea, Your... Allayne. And if my brother and his family don't want it, there are plenty of people here who could use the extra food."

Rufan brought my bag back and handed it to me. It was considerably heavier than when I had brought it downstairs.

"Thank you," I said.

He nodded at me. "Safe travels." He then turned to his sister, holding out a shiny new hair ribbon in pale blue. "I nearly forgot, Taryn. A gift from Patrice and me. She pointed it out to me this morning lying on our dresser, reminding me to give it to you; I'd never hear the end of it if I forgot after her reminder."

Taryn laughed and took the ribbon with obvious delight. Immediately tying her hair back with it, she said, "Thank you, I love it. Blue is my favorite color."

The three of us exited the house. I hefted the knapsack onto my shoulders and shaded my eyes, scanning my route. I was to go through the town and follow the road into the countryside, which would eventually take me to Orchwell. Taryn was to go back the way we had come, back to the castle.

"How will I contact you to find out how things are back in Calia?" I asked Taryn. "It's not like I can send you letters from where I am. I don't even know where I'm ultimately going."

"Did you not learn anything over the last year?" Taryn teased me. "Use a calling spell, and you'll be able to connect with me."

"I don't know how good I'll be," I said ruefully. "I only started learning that spell one month ago."

"So practice," she said. "I tucked your spell book in your bag."

I smiled. Of course she had. Taryn always knew what I needed before I knew it myself.

She stepped toward me, then stopped, hesitating. I crossed the two extra steps and enfolded her in a hug. "Taryn, thank you," I said to her. "For everything."

"Be well, Princess," she said, forgetting to drop my title. "Come back to us soon."

I gazed down the road to Orchwell again, then the road that would have taken me back home to the castle. I looked back at Taryn. "Take care of my mother."

Chapter Eight

SETTING OFF SOUTHWARD, I could feel the eyes of Taryn and Rufan on me as I walked away. I hadn't made it very far when someone screamed. All of sudden the sleepy morning was punctuated by more yells and shouts as people ran toward the distraught and horrified woman, who was pointing down an alleyway just a few feet away from Rufan's house.

Someone grabbed my arm. I nearly screamed myself, biting it back at the last minute when I saw Taryn at my elbow. Rufan was right behind her. "What's going on?" I asked them.

"I don't know, but let's find out," Taryn said. The three of us hurried toward the growing crowd at the alley entrance.

Rufan approached a man at the back of the crowd, who was craning his neck to watch the events unfolding. "Jarrod! What's happened?"

The man turned around when he heard his name. Seeing Rufan, he clapped him on the shoulder, greeting him and pulling him closer at the same time. "When Mistress Karna went out this morning to throw away the scraps for the dogs, she found someone lying in the alley."

"Another one?" Rufan asked. I was briefly confused about Rufan's comment, until I recalled what Taryn had told me the other day about the palace kitchen maid, Sava, and how Sava's brother had been found near Rufan's house.

"Yes. But this... this one's not crazy. This one is dead." Jarrod shuddered, looking sick. Rufan and Taryn had similar looks on their faces.

"Was it..." I couldn't even bring myself to finish. *A murder?* But, to my knowledge, Calia rarely had problems with violent crimes. Of course, people argued, and not everyone got along with one another. But, as a largely magical society, most people didn't resort to physical or even magical violence to solve issues. We were the intellectual lot of the Gifted Lands — or, the know-it-all snobs, if other kingdoms were feeling uncharitable in their description — more likely to take someone to trial to win an argument instead of punch them. And there were harsh laws in place to prevent violence against those who didn't have magic. I hadn't heard of a murder happening in Calia at all in my lifetime, and possibly longer than that.

Noticing Taryn and me for the first time, Jarrod nodded his head at each of us, touching the brim of his hat in a gesture of respect. He frowned at me, as if trying to figure out where he had seen me before. I stiffened and ducked my head slightly, stepping behind Taryn a bit so she would draw his focus.

"It's hard to say," he said. "From what I've heard, there's not a mark on her, but her face was frozen with her eyes wide open, looking like she had seen something awful."

"Her? It was a woman?" Taryn asked.

"Yes, miss. Can't be much older than either of you," he said sadly.

"First Sava's brother, now this woman," Rufan said. "And wasn't there that weirdness with Cantin two weeks ago?"

"Yes, but Cantin's mind was already getting a bit unhinged as he's gotten older," Jerrod said.

Taryn and I stepped back from the crowd as Rufan continued to ask Jerrod more questions. Taryn's eyes were frantic as she gave me another fierce hug. "There's something strange going on," she said. "I don't like it."

"I'll be careful," I promised her. "I'm more worried about you back here."

"Contact me as much as you can," Taryn said. "I'll feel better if we're able to talk often."

I agreed, and set off again. I was eager to put as much distance as possible between myself and the strange goings-on in the town, as if running away from the problem would keep it from affecting me.

SEVERAL HOURS LATER, I was still on the road to Orchwell when I heard hoofbeats on the road behind me. It had been a pretty uneventful day — the only other travelers I had passed were people like me: common folk headed to either Orchwell or Calia.

But these riders were coming down the road fast. I paused and turned, curious to see who had such urgent business.

I caught a flash of a silver and blue caparison — the colors of Calia. Remembering my mother's warning, I looked around for a place to hide. The road was fairly open here. There were no convenient trees or even a rock to hide behind.

There was, however, a shallow ditch to the side of the road. I dove into it, hoping the Calian riders hadn't seen me up ahead of them on the road. Dirt covered my clothes and face and I sneezed right as the riders reached my hiding spot.

The horses stopped. I heard one of the riders dismount. And then, a male voice above me: "Miss, are you all right?"

Of all the times for them to be chivalrous! While I was glad that the knights of Calia were decent and honorable men, I was also cursing that very quality of theirs right now.

I slowly sat up, trying to keep my face hidden from the men without being obvious about it. The knight who addressed me was holding out his hand to help me out of the ditch. I took it gingerly and stood, trying to keep my distance. I felt hot and feverish, and I was sure my nervousness was radiating from me like a beacon.

"Thank you, kind sir," I said. I pitched my voice lower, hoping to disguise it.

"Are you hurt, miss?" The man indicated his horse. "We're headed to Orchwell, and would be happy to escort you somewhere if you need assistance."

One of the man's fellow riders shifted his horse uneasily. "Sir, do we have time...?"

The man waved him to silence. "There's always time to help someone."

"I'm fine, sir," I said. "I just tripped and fell when you came by. My home is nearby, and I'll be glad to get back and clean up."

The man laughed and remounted. "Of course, miss. Take care, then." He was about to lead his men away, when he stopped and gave me an appraising look. "You know, you look a bit like Princess Jennica of Calia."

My heart stopped. My mind screamed, *Please don't recognize me, please don't recognize me!*

"She's about as tall as you," he continued. "But she has dark hair and dark eyes. Ah, maybe I just think that you look like her because we are on our way to spread the good news: our princess is getting married in one month's time." He nodded to me and turned his horse's head toward Orchwell. "Farewell, miss!"

The royal riders continued on their way. I touched my face, smiling at the copious amount of dirt that was smeared on my fingers when I pulled them away. Thank goodness I had "tripped" when I did. In my commoner's clothes, with the dirt of the road all over my face and dress, they didn't recognize me. But Father — or, I amended, King Hendon; it was actually a relief not to think of him as my father anymore — would be livid if he learned that I was missing. A royal wedding with no bride would be the ultimate insult to all the rulers of the other realms that were sure to be in attendance at the event.

My hair was sticking to the back of my neck, so I gathered it up and shook it out. I idly ran my dirt-streaked fingers through it, trying to comb some leaves and twigs from it. And then, I stopped, amazed. My normally jet black hair was much, much lighter. It looked as if there were thick streaks of gold in it. A trick of the sunlight? Whatever it was, I was grateful for the optical deception that kept the knights of Calia from recognizing their princess.

Even though by this time the riders were long gone, I stared down the road after them for some time before I started walking again.

THE SUN WAS BEGINNING its descent when I realized I should find shelter. Rufan had pointed out places I could possibly stay, but I hadn't thought to ask how long it would take to reach any of them. I was tired, dusty, and extremely thirsty.

Rufan had packed a small waterskin in my pack along with some other food, but I had finished the contents hours ago.

Just when I thought I couldn't walk another step, I saw a modest farmstead up the road. I quickened my pace. Before approaching the door, I shook the dust out of my dress as best as I could, and tried to straighten my hair.

My knock was greeted with a boisterous, "Yes, yes, I'm coming!"

The door swung open abruptly. A tall, lean man was on the other side. His brown hair and beard were beginning to show signs of gray.

"Good evening, sir," I said. "I'm on my way to Orchwell and need a place to stay for the night. I wondered if you had an extra room I might rent?"

"Who is it, Marchand?" A woman with a baby on her hip came to the door. She was nearly as tall as her husband. A little girl clung to the woman's skirts, thumb in her small mouth. When I smiled at the little girl, she hid behind her mother, then peeked out from behind her mother's legs and shyly smiled back at me.

"It's a traveler, Asra," he told her. To me, he said, "What's your name, girl?"

"Allayne."

"Come on in," he said. He stepped back to allow me in.

"Thank you," I said, a bit surprised. I thought I would have to apply more persuasion, but perhaps they were used to entertaining strangers from the road.

"We're happy to help those traveling by," Asra said, confirming my hunch. "It's always nice to meet new people. And it's a great way to get news from the kingdoms."

"Today's been an exciting day though," Marchand said. "In addition to your visit, riders from Calia passed through earlier."

"They passed me on the road earlier today," I said. "It seems the princess is getting married?"

"That's what they said," Marchand confirmed. "To Prince Anders of Rothschan. The king's riders are bringing invitations to the royalty and nobles of neighboring kingdoms."

"What a celebration it will be! Can you imagine, all those fancies in one place?" Asra said, shaking her head. "I don't think anyone invited would dare turn down King Hendon's invitation. And with Prince Anders set to become the next king of Calia, no one would want to anger Rothschan either."

"Prince Anders would become king of Calia?" I asked, confused. I had assumed that a marriage to Prince Anders meant I would leave Calia and move to Rothschan to eventually become queen there.

"Prince Anders is a second son," Marchand said. "The Crown Prince of Rothschan is in good health and just married a year ago. His wife is expecting a child. The possibility that Prince Anders could inherit the throne of Rothschan is slim."

I had vaguely remembered hearing something about this, but as King Hendon didn't think that politics was something for a princess to learn, I hadn't really paid attention. I now began to wonder if the king had kept me in the dark deliberately.

I was also surprised to learn that the king was fine with Prince Anders eventually taking his place. No one lives forever, of course, but Hendon wasn't the type to happily acquiesce power. By marrying me off to Anders, the king would be somewhat closer to his homeland of Rothschan by alliance, but his power would remain firmly in Calia.

"A royal wedding will be good for business, I hope," said Asra. "We'll have to dip into our stores to supply it, but it will be worth it. Ah, well, enough gossip. I'll go get your room ready."

I gave her a small smile, feeling guilty that my escape might potentially cause them misfortune. Asra, along with the two children, walked down a hallway toward the back of the house.

I stood at the door awkwardly. Marchand said conversationally, "So you're headed to Orchwell, eh? You must be coming from Calia, then? I bet the kingdom is busy with preparations for the wedding, yes?"

"They will be soon," I said, trying to be truthful without giving too much away. "Since it was just announced, no preparations are truly underway yet."

"Are you from Calia? What will you be doing in Orchwell?"

Luckily, I was spared from answering by Marchand's daughter. The little girl came bounding down the hall and stopped just a few feet from us. "Momma told me to tell you and the lady that the room is ready," she said to her father. Her message delivered, she promptly stuck her thumb in her mouth again.

Marchand laughed and picked up his daughter. She giggled as he swung her around. Balancing the little girl on one side, he pointed with his free hand. "Just go down the hall, second room on the left," he said.

"Thank you," I said, and walked in the direction he pointed.

Asra was tweaking the coverlet when I walked into the bedroom. It was a simple room, with plain white walls and a brightly colored quilt on the bed.

"What a beautiful quilt," I commented.

Asra turned around, saw me, and beamed proudly. "My mother and I made that together when Marchand and I were engaged. It was weeks of hard work, but spending the time with my mother made it worthwhile. Even if I pricked my finger more than I care to admit. I'm sure there are still bloodstains on the fabric," she finished, laughing.

I laughed with her, but my mirth was tinged with sadness. I wondered when I'd be back with my mother, working on a project together or even just drinking tea and talking.

Asra saw the tightness in my face and thankfully mistook it for something else. "I'm sure you're tired after your journey," she said. "There's a pitcher and bowl on the nightstand to wash up. Do you need anything else?"

"If it's not too much trouble, something to eat and drink would be lovely."

"Of course. I'll bring something by in a few minutes."

"Thank you."

Asra bustled out of the room, shutting the door behind her.

I surveyed the room and put my pack on a chair in the corner. I rolled my shoulders, glad to get the weight off my back. I crossed to the pitcher, poured some water into the bowl, and splashed the cool water on my face. I could feel the dust falling off my skin. It was only day one on my own, but I already missed the luxurious heated baths I used to take nightly at the palace.

There was a light knock on the door. I opened the door to find Asra holding a simple wooden tray with some food and a small glass of water. "We're lucky to have our own well nearby," she said as she handed me the tray. "Freshest water for miles. Sleep well, and we'll see you in the morning."

I thanked her and shut the door, putting the tray down next to the pitcher. I bolted down the food and drink, glad no one was around to see me eat so inelegantly. My hunger and thirst abated, I was ready to settle in for the night.

I opened my pack and rummaged through it, looking for the journal that contained the spells I was learning and other handwritten notes. I found the comb and ribbons Taryn had mentioned, as well as a second dress and a small bag of coins. Opening the bag, I gasped when I saw how much money my mother and Taryn had thoughtfully provided for me. I had been carrying a few coins, enough for tonight's stay and perhaps a meal somewhere else, but this pouch would definitely take me further. With this money, I would be able to afford a few comfortable nights at an inn and, if I was careful enough, some extra supplies or food.

My fingers brushed against my mother's letter, and my fingers briefly tightened around the papers. I was extremely curious, but I was also afraid of what I would read. The room felt too small and dark to learn the truth of my mother's story.

Dropping the letter, I instead pulled out a slim leather-bound volume from my bag. I tossed the book onto the bed and took off my dress. Clad only in my shift, I climbed into bed and grabbed the book. There was a small candle burning on a stand next to the bed, but I conjured a light spell so I could read a little better. I hung the light above my bed and settled back into the pillows.

I flipped through the pages until I found the calling spell Taryn suggested. Reading over the instructions carefully, I prepared to cast the spell. I focused on Taryn in my mind, willing her to sense my summons. Touching my lips with my index and middle finger, I moved my fingers about an inch from my face and blew on the tips.

Taryn's face appeared in front of me, level with my own. I smiled at my success.

The Taryn image smiled back. "Good job, Your Highness," she said to me. "I knew you could do it."

"You're the only one who was sure," I said.

"Don't cut yourself down," she said. "You have a knack for magic. In your lessons, even if you were just learning a spell, you mastered it quicker than expected."

I nodded in thanks. "How are things back home?"

"All is well," she said. "The king asked for you this morning, but Queen Melandria convinced him that she changed your mind and you've accepted the match. So he thinks you're in seclusion preparing for the wedding, and he's gone ahead with preparations of his own."

"Yes, I saw some Calian riders earlier today," I said. "And the farmer who was kind enough to let me stay for the night mentioned that formal invitations for the wedding are currently being sent out."

"We're all taking on extra responsibilities for the wedding, in addition to our regular duties," Taryn said. "King Hendon boasts that this will be a celebration like none in the Gifted Lands has ever seen before."

Calia had never been overly friendly with the other kingdoms. At best, we were neutral with the other countries. In actuality, on the rare occasions they fought their wars or had their problems, we turned a blind eye to them. I supposed a royal wedding was a perfect reason to try to build good relations with our neighbors, but the king had barely been civil to *me* growing up. Why would he want to be friendly with strangers, even for a political advantage?

"How is my mother?" I asked. "Is she well?"

"As well as we could hope for," Taryn said. "She's being watched."

I suspected as much, but hearing it affirmed made my heart sink. "What happened?"

"The king himself came to visit her as we were making our way out of the palace," she told me. Which in itself was suspicious, since in recent years the king and queen didn't try to hide the fact that theirs was a loveless marriage. They put on a good show for the public, and sometimes even for the palace staff, but those closest to them knew the truth. "He wanted to talk to her about the dinner and the engagement. Your mother thought she had misled him well, but she's noticed that there have been more guards near her rooms lately."

"She'll be okay." I tried to sound confident, but Taryn heard the unspoken question and tried to soothe me.

"Yes, she will be. The queen is clever, and she's aware of the king's spies. Don't worry."

Taryn filled me in on some of the other things happening around the castle, but we didn't talk much longer. She was afraid of possible spies. For now, she said, I should contact her as often as I could, but if things got worse at the palace she would warn me to cut down on our communication. We said goodbye, and as I ended the calling spell, Taryn's image winked out.

Now alone, I thought this would be a good time to brush up on my magic lessons. I leafed through the book, reading carefully. But I was exhausted, and soon the day's walk caught up to me. I was halfway though studying a spell when my heavy eyes gave in to sleep.

Chapter Nine

SUNLIGHT STREAMED THROUGH the windows, hitting my eyes and waking me. Turning, I felt something hard beneath my arm and realized I had fallen asleep on my spell book. I sat up, still a bit groggy, and reluctantly got out of bed.

After a quick wash from the basin, I pulled on my dress and shoes and pinned my hair up to keep it out of the way while I walked. It wasn't as neat or nicely done as the way Taryn dressed my hair, but it would do the job well enough. After packing my bag, I left my room. I wondered where my hosts were, since the house seemed so quiet. As I poked my head around the hallway, Asra spotted me.

"I hope you slept well," she said.

"Extremely well," I said.

"Did you want breakfast before you go?" she asked me.

Food sounded great, but I was eager to be on my way and cover as much distance as possible. "Thank you, but I'll just head out now." I pressed a coin into her palm. "Thank you for your hospitality."

Asra looked at the coin in her hand and whistled. "Thank *you*, miss. This is more than enough for one night's lodging. Wait here, don't go just yet."

She hurried away. A few moments later, she came back holding a small basket covered with a cloth. She held it out to me.

"Oh, I couldn't — " I started to protest.

"Please do," she said. "What you just gave me more than covers it."

I thanked her for her generosity. She saw me out the door, waving as I left. "Safe travels, miss. Stop by if you come back this way."

I waved back and headed down the road.

THE REST OF THE DAY passed uneventfully. I walked and walked, stopping around noon to eat the food Asra had packed for me. I should say, overpacked — I ate until I was full and there were still items left in the basket. There were two cloths in the basket; Asra had wrapped the food in one, and used the other to cover the basket. I tied one around my hair as a headscarf to keep my hair somewhat tidy during the rest of my walk.

While I was stopped, I pulled my mother's letter out from my pack and smoothed it out.

I had put it off as long as possible, afraid to know what she had kept from me for years. But the cheerful, bright sun chased away the shadows of apprehension around my heart as I read.

MY DARLING JENNICA,

There is much to tell you, and so little time. Hendon grows suspicious of my every move, and once my theft has been discovered, he will surely punish me in some fashion. But I get ahead of myself. Let me speak plainly.

Jennica, Hendon is not your father. The stories you have been told surrounding our courtship and marriage have all been lies.

Many years ago, a dragon did come to Calia. His name was Joichan, and he was searching for something that had been stolen from him. A gold necklace with a moonstone pendant. Hendon had stolen it from Joichan, and Joichan had tracked Hendon across the Gifted Lands trying to find him and reclaim the necklace. Joichan's search ultimately led him to Calia, where he lost the trail. So he took up residence in our kingdom while he continued to search the area.

But people are superstitious. It was assumed that a dragon's presence in Calia meant he would ravage the land until he had been appeased by an offering. A maiden every year, that sort of thing. Utter nonsense, but we believed it. To prevent any of our people from going to their deaths (or so we thought), I ran off to sacrifice myself to the dragon, hoping to stop any future sacrifices.

It did stop any sacrifices from happening (and Joichan was very grateful that my presence meant he didn't have to figure out what to do with an influx of maidens), but it caused a new problem: my father the king sent word to all the knights and princes of the neighboring realms to battle the dragon to save me, win my hand in marriage, and win the kingdom of Calia. This went on for two years, by which time I didn't want to be saved — the dragon and I had fallen in love.

Joichan is a shapeshifter, and can assume dragon or human form. We had planned on leaving Calia, when Hendon showed up. He was able to best the dragon, for he had Joichan's moonstone necklace, and was able to use Joichan's magic against him. Weakened, Joichan could only fly away and leave me, or be killed by Hendon.

With his victory, Hendon claimed me for his bride and won the kingdom of Calia. I was pregnant with you, and it was safer for me to marry Hendon and raise you as his daughter rather than try to find Joichan. But I never forgot Joichan, and I never forgot what you are, and what you are capable of.

The moonstone necklace is your birthright. With it you will be able to tap into the magic of dragons. Just as Hendon stole it from your father Joichan, I stole it from Hendon to give to you. Keep it safe, and bring it back to Joichan. He will be able to help us take the kingdom back from Hendon. Hendon has some dark plan, I fear. This marriage alliance is just his first step to conquering all of the Gifted Lands. And he somehow has even darker magic at his disposal.

I will be counting the days until both you and your father return to me safely.

MY MOTHER'S WORDS SWAM before my eyes. A tear slipped down my face and plopped onto the page, smearing the ink into an illegible blotch. I blinked my tears away, wiping my eyes with the back of my hand. Carefully, I refolded the letter and tucked it away in my pack, burying it at the bottom so it wouldn't accidentally fall out if I needed to get something out of my bag. Standing up, I stretched my back after the long lunch.

To think that all these years my mother had been living a lie. No wonder she supported my feelings against the wedding to Prince Anders. She didn't want her only daughter to get trapped like she had. But something else was going on as well, something more sinister. *Hendon has some dark plan... and even darker magic.*

What could the king be planning? And who was helping him? Hendon despised magic, and shared the Rothschan belief that it should be eradicated. The one thing I knew from growing up in Hendon's shadow: he was a strong-minded man, a very black-and-white thinker. It seemed impossible that he would be willing to compromise on such an ingrained belief.

I shouldered my pack to continue on my way, shuddering despite the sunlight shining down on me. Whatever Hendon was planning must be dire indeed.

Chapter Ten

CLOSE TO THE DAY'S end I came across an inn just off the road. When I entered the place, it wasn't too crowded. There were two people sitting at a table, eating, but no other customers. The innkeeper spotted me and came over to talk to me. It was easy to secure a room for the night, and I was happy to learn that the price also included a meal.

"I'll show you to your room," the innkeeper said to me. He started up the stairs, with me trailing after. He stopped at the second room down and opened the door. The modestly furnished room lacked the homey touches of Marchand and Asra's house, but it had everything I needed.

The innkeeper handed me the room key. "Dinner is ready whenever you are. Just come on back down."

He left me standing alone in the middle of the room. After I put my things down on the bed, I quickly washed the road dust from my face and hands and readjusted my headscarf. I dried my hands thoroughly and got my spell book out of my bag. Flipping through the pages, I found what I wanted near the middle: a locking spell.

This bit of magic would be a little tricky. There was a certain hand motion to lock something, and to undo the lock, I only had to do the hand motion in reverse. But a universal lock spell meant that any magician would be able to undo someone else's lock; therefore, the spell had to include something specific to me so the item I was locking knew to only lock and unlock for me. I knew the spell in theory, but had never added the personal element. The easiest way to do that would be to add in a small, extra hand flourish of my own design.

I read and reread the spell until I was sure I had it, trying the hand motions as well. When I was sure I had it, I looked around for something to practice on. By the door sat a wooden chest, with a key on the table nearby. *That's a nice touch*, I thought. Although it wouldn't deter an extremely determined thief, it provided a bit of security for a guest's belongings.

Focusing on the chest's metal lock, I reached out my right hand like I was twisting a doorknob and softly said, "*Obfirmo*." I thought I heard a slight sound, like the lock mechanism was clicking into place. I tried lifting the chest lid and found, to my disappointment, that it opened easily. Placing it back down, I repeated my spell. This time I definitely heard a click. When I tried the lid again, it wouldn't budge. I smiled in satisfaction. I reached out and reversed my doorknob twisting hand motion. "*Recludo*." The chest lock clicked again, and the lid opened easily at my touch.

I practiced a few more times until I was satisfied I had mastered the spell. I placed my belongings in the chest, locked it with magic, and took the key just to be safe. When I left my room I used my room key, and surreptitiously spell-locked the door as well. Then I headed downstairs to dinner.

The common room was much fuller now. I scanned the room, looking for an empty seat. There was one, toward the front of the room nearest to the inn's door. I picked my way across the room and sat down.

The innkeeper's daughter, a girl of about twelve, appeared almost immediately. "Evening, miss," she said. "What'll ya have? There's a meat pie, or beef stew."

I requested the pie, and the girl moved away to the next patron. I looked around the room, wondering if I was unsafe as a woman traveling alone. I needn't have worried. Although the room was primarily filled with men, there were a few women present. Mostly wives, it seemed, although I saw one family with three young children nearby.

The innkeeper's daughter returned with my meat pie and a glass of mead. The pie was so fresh that steam was rising from it, so I sipped at my mead and waited for my meal to cool a little so I could eat it comfortably.

I had just popped a bite of pie into my mouth when the door to the inn opened and Prince Anders strode in. I nearly choked on my food and hastily grabbed my glass to wash it down. When I was able to swallow, I looked up at the prince, who thankfully hadn't noticed me.

The innkeeper rushed up to the prince, who was surveying the room with distaste. I slunk lower in my seat, wishing I had a hat or a hood or *something*. Hopefully with the kerchief tied around my hair I blended in with everybody else. I tried not to make eye contact with Prince Anders while still keeping an eye on him, which was not easy.

"Milord, how may we be of service?" the innkeeper said to the prince.

"I require a room for the night," he said. "Two rooms, if you have them. If not, then a room large enough to accommodate myself and my valet."

The innkeeper said, "I do have two rooms, milord. I've a guest staying in the room between you, but I daresay you'll be close enough if you need your man, sir."

Oh, great! I was going to be sandwiched in between the prince and his entourage! How would I come and go without them seeing me?

"That will do nicely," Prince Anders said. He gave the man some coins. "I trust that will be enough for the rooms, and for our horses lodging in your stable?"

"You're very generous, sir," the innkeeper told him. "Meal's included, too. If you'd like to sit down we can serve you shortly."

The prince nodded to the innkeeper and strode past my table. I brought a huge spoonful of meat pie to my mouth, hoping this would help disguise me. I didn't dare turn around, in case the prince saw my face and recognized me, but I heard his footsteps stop somewhere behind me and to my left.

The door opened again and the prince's valet entered. He spotted the prince and joined him at his table.

"The horses are settled, Your Grace," the valet said. I nearly jumped. His voice was so close; I was pretty sure the prince and his man were seated right behind me.

"Very good," Prince Anders replied. His voice was equally close. *Drat! How would I get back to my room without them seeing me?*

I heard the innkeeper's daughter approach and ask them for their orders, then leave again after each man had spoken. I started eating my food as quickly as I could, hoping to leave the room while the prince and his man were distracted with their meal.

"I'll be glad when we're back in Rothschan," Prince Anders said. "I despise traveling."

"Understandable, Your Grace," said the valet soothingly. "Unfortunately, we'll barely be home before we have to turn right around and come back to Calia again."

"Unfortunately," the prince agreed. "I'm glad Mother had the foresight to start the wedding preparations before we came here. This visit was merely a formality."

"Like there was ever any doubt that King Hendon would turn down your suit. All you really had to do was finalize the details."

"And make sure the princess of Calia wasn't an ugly cow. Hendon was very eager to wed his daughter off. But for the price of a future kingdom, I can hardly complain, can I?" Prince Anders laughed loudly, his valet joining in. At my table where I sat eavesdropping, I bristled.

"You'll make a fine king of Calia, Your Grace," the valet said.

"I hope sooner rather than later," the prince replied. Both men laughed again.

The innkeeper's daughter returned with food and drink for the prince and his valet. I had finished my own meal by that time; it was delicious, but I had hardly tasted it in my haste to get out of there.

I stood up, intending to go the long way around the room and up the stairs. *Hmm, like* that *wouldn't be suspicious.*

Just as I skirted the table to cross to the other side of the room, the family of five headed to the door. The father and mother talked with the innkeeper while the children played an impromptu game of hide and seek using their parents' legs, the table, and nearby chairs.

With my way blocked, I now had no choice but to pass by the table where Prince Anders and his valet sat, noisily eating and drinking. I took a deep breath and turned around. I tried hard not to look like I was hurrying as I started to walk by the prince's table, keeping my face turned away from the two men as much as I could without looking obvious.

Step by excruciating step, I had nearly passed their table when I heard the prince say, "Miss? Wait... Don't I know you?"

Chapter Eleven

MY STEPS FALTERED. My heart raced. What should I do?

The prince's valet pushed his chair back so he was partially blocking my path. "His Royal Highness, Prince Anders of Rothschan, is asking you a question, young woman."

I swallowed hard, fighting the rising sense of panic in my chest. My face flushed, and I was breathing hard like I had just been running. This was it. My journey to find my father was over before it had even really begun. Prince Anders would bring his reluctant bride back to Calia and King Hendon would lock me up until the wedding. My mind raced. Should I throw myself on the prince's mercy?

I slowly turned to face Prince Anders. We stared at each other. Just as I was about to speak, the prince said, "I am mistaken. I thought you were my intended, Princess Jennica of Calia, but... you look nothing like her." He snorted rudely. "Thank goodness."

I look nothing like her? But I AM her! Perhaps the prince had too much to drink, or was exhausted from his travels. However, I wasn't going to question my good fortune. I sketched a quick curtsy toward the prince. Hurrying past their table, I practically ran up the stairs to my room.

Once I was at the door, I said the spell to undo the lock as I was hastily working the key in the lock simultaneously. With both magical and mundane locks open, I slipped inside. There was no bar inside for the door; I supposed perhaps guests normally pushed the wooden chest to block entrance into the room at night. I tried moving the chest, but couldn't get it to budge. Instead, I locked the door magically and with the key and then sat down on the bed, trying to calm my frantically beating heart.

I hadn't realized how afraid I was until I had seen my hand shaking while trying to do the spell. I thought it was a trick of the dim light in the hallway, but once I lit the lamp on the bedside table, I saw that my hand looked different. In fact, my whole arm looked different. My normally olive-toned skin had deepened a few shades, and my skin seemed to have a deep golden metallic sheen to it. There was a faint pattern on my arms, too, but I couldn't quite make it out.

I unpinned my hair, shaking it loose so it fell around my shoulders. Grabbing a fistful of hair to examine, I saw that my dark hair had golden streaks running through it again. But that couldn't be right. When I combed through my hair this morning, it was as solid black as it had always been.

Mentally I ran through my options. I could leave tonight, but that would leave me without a place to sleep. Besides, I had already paid for the room. Since I didn't know the prince's plans, I didn't know what time he intended on leaving the next day. But since he was going home to Rothschan, which was about a three days' ride from Calia, it seemed safe to assume that he and his valet would want to travel at first light. Fortunately I wasn't going as far; Orchwell was only about a half day's walk away from where I was currently staying. I decided to wake before sunrise and get back on the road. Hopefully I would be well away from the inn before the prince woke up and started his journey again.

Now that I had a plan in mind, I felt a lot calmer. I unlocked the trunk and fished out my spell book. After an hour or so of study, I put the book down on the bedside table, trimmed the lamp and went to sleep.

I was awakened by the sound of someone trying to get into my room.

Chapter Twelve

I SAT UP IN BED, TOO scared to make a noise. I wasn't sure how long I had been sleeping, but the moon spilled through the window across the room and created a pool of light just by the door.

A key turned partway in the lock, then stopped, unable to move further. The handle of the door rattled. I reached out and felt around the bedside table, wondering if I could use the lamp as a weapon.

"Why won't this stupid door unlock? Why won't my key work?" The voice, although a little muffled by the door, was unmistakably that of Prince Anders.

I slipped out of bed and grabbed the base of the lamp, holding it close to my chest.

The door handle rattled again. "Where's the innkeeper? This door is broken. Why won't it unlock?" The prince's voice was louder now, and slightly slurred.

Footsteps came hastily up the stairs. "Here, Your Grace," I heard the valet say smoothly. "Let me bring your to your room. I'm afraid that's not the right one."

"But it is!" Prince Anders was definitely drunk. "I counted the doors. One. Two.... One."

There was a *thump* as something heavy fell against my door. I almost felt bad for the valet.

"Come now, Your Grace," the valet said. He sounded a bit labored, like he was carrying something — well, someone — heavy. "Just a few steps more."

I heard some slow, uneven steps as Prince Anders and his valet made their way a few paces beyond my room. The door to the room next to mine opened and shut. After a few moments, I heard snoring coming from that direction.

The door of the prince's room opened and closed again, and I heard the valet's footsteps as he passed by my room to his, which must have been the first one at the top of the stairs.

"Idiot," I heard him mutter. "Rothschan's well to be rid of him. Heaven help Calia." The valet's door opened and shut, and then all was quiet in the hallway once again.

I put the lamp back down on the bedside table and climbed back into bed. While my heart was still racing, I was also proud of how well my lock spell had worked.

I slept fitfully until it was time to get up and leave in earnest. Prince Anders was still snoring loudly in the room next door, which eased my mind about potentially running into him. I hoped the valet was still abed, knowing that the two of them wouldn't be getting an early start with his master in that state.

I carefully made my way downstairs, where the innkeeper was just building up the fire in the hearth, preparing for his own busy day. He unlocked the door for me and I started down the road toward Orchwell. The stars were gone from the sky and there was a faint orange glow at the horizon when I left.

About an hour later, the sun had risen and I was well on my way to Orchwell. There was no chance now of seeing Prince Anders; he would be taking a different road from the inn since Rothschan lay to the west, and I was headed straight south.

When the sun was almost directly overhead, I noticed there was more traffic on the road. I quickened my step, knowing I was close to my destination. Less than an hour later, and I was there: Orchwell, the Land of Seekers.

Chapter Thirteen

EACH OF THE REALMS in the Gifted Lands has its own unique properties. Calia, for example, produces some of the finest magicians in the world, something that its ruler, King Hendon, barely tolerated. I had always assumed it was because he originally hailed from Rothschan, a land known for its military prowess. The people of Rothschan had a distrust of anything mystical — if it wasn't logical and easily understood, then it was dangerous and to be avoided. An alliance between Calia and Rothschan seemed unlikely, although with my mother and Hendon's marriage, it now had precedent. A union between the two kingdoms meant others would be unlikely to oppose us — the combination of might and magic would be formidable.

And now I was in Orchwell, our closest neighboring kingdom. An easy day's ride away, it had taken me about two and a half days of walking. I was fortunate that the long summer days gave me extra time for traveling.

Orchwell was also called the Land of Seekers. I wondered how the ability to seek worked. Did you have to study and practice it, like magic? Or were you just able to execute your skill flawlessly from birth?

And what if what you sought did not want to be found? With his abilities, my shapeshifting dragon father could easily hide if he wanted. I just hoped that once he realized who I was, he wouldn't want to hide from me. While I was determined to find Joichan, I only had one month to stop the wedding, dragon or no dragon.

I joined the crowd of people entering Orchwell's gates confidently, sure that the Calian riders were long gone. The throng of villagers, merchants, and other visitors pushed forward. Soon, I was inside the gates of Orchwell's capital.

Once inside, I gaped at the city around me. I had only been here once, when I was very little. And even then, I had been in the royal carriage, curtains buttoned up against the outside world. We had gone straight to the palace, not taking any time on our visit to tour the kingdom of Orchwell at all.

Everywhere I looked, I saw brightly painted signs. On the doors, in the windows, on wooden slats hanging over entryways. It seemed that seekers were not coy about being found. Each sign advertised what, exactly, the occupants of that particular location were good at finding. This person specialized in jewelry; that one's focus was on finding a child's hidden talent. Some seeking talents seemed very broad, while others had only one highly specialized skill. Yet as I looked all around me, lost in the colorful signage, I couldn't find anything that screamed *I find dragons!*

I wandered down the street, taking it all in. I was so caught up in the spectacle around me that I didn't notice the produce woman until I bumped right into her.

"Oh my goodness!" I said in dismay. In my absentmindedness, I had run right into her and nearly tipped over her little wheeled stand of fruits and vegetables.

I reached out to steady her cart before any of her produce could fall into the street. "Please excuse me, madam. I was so busy looking up I didn't look where I was going."

The middle-aged woman laughed good-naturedly. "You must be a visitor, then. Newcomers always gawk when they get their first look at Orchwell's capital city."

"It *is* overwhelming," I admitted. "How does one seek a seeker when there are so many of them?"

"You could spend days looking at all the signs, trying to find the one you're looking for," she agreed.

"Are you a seeker?" I asked, eyeing her cart. What would she seek? The perfect vegetable?

The woman laughed. "Contrary to the rumors, not every citizen of Orchwell is a seeker," she said. "I'm just a mere farmer. Many of my friends are seekers of some sort, however. After seeing what they go through, I'm happy to be 'only' a farmer."

"Oh?" I wondered what she meant.

She motioned me closer and pitched her voice lower. "Seeking is a double-edged sword. It's a rare and wonderful talent, but it can also drive a person mad if they don't use their gift regularly. Sometimes it can lead them into physically or emotionally dangerous places. Like it or not, the things a seeker seeks must be found. And sometimes it's better to leave things lost, if you take my meaning."

She leaned back and spoke in her regular tone. "But I'm sure you didn't come to Orchwell just to sightsee. No one ever does. Are you looking for someone or something in particular?"

"Yes, actually," I said. "A man — or woman — named Kye. Have you heard of this person?"

"Oh, Kye," she said, smiling. "He's easy enough to find. Just continue down this way, turn right at the first street you can, and you'll find his home on the right. He's got the dragon sign on his door."

"Thank you," I said. To show extra appreciation, I decided to purchase an apple from her stand. As I was paying her, she said, "Funny, though. You don't look like the adventuring sort."

What did that mean? Before I could ask her, she turned away to talk to another customer. I shrugged and started walking down the street, eating my apple as I went.

I had finished my apple just as I found Kye's house, following the woman's directions. Sure enough, there was a picture of a golden dragon on the weathered gray door. I studied the picture, admiring the artist's work. The dragon was fierce, but majestic and beautiful as well. Was that what my father Joichan was like?

I knocked on the door. A panel slid back in the door and a pair of rich brown eyes suddenly stared at me from the golden dragon's face. I stepped back, startled.

"Yes?" A muffled male voice spoke from behind the dragon sign.

"Ah... hello," I said hesitantly.

"Can I help you?"

"Yes," I said, trying to gain confidence. "I'm looking for Kye. I was told I could find him here?"

"Kye doesn't seek anymore," the voice said.

"Please. It's important."

The brown eyes regarded me, expression hard and unreadable. Then: "Fine. Six hundred pieces of gold, half of the money up front."

"Three hundred pieces of gold?" I said in dismay. While my mother had been generous, that amount was considerably more than all the money I carried. "I... I don't have *that* much money."

"Too bad, then," the voice said. The panel started to slide shut.

"Wait!" I called out. The panel stopped mid-slide and slowly opened again. "Please. I need Kye's help."

"Three hundred gold," the voice said. "Or don't waste my time."

"Queen Melandria of Calia sent me to find Kye," I said desperately. "My business with him is most urgent."

There was a pause as the brown eyes sized me up. The silence stretched out longer as I stood on the doorstep awkwardly. Finally, with a decisive *bang*, the panel slid shut and the brown eyes disappeared.

I turned to go, my eyes stinging with sudden tears.

The door swung open behind me. I turned around and was face to face with those brown eyes again. They were set in the face of a man who looked near my age, or maybe a few years older. His dark brown hair fell over his forehead and he pushed it back impatiently as we stared at each other.

"Well? Come in," he said, and held the door open for me.

Chapter Fourteen

AS I ENTERED THE HOUSE, my eyes were drawn to all the fantastic things on display. Whoever lived here was obviously well-traveled, as souvenirs from all over the Gifted Lands and beyond were featured all over the room. I spied a small square of stained glass layered on the window, its rich blue and green rays of colored light illuminating the wooden carvings on a table nearby. A lush red silk robe hung on one wall, and an impressive tapestry of the night sky hung on another wall. I longed to examine it up close. And everywhere I looked — on bookshelves, on the mantle, even on the windowsills — there were little painted figurines of various kinds of dragons.

But even though all these interesting knick-knacks initially drew the eye, they couldn't disguise the peeling paint on the walls, the warped wooden furniture, or the fraying fabric curtains drawn back from the windows. This sad backdrop to the bright and beautiful objects surrounding us made me feel that, instead of a proud display of a well-lived life, they were testaments to a faded glory.

The young man observed me as I gaped at everything. "That's the usual expression people have when they first come here," he said.

"These are amazing," I said, giving into the temptation to study the celestial sky tapestry. I stopped myself from running my fingers down the intricate weaving. "Everything here is so beautiful. You must have traveled everywhere, Kye."

"I'm not — " he began to say, when he was interrupted by an older gentleman who hobbled into the room, leaning heavily on a cane.

"Who's here, Beyan?" the man asked my host. He had the same features as Beyan, but there were gray streaks through his brown hair and at his temples, and his face had a more weathered look. His right leg was deformed, twisted in a way that was unnatural. He subtly winced with each step; even though the injury looked old, I could see it still hurt him. Despite his infirmity, he gave off the sense that he was still very capable.

"A potential patron," said Beyan. "Says Queen Melandria of Calia sent her to find you, Father."

The older man smiled. "Now there's a name I haven't heard in a long time. But when I met her, she was still Princess Melandria, you know. She wouldn't become queen until years later, when her father passed away."

"You're... Kye?" I asked the older man.

"That's right," he confirmed.

"Can you help me? The queen specifically told me to seek you out. I'm looking for a dragon," I said.

Kye laughed. "Of course you are, or you wouldn't be here. But I'm retired, and have been for some time now." He gestured to his leg with the cane. "I never really recovered from my last seeking engagement. Not much use in the field now."

"I don't suppose I could convince you to come out of retirement?" I asked doubtfully.

"No chance whatsoever," Kye said cheerfully. "I'm quite happy at home, painting dragons instead of chasing them."

So the dragon figurines were his creation.

"I saw all of those miniatures when I came in. They're beautifully done," I said.

"They're not just little show pieces," he said. "Each figurine is a dragon I was commissioned to seek."

"Really?" I took a second look around the room, now paying closer attention to the colorful statuettes.

"Sure," Kye said. He pointed at a blue dragon. "That was an ice dragon I was tasked to find in the frigid north. What an expedition! I thought my limbs would all freeze off before we found her." He indicated a purple dragon figure. "This was my first ever seeking engagement. Just a little earth dragon, but he was a feisty one."

My eye caught a golden dragon, similar to the painting on the door. This figurine was larger than most of the other dragons. "What about this one?" I asked.

Kye's expression clouded over. "He's a fire dragon, with a fair amount of magic as well. His name is Joichan."

My eyes widened. So this was my father!

I studied the figurine closely. Larger than most of the other figurines, it seemed more alive than the other carvings on the shelves. Perhaps it was the proud stance, or the wise expression. Or maybe it was the majestic tilt of the head, the way the flight-ready, curved wings spoke of power simmering under the surface.

"It's a remarkable likeness," I murmured.

"Thank you," said Kye. "It's something to amuse me in retirement, and I make a bit of money selling them off."

I turned back to Kye. "Your injury... so you fought the dragons you were tasked to seek?"

"Goodness, no," Kye said with genuine revulsion. "Everyone in my direct family line has been a dragon seeker for at least five generations back. Seekers are peaceful. Our job is to find them, not hurt or kill them. That would be a perversion of our gift." He became more animated as he spoke, waving his cane around. When he put his cane back down, it slipped and Kye wobbled with it.

Instantly Beyan was at his side, arm around Kye to support him. "Let's get you sitting down and settled," Beyan said. He started to walk Kye out of the room. Over his shoulder, he called to me, "Just wait there, I'll be right back."

While I waited, I studied the Joichan figurine once more. Without Kye's help, how would I find Joichan?

Beyan walked back into the room. "My father is a very passionate person, especially when it comes to dragons," he explained. "Well, when you grow up surrounded by the exciting stories, and it's your livelihood... It was a hard adjustment for him, having to retire from seeking when he was in his prime."

"I'm sorry to hear that," I said politely. "Well, I seem to have hit a dead end. Are there any others in Orchwell who seek dragons?"

"None as fine as my father," said Beyan.

Naturally. Why couldn't it be easy — find Kye, find Joichan, save Calia? I sighed. I now had to decide if I should return home, or try to continue on by myself. "Thank you for your time."

My disappointment must have been obvious, because Beyan stopped me as I turned to leave. "Who is it you're looking for?"

I reached out toward the Joichan miniature, my fingers just shy of actually touching the majestic dragon carving. "This one."

Beyan's eyes flashed. "I will take you."

"What? I thought — "

"I said none could seek as well as my father. But I didn't say that I am not a dragon seeker."

Hope flared in my heart. "If you could help me, I would be so grateful."

"My father is injured, as you can tell. In the last few years it's gotten worse; he needs my help almost daily. I try not to take jobs that take me away from his side for longer than a day or two, but those don't pay much, nor do they come along often. Your task sounds promising, but I'll be gone for at least a week, possibly longer. I need to make sure the time away from my father will be worth my while."

The little flicker of hope died out. "I can't pay the fee you requested. I have some money for my journey, but not that much."

He studied me silently for a long moment, as if trying to uncover all my secrets with his eyes. I shifted uncomfortably under his gaze.

"You said Queen Melandria of Calia sent you?" he asked me.

"Yes."

"I'll forgo the advance payment, if the queen will pay twice the entire amount immediately once we complete this task."

I hesitated. It was quite a lot of money, and Mother hadn't given me instructions on what to do *after* I found Kye. Besides find my father, of course.

"Unless your task is not as urgent as you make it seem." Beyan began to turn away. "Obviously, you're not authorized to — "

"Done." *On my word as the Crown Princess,* I thought. But I couldn't say that to him. "Twelve hundred gold for taking me to Joichan. With an additional twelve hundred as a bonus."

Beyan was definitely interested now. Then his lips thinned and his eyes narrowed. "How can I trust your word?"

I tugged a simple gold ring from around my little finger. It was surprisingly plain for royal jewelry, but I loved it nonetheless. It had been a birthday present from my mother on my sixteenth birthday, and there was a small engraving on the inside with my initials. I ran my thumb over the little gold ring, sad to let it go. Holding it up so Beyan could see it, I said, "If I am not present when you meet with Queen Melandria, ask for a woman named Taryn to help you gain an audience with the queen. Give this to the queen as a token of my word. You have my assurance that she will honor our agreement."

"Really? And you are?"

I realized belatedly that I had never introduced myself to Beyan or his father. "My name is Allayne." I had to trust that Taryn would recognize my "name" and help Beyan if I wasn't there with him.

Taking my ring, Beyan placed it on a leather cord that he grabbed from the table nearby. He tied the cord around his neck and tucked it under his shirt. Then he held out his hand toward me. I took it gingerly, unused to the custom of shaking hands. His grip was cool and strong.

"Perfect." For the first time since we met, he smiled. It transformed him from a sullen young man to an eager seeker, ready to start his quest. "We leave in the morning."

Chapter Fifteen

I APPROACHED THE CITY gates right as the sun streaked over the horizon. I was carrying considerably more than when I had arrived, as the rest of my time in Orchwell had been spent purchasing things for an extended trek across the Gifted Lands. The supply of money that Taryn had put in my pack was dwindling, and I hoped there wouldn't be too many more expenses on the journey.

Beyan was not the only one waiting for me. A quick round of introductions let me know who my new traveling companions would be. Rhyss was as tall as Beyan, but with freckled skin and a shock of red hair. Farrah's ebony skin set off her gorgeous lavender hair and striking violet eyes, marking her as half Fae, half human.

Rhyss and Farrah held the reins to their mounts, already carrying their gear. Beyan had two horses — his own, and a hired horse for me. He handed me the reins, saying, "Her name is Dorie."

"Hello, Dorie," I said, patting the horse. She nickered softly, turning her big brown head toward mine.

Beyan loaded Dorie with my extra gear and knapsack. "Can you ride?" he asked me.

"Of course," I said, bristling somewhat. I had learned to ride a horse practically as soon as I could walk. But the curious looks from the group clued me in to the realization that, while every noble might know how to ride, not every commoner would.

I made my tone meeker. "I was lucky. I grew up helping the stable master at the palace in Calia."

That was somewhat true. Although if you asked the stable master, he would say my "helping" him was more like "getting underfoot" all the time.

Farrah and Rhyss nodded, tending to their own horses. Beyan narrowed his eyes at me, but didn't say anything. After a moment, he turned back to Dorie and double checked that my gear was secured properly. Internally, I winced at my potential gaffe. I would have to be careful with my words, or I might accidentally give myself — and my identity — away.

We mounted our horses and began the journey south, toward Annlyn. The southernmost kingdom of the Gifted Lands, it was famous for its expert jewelry makers. Often pieces made by Annlyn craftspeople were expensive but highly sought after.

Our route would take us directly to the kingdom of Annlyn, where we would restock and get ready to find Joichan. Somewhere nearby Annlyn was the last known lair of Joichan, where Beyan's father Kye had faced the dragon. Once we were closer to Annlyn, Beyan assured me that his seeker abilities would help him find Joichan's exact location, and even if Joichan had since moved on, we might be able to get information on where the dragon had gone. With no other leads, heading south seemed to be our best option.

Our little group of four fell into pairs: Rhyss and Farrah leading, with Beyan and me riding behind them. As we rode, I noticed that everyone carried a weapon of some sort, and I wondered if I should have purchased one yesterday. Too late now, though. The shops wouldn't open for a few more hours, and we were going to be on the road by then. Besides, even if I did have a weapon, I wouldn't know how to use it.

Beyan followed my gaze. He reassured me, "It's handy if you have a weapon, but we don't expect our patrons to be armed."

"That's what we're here for," Rhyss called back cheerfully.

Farrah turned around briefly to roll her eyes at me. "Rhyss will tell you he's the muscle of the group," she said, before turning back to poke Rhyss's arm. He yelped in surprise. "But if he's so good, why am I constantly patching him up?"

"So you're not all seekers?" I asked, confused.

"Thank heavens, no," Farrah said. "That's not the life for me. Rhyss and I aren't from Orchwell originally. I'm from Shonn, and Rhyss grew up in Bomora." She named two more countries that were part of the Gifted Lands. Bomora was to the west, beyond Rothschan. Shonn was Calia's eastern neighbor. "No, Beyan and Rhyss and I have been friends for years, and when he has a job he brings us along to help."

"You mean in case there's trouble?" I clarified.

"Or to bring home the bounty," Rhyss said jauntily.

Before I could ask Rhyss what he meant, Farrah spoke. "Don't worry, Allayne." It took me a second to remember that was my name now. "Whatever happens, we'll take care of it. We haven't lost a patron yet, and we don't expect them to do too much."

"I'm not entirely useless," I said, stung. "I can do *some* things. Like magic. Although I'm still learning."

"I figured if you're from Calia then you must know some magic," Farrah said. "That could come in handy."

"Farrah is our resident magician," Beyan explained. "But her way of doing magic is different than most people's."

"It's my Fae blood," she said. "Magic comes to me as easily as breathing. I don't have to learn complex spells or another language to conjure something; I just have to will it into being."

"I've never met magicians from other disciplines, since I've only studied Calian theory," I said. "Are you able to explain how you perform magic? I'd love to learn, even if I can't replicate what you do."

Farrah looked thoughtful. "Well, my ability is rather limited. I can create things, but I can't destroy them. It makes me a terrific healer, but not much use in a fight. But, if you're interested..."

"Oh, yes."

Farrah dropped back to ride beside me. She launched into a description of her approach to magic. Beyan and Rhyss rode on ahead, uninterested in a discussion on magical theory.

I found Farrah's way of doing magic fascinating. In Calia, magicians often had to use hand gestures and words as a way of focusing magic and making it useful. But because Farrah was innately magic, thanks to her heritage, she could see magic all around her. In fact, growing up, she said, she had to learn how to turn off her magical ability because she would frequently conjure things accidentally.

"Now I have to deliberately access my magic, just like you would deliberately open a door," she said. "It's not hard, though. I can do it in an instant. It's just a conscious decision now whereas when I was younger, it wasn't."

"Would all offspring from a magical and human union have innate magical ability?" I wondered.

"To my knowledge, yes," Farrah said. "The magical side always breeds true. Only humans need rituals or spells to use magic; any creature or the Fae would be able to tap into magic naturally. I know many others who are like me, half Fae and half human, and we all have the same magical talent."

"What about children of other unions between humans and other kinds of magical beings?"

"I know of none."

"Really?"

"I don't think such a thing is possible. Faerie and human, yes. Other species? No. But who's to say? Just because no one's ever heard of such a thing doesn't mean it couldn't happen. It just seems unlikely."

I wanted to debate the issue more — after all, I was a child of a supposedly impossible union — but Farrah delved into more magic theory. It really was interesting, and we kept coming back to the topic all throughout the day. Our impromptu lesson helped pass the time on the road, up until it was time to make camp for the night.

Chapter Sixteen

THE DAYS PASSED BY in a similar rhythm. Covering the seemingly endless miles on horseback, Farrah and I would spend the days discussing magic theory. Through her tutelage I became better at using my magic skills.

Before falling asleep, I'd either read my spell book and practice, or listen to the stories my companions told. They had an easy camaraderie that I envied. Being royalty meant that people around me were always guarded, either on their best behavior or seeking something to help them advance. I had few truly real friends. But these three didn't have those inhibitions in place. I learned that Farrah's family had moved to Orchwell when she was five, and she and Beyan had grown up together. Rhyss had moved to Orchwell later, as a teenager, and the three of them quickly become inseparable.

I enjoyed getting to know my companions, although I remained wary. Once or twice I caught myself before I let something about my true self slip. Luckily, none of them seemed to notice.

One night, when we all were gathered around the campfire, Beyan asked me out of the blue, "So, Allayne, why are *you* looking for Joichan? I would think Queen Melandria of Calia could engage any of her knights to search, instead of sending an unarmed woman after a dangerous dragon."

I had been hemming one of my dresses, which was a painstaking process. One dress, which would have taken Taryn just a few short hours to hem, was, so far, taking me the entire journey to fix. Beyan's question startled me, and I jammed my finger with my needle. Blood welled up on my forefinger, and I pressed it against my thumb, hoping to stanch the flow immediately.

Seeing what had happened, Farrah said, "Oh, you've hurt yourself!"

"It's nothing," I said, as she fussed over my finger. Secretly, I was glad for the distraction, as it gave me a chance to think about how to answer Beyan.

Farrah held my hand, palm up, in hers. In seconds, she had magically sewn the wound shut. My finger was smooth and clean, no scarring, as if the gash had never been. Even the blood on my thumb and index finger were gone.

"Thank you," I said, marveling at her handiwork.

She shrugged modestly, but I caught the hint of a pleased smile teasing the corners of her mouth.

Beyan was still watching me, patiently waiting for an answer to his question. What was it that Taryn had said? *The best lies have a bit of truth in them.*

Cautiously taking my needle up, I said, "My father was one of the knights who went forth to fight the dragon Joichan." I didn't have to say *which* knight. "I was just a baby." Still true. Somewhat. "He... he perished in the attempt. When I was old enough, I went into service at the palace to help my family. Because of my history, when the queen decided to track down Joichan, I volunteered." Somehow I had said the rest of that without lightening striking me, and I sounded convincing. I hoped.

"You volunteered?" Rhyss said. "Why?"

"Volunteer might not be completely accurate," I allowed. "I wanted to go because I hoped it will help my family gains." Like by helping me gain a family.

The others nodded. As adventurers-for-hire, they could understand taking on a quest solely for financial reasons.

"What about all of you?" My eyes swept over each of them in turn. "How did you get started in all of this?" I waved my hand around the campsite, encompassing Beyan poking the fire with a stick, Rhyss sharpening his daggers, Farrah lounging against her pack, and our four horses tethered and placidly chewing on grass nearby.

Farrah shifted lazily. "When Beyan started his seeking trade, I went along with him. Partly to see the world, partly to make sure he came home in one piece."

"Be honest," Beyan grinned. "I was just your excuse. It was completely to see the world. Making sure I got back safely so you could go on future travels was just an advantage."

"You said it, I didn't," Farrah teased back.

"After a while, the jobs started getting harder," Beyan said. He held up his left arm in the firelight and pulled back his sleeve. A nasty slash of a scar ran from his wrist to his elbow. "Nearly didn't make it back from this one."

"I remember that," Farrah said, a faraway look in her eyes. "It took all I had to heal you, I've never been so drained. As it was, I couldn't completely heal you. I worried that we would have to amputate."

"So naturally they asked me to come along and help," Rhyss said.

"You begged us," Beyan and Farrah said together, then laughed. Rhyss and I joined in.

"It sounds like between the three of you, I'm in safe, capable hands," I said. "I'm glad I have nothing to fear. From any dragon."

Beyan, who had been smiling just moments ago, dropped his stick into the fire and abruptly stood up. "I'm going to find more wood for the fire," he said, and disappeared into the trees surrounding us.

I looked at Farrah and Rhyss. "Did I say something to offend Beyan?" I asked.

Rhyss seemed to be concentrating extra hard on sharpening his weapons, which, to me, already looked pretty sharp. Farrah heaved a deep sigh and shifted her weight again.

"He'll be okay," she told me. "Beyan is a very experienced seeker. It runs in his blood, and his father Kye was one of the best. Beyan would never admit it, but this particular commission has him worried."

"But why, though?" I asked. "If Beyan has done so much already, this is just another routine job."

Neither Rhyss nor Farrah said anything, or would even look at me.

"Isn't it?" I whispered.

"You've met Kye, right?" Farrah asked. I nodded. "So you know he had to retire from seeking because of an injury."

"Kye mentioned that," I said.

"When Kye got injured, Beyan was only about four or five years old," Farrah explained. "While many seekers train as children, most don't start their careers right away. It takes years of study and apprenticeship before they go out on their own. At seven, Beyan was the youngest ever seeker — of any type. He'd just do local jobs as they came up, and eventually as he got older he moved into more lucrative jobs that required travel.

If his father hadn't gotten hurt, they would be doing these commissions together.

"At first it wasn't so bad. Beyan would be gone for a few days, but his mother was there to look after Kye, and she worked as a seamstress to help bring in money. But then she fell ill a few years ago — the cost of the medicines she required ruined what was left of their family's finances. And in the end, it didn't help. After she died, Kye's condition seemed to worsen overnight. Beyan doesn't like to leave Kye alone too long, but then it limits how much he can earn, because he's forced to turn down so many jobs."

"That does sound difficult," I sympathized. "For Beyan to be forced to grow up so fast, to lose a beloved wife and mother, and for his father to have to send his son into danger alone. But I still don't see — "

"Ever since he was a child, Beyan has wanted to find Joichan," Farrah said. "Joichan is the one that gave Kye that career-ending injury. I think it's best if Beyan leaves well enough alone; that dragon has caused enough trouble for their family. But Beyan wants to finish the job his father couldn't."

Chapter Seventeen

WE WERE GETTING CLOSE to Annlyn. Not only because we had been on the road for nearly a week, but also because the weather had steadily been getting hotter. A Calian summer was marked by pleasantly mild days and chill nights. But here in the southern reaches of the Gifted Lands, it was scorching. My cloak had been relegated to the bottom of my pack, unneeded except as a blanket at night. As we traveled under the relentless sun, I sweltered in my borrowed dress. Too bad Taryn hadn't packed a lighter one from her closet. At this rate, I'd be riding into Annlyn wearing nothing but my shift, propriety notwithstanding.

In the skies, we'd spot the occasional dragon winging through the air. There was a medium-sized crimson fledgling, trailing after its darker maroon-colored mother on unsteady wings. A majestic coffee-colored dragon leisurely glided above us, casting a long shadow for miles. But there was no sign of the metallic golden dragon that was Joichan.

Initially I had thought I would find the journey rough. I had never traveled this far from my home, and on the few occasions I had left Calia, there were always servants present to do the packing and the cooking and the cleaning. And of course, I had either been on horseback or in a carriage. But I was determined not to be a burden to the rest of the group.

In addition to my magical studies, I pestered Beyan or Rhyss to teach me basic fighting techniques. Because of my interest, Beyan produced a spare dagger he insisted I keep. "That way you're not such a liability," he said, but he looked pleased.

Solemnly, I accepted his gift and then turned away so he wouldn't see the smile quickly blooming on my face. We both knew that sarcasm was just his favorite way of communication.

While Rhyss was a capable fighter, he was a bit too flighty to be a good teacher. Farrah often made fun of his distracted nature. "It's amazing your neck is still on your body, with the way your mind wanders so much," she'd laugh.

Beyan, on the other hand, was a surprisingly patient instructor. In addition to his skills as a dragon seeker, he had observed and absorbed his father's gift of teaching. It made sense, as each generation of seekers was supposed to teach the next. Over the course of our journey, my skills with the knife also increased, to the point where Beyan deemed me "competent." High praise, coming from him.

Aside from the occasional hunt for small game, no one in the group had been called upon to actually use their fighting skills. I was actually quite grateful about that. I was afraid that, should the situation warrant it, I would react poorly in a fight. And I didn't think I had it in me to end someone's life, even in self-defense.

The fighting lessons seemed to be helping not only me, but Beyan. I don't mean that Beyan needed to improve his skills with a weapon — he obviously knew what he was doing, or he wouldn't have been able to teach a beginner like me. But I noticed that he was unsettled, and our lessons helped provide a distraction. I couldn't understand what was wrong as I observed him surreptitiously while we traveled. He was shaky, from more than the jostle of riding a horse. Sweating profusely, even if we were sitting in the shade. Restless in his sleep at night. Farrah took to riding next to him, speaking to him in a low, calm voice.

We stopped to refill our canteens more often, as Beyan drank more than all of us combined. Farrah constantly supplied him with cool, damp cloths to put on his arms and forehead. Even cheerful, oblivious Rhyss grew somber and quiet, careful not to offend the now temperamental Beyan.

As we traveled further south, I noticed that the roads going north were heavy with travelers. When I commented randomly on this, Beyan frowned. "It's unusual. Perhaps people want to holiday in the northern kingdoms to escape the heat down here."

"I suppose," I said doubtfully. "But I know Calia never gets that many visitors from the south. We're so far away; it's the same reason most Calians wouldn't travel all the way down here."

"Maybe they're headed somewhere else. To Orchwell? Although Orchwell doesn't get that many southerners visiting, either."

Farrah laughed at his statement. "It's amazing how you can be so observant and so dense all at the same time."

Beyan's frown deepened. "What's that supposed to mean?"

"Didn't you notice the colors on the carriage that just passed by? Or how fine the horses are?"

"What of it?"

Farrah rolled her eyes. "These aren't just everyday travelers. It's the royalty and nobles of the southern kingdoms, headed north for a special occasion."

And the only special occasion was the wedding of Calia's princess to the prince of Rothschan.

I kicked myself mentally for not keeping up with what was going on back home. Since our contact my first night away from Calia, I hadn't gotten back in touch with Taryn. Although, truth be told, it was a bit hard to sneak away from my companions at night. Still, I decided that that night I would find a way to talk to Taryn, if only to reassure myself that all was well.

THE CAMPFIRE HAD BEEN reduced to mere embers when I cautiously propped myself up on my elbows and looked over the group. Everyone seemed to be asleep, so I slowly and quietly got up, being careful where I stepped. The horses, tethered to some trees nearby, sidestepped and nickered softly at my movement, but settled down quickly at a quiet, placating word from me. I had just reached the edge of the camp when I heard a quiet voice right behind me in the darkness.

"Where are you headed, Allayne?" I turned slightly to my right. Although I couldn't see him clearly in the dim light, I knew it was Beyan.

"I didn't mean to wake you," I whispered.

"I wasn't sleeping," he said.

"Well, I just need to... to relieve myself," I said, scrambling for a plausible excuse.

"You shouldn't go by yourself. Let me wake Farrah."

"No!" I spoke a little louder than I intended. Hastily, I glanced over at Farrah and Rhyss. Rhyss stirred in his sleep a little, but Farrah still slept soundly.

"No," I brought my voice back to a whisper. "I'll be okay by myself."

I could sense Beyan frowning, even though I couldn't see it. "All right," he conceded. "Don't go far. If you're gone too long, I'll come find you."

I nodded, then remembered Beyan probably couldn't see the motion in the darkness. "Sure," I said aloud for his benefit.

I conjured a light, then moved farther away from camp. When I felt suitably hidden from eyes and ears, I stopped and leaned against a nearby tree. I listened intently for a few moments, but it didn't seem like Beyan had followed me.

Quickly I created a calling spell, concentrating on Taryn's image in my mind's eye. But Taryn didn't appear when I completed the spell.

Frowning, I waved my hand through the haze where Taryn's face should have appeared, ending the spell. I'd never had a calling spell fail before. To my knowledge, the person being summoned would feel the magical pull and had the option to accept or deny the spell. If that other person didn't want the connection, the spell would ricochet, sending small fragments of magic back to alert the initiator that the connection was denied. Either way, *something* should happen.

I tried the spell again. This time Taryn's face appeared level with my own.

"Taryn!" I said, relieved. "There you are! Why didn't you — "

"Shh!" she said, looking around her warily. "I don't have much time, Your Highness. I'm sorry I couldn't answer you before, but... oh, it's gotten so bad here."

"What? What's happening?"

"King Hendon broke protocol and demanded a visit with you, even though you're still in your bridal month seclusion. When he discovered you were missing, he questioned Queen Melandria, who of course wouldn't say where you had gone. He threatened her — "

I gasped.

"Don't worry, she's fine." Taryn was quick to assure me. "But whereas before we only suspected she was being watched, now the king has set a definite watch on her."

I remembered the traveling nobles on their way north. "We've seen the kings and queens of the neighboring kingdoms headed north, though. Surely it's not for the wedding. If King Hendon knows I'm not there, he's probably cancelled it, right?"

Taryn shook her head. "No, to the contrary. He's sent out envoys to all the kingdoms, inviting all the leaders and their people of rank. Even Prince Anders thinks the wedding is still happening. So here in Calia we are still preparing for a royal wedding, even while the king has riders out looking for you."

"When? When did this happen?" I asked urgently.

"Just a few days ago," she said. "You have a good lead, but not for long."

"Thank you for telling me this," I said.

"There's more," Taryn added. "It's not really related, but..."

"What? What's happening?"

"Remember I told you about the kitchen maid Sava, and how her brother went missing but returned with a damaged mind? The boy disappeared again, which was bizarre, because he refused to leave the house since his return. And Sava has gone missing as well. Their parents are sick with grief over losing both of their children."

Taryn was right. It was palace intrigue that wasn't really related to the wedding or my mother, but it was still interesting news nonetheless. "Did the girl run off to find her brother?"

"Unlikely. They both disappeared at the same time."

I shook my head, unsure what to make of it. "Hopefully they turn up soon."

"I'll try to contact you again soon, let you know what's going on around the palace," Taryn said. "It might be easier than you contacting me."

I nodded. "Be safe, Taryn."

"You as well, Your Highness." Her face disappeared.

I stayed at the tree, thinking about everything Taryn had told me. A snapping branch caused my head to jerk up. Feeling for my dagger, I realized that I had left it at the camp. I tried to survey my surroundings, but in the dim moonlight there wasn't much I could see. Someone stepped toward me.

"Allayne?"

"Beyan! Did you... were you following me?" Had he heard any part of my conversation with Taryn?

"You've been gone for at least three quarters of an hour. I told you I'd come looking for you if you were gone too long," he chastised me.

I exhaled slowly, trying to calm myself down. "You're right. I'm sorry. Let's go back," I said.

As we started to head back to camp, Beyan asked, "Can you create a light?"

I obliged, and we walked in silence for a while. In the glow of the magical sphere, I studied Beyan's face. So young, and yet in many ways he seemed so much older than Rhyss, Farrah, or me.

Beyan broke the silence. "What?"

"Huh?"

"You're staring at me. What is it?"

"Oh." Flustered, I stalled for time. "I was just wondering... when do you think we'll find Joichan?"

Beyan didn't answer me right away. Then, "It depends. You've seen the dragons flying overhead; technically we're in fire dragon country. They usually don't live near the kingdoms, for obvious reasons. Except for Joichan, apparently. Being so close to so many dragons is difficult. I can feel the pull of their magic, and since they're fire dragons, my body is constantly overheated."

"That's what it was!" I had seen the obvious signs, but hadn't pieced it all together.

Beyan nodded. "Every seeker's ability works differently, but the way it affects me is that I not only feel drawn to dragons, but I somehow mirror their essence. So if it's an ice dragon I'm seeking, I feel the chill. And if it's fire..."

"I can imagine that's extremely unpleasant."

"It was, when I was younger and untrained. I'm able to control the feelings better now. But every so often, the sensations can get a little... intense."

"If you're sensing every dragon in the area, how will you find Joichan?"

"Every dragon has a magical signature, even if they share a common essence. Luckily, my father told me how to spot Joichan's signature. But it's been a long time... We have to hope that Joichan still lives in the same place, or nearby."

"If you don't mind my asking..." I started.

"You're wondering why I said I'd take you to find Joichan?" Beyan finished.

"Yes. I mean, besides the money you'll receive in the end. I got the sense that if it was any other dragon I wanted to find, you wouldn't have taken the job." I trailed off, wondering if I had offended Beyan. "We don't have to discuss it if you don't want to."

Beyan drew in a deep breath. "No, you're right. I specifically wanted to find this dragon. Need to find him. It's not exactly a secret. It's just not something I like to be reminded of."

We had just about reached the camp. Beyan stopped suddenly, grabbing my arm to stop me from moving forward.

"What — ?" I began.

"Shh." He motioned me to silence. In a low voice, he hissed, "Extinguish the light."

Hastily, I brought my palms together and the light instantly went out. Beyan whispered, "There's someone at the camp. Come on."

He moved forward, so stealthily I couldn't hear his footsteps. In the near dark I couldn't follow his movements with my eyes. Cursing him mentally, I carefully picked my way after him, hoping I would be able to stay just as silent.

In the embers of the firelight I could see some shadowed figures moving through our camp. I quickly counted four individuals. I eyed my pack in the distance, wishing I hadn't left my dagger in my bag. Even if I wasn't as adept with a weapon as the others, I would have felt a lot better with one in my hand.

Heart beating fast, I could feel the blood pounding behind my temples as I tried to calm my breathing. Panicking wouldn't help any of us now.

And then I saw a glint of metal as the moonlight reflected off the upraised knife one of the intruders held. Blade raised high, he was about to slit the throat of the sleeping Farrah.

There was a whistle of air to my right, little dull flashes of light, and then a strangled gargle from the man as he fell to the side. Beyan straightened from his throwing stance and ran into the camp, any pretense of quiet discarded. I ran after him.

Immediately alert, Farrah and Rhyss both jumped out of their bedrolls. Rhyss grabbed for his sword, barely parrying a blow from another bandit. Farrah pointed at the fire pit, and the blaze roared to life, illuminating the area and exposing the men who had snuck into our camp. Our horses, still tied to the trees, neighed in alarm at the sudden movements. Looking around, I tried to assess the situation.

Rhyss seemed evenly matched with the assailant who had engaged him in combat. Even though Farrah had said her magic was useless in a fight, she had a dagger in her hand and she and Beyan were harrying another thief. A man lay unmoving by the fire pit, having had the misfortune of meeting Beyan's knife.

That left one thief unaccounted for. Where was he?

A hand grabbed my arm. I shrieked. The bandit smiled at me, his grin revealing a row of dirty teeth. His unkempt and wild hair matched his equally disheveled clothes. I tried to tug my arm away, but the more I pulled, the harder his grip became.

"Ooh, a feisty one," he leered. His breath was as disgusting as his clothes. "Don't put up a fight, pretty, and I promise it'll go easier on you."

He grabbed at the front of my dress. The collar and part of the bodice ripped, revealing my gold necklace with its moonstone pendant. In the light of the fire, the jewel glowed unnaturally.

"What's this?" The man eyed my necklace with interest. I tried to kick him, but failed to make contact as he easily sidestepped my blows. Greedily, his filthy fingers reached out toward the pendant.

I shouted. Not a spell; I wasn't thinking straight enough for that. I just knew I did *not* want this man getting a hold of my necklace. It was more than a pretty bauble. It was a part of me, part of my soul, and I couldn't risk losing it to him or to anyone.

And yet, even though I was yelling incoherently, something happened. The man stopped mid-reach and looked at his hand — the one gripping my arm — in horror. His fingers were bright red and smelled like smoke. The color traveled into his hand, up his arm, blanketing his whole body. His terrified eyes met my equally alarmed ones right before he burst into flames that quickly consumed him. Within moments, all that remained of him was a sorry pile of ash at my feet.

The entire camp went deathly silent. Stopped in mid-fight, both my friends and our foes were staring at me. I stared back at them, then at the ashes. Did that really just happen? And had I truly been the cause of it?

Turning toward my friends, I took a step forward. I didn't know what I would do — grab my weapon? try doing deliberate magic? run away? — but when I broke the spell by moving, the other bandits dropped their weapons, their packs, and anything else they were holding in their hands, and fled into the forest. Part of me felt empowered, like nothing could stand against me. And part of me wanted to call after the men, even though they had threatened our lives, and tell them I wasn't normally like this.

Except I didn't know what was normal anymore.

Chapter Eighteen

THE BLOOD WAS STILL pounding in my ears, not from adrenaline, but from worry. My friends were still frozen in place where they had been when the bandits ran off. I looked at each of them in turn. Farrah looked thoughtful; Rhyss looked a little frightened, but also excited. Beyan's expression was hardest to read.

Rhyss broke the tension by shaking his head in amazement and saying, "Wow, Allayne. Didn't know you had it in you."

I laughed, shakily. "Me neither."

"You saved us," he said more seriously. "We were barely holding our own against those men until you did that. Scared them right off."

I nodded and shrugged numbly. I didn't feel much like a hero.

Farrah crossed over to me and put her hands on my shoulders. Studying my face, she asked, "Are you okay?"

"I... I think so."

She shook her head. "I don't think so. I think you're in shock."

"Maybe? I don't know? I've never done that before."

"Never used your magic in that way?"

"Never... never killed someone."

Farrah pulled me into a hug. "It is unsettling," she agreed. "And it doesn't get easier if and when it happens again. But you weren't doing it in cruelty or malice. You were defending yourself. That man would have robbed you, or worse, if you hadn't used your magic against him."

Or worse. I shuddered.

Farrah turned away and rummaged through her pack. Finding a shawl, she held it out to me. Wordlessly, I took it and wrapped it around myself, willing it to be armor against my jumbled emotions instead of just flimsy fabric.

"What *did* you do, exactly?" Beyan asked.

"I'm honestly not sure," I admitted. My fingers grasped the pendant. There was no point in keeping it secret anymore, since the entire group had seen the bandit try to take it. "That man — " I tried not to look at the pile of ash " — wanted it, I didn't want him to have it, and the next thing I knew... well, you know."

Beyan tried to study the necklace without studying anything else about me, which was kind of hard, given that my dress was half torn. I appreciated his chivalry, and would have found the situation amusing if I wasn't so stunned by the night's events.

"A soulstone," Beyan said. "I didn't think there were any left. I thought they were just legends or fantasies."

Soulstone. When Beyan named the jewel around my neck, something settled into place in my heart. It made sense, the way my moonstone and I were tied together, the way I felt so strongly about it.

"Where did you get it?" Beyan asked me. I hesitated, trying to think of what I could say that would sound plausible but not give away any more secrets.

A slight breeze danced through the camp, stirring up the ash at my feet and blowing it past my face. I sneezed.

"You can satisfy your curiosity later," Farrah chided Beyan. "We have a few things to take care of first." To me, she asked, "You have a change of clothing, right?"

"Yes."

"Good. Go get it and change into it, and give me the dress you're wearing. I can fix the tear," she said. "I'll go with you as lookout."

Rhyss snorted. Farrah shot him a dirty look. I relaxed a little. At least things were beginning to get back to normal.

"And you two boys can clean up the camp," she said, indicating the items lying around from the bandits' flight.

"If I wanted someone to boss me around, I would have brought my mother," Rhyss said, but he started picking up weapons and putting them in a pile by the fire. Beyan retrieved his knife from the fallen bandit and cleaned it off.

I went to my pack to get my other dress. My dagger was on top of all my other things, and I slipped it into my boot, determined never to go anywhere without it again. Farrah and I went into the forest just at the edges of our camp, and I quickly changed into my new dress. Farrah took my ripped gown from my arms as we walked back.

While Farrah stitched by the firelight, I helped Rhyss gather the bandits' things, returning the items they had stolen from us and going through their bags to see what spoils we had gained. Beyan took care of the more distasteful tasks, sweeping the ash out of the area and dragging the dead bandit away from the camp and into the forest.

Our chores finished, Beyan and Rhyss joined Farrah and me by the fire. Farrah had put her sewing tools away, and we both sat starting at the bounty left by the bandits. They had apparently robbed other camps before ours, as their bags were full of money, small valuables, and food. Knowing that others may have died in their nighttime ambushes, I felt a little better about what had happened.

Rhyss let out a slow whistle. "Nice," he commented. "Raises for everyone?" He raised his eyebrows at Beyan.

Beyan shook his head. "It's blood money. I'd feel bad keeping it."

"It's not like we can give it back," Farrah pointed out.

"True," Beyan said. He sighed. "We needed some supplies anyway. We're running low on food, but I don't necessarily trust what's in the bandits' bags. And we should probably outfit ourselves better before facing Joichan. I suppose we could use the money that way."

"It's a gift from the gods, I say," Rhyss said. "We shouldn't deny their bounty. It would only make them mad."

Farrah snorted. "Superstitious nonsense." Her Faerie heritage didn't easily lend itself to religious beliefs, as some humans actually revered the Fae and practiced rituals to either appease or entice them.

Farrah had once commented, during one of our conversations on magic and heritage, that it was hard to believe in a deity of any sort when she was, in theory, supposedly part deity herself. "It's kind of weird to believe in yourself," she had told me.

"Say what you will," Rhyss said loftily. "It's a sign. We should use it to bribe the dragon."

"Maybe," Beyan said. "But from the stories I've heard, I don't think Joichan is so easily swayed."

Now that everything was in order, Rhyss and Farrah settled back into their bedrolls. I made no move to go to sleep. Beyan looked at me curiously.

"I'm still too jittery to sleep," I said. "I can keep watch, if you like."

Beyan laughed. "Somehow, I don't think they'll be coming back, but we should keep a watch anyway."

He kindly didn't say that it was because of my leaving, and him coming after me, that the camp had been left undefended in the first place. Still, I felt the shame of it acutely.

Farrah yawned. "Fighting always makes me sleepy. Or hungry," she said. "Wake me up after a few hours, I'd be happy to take over."

"Okay," I said, knowing I probably would let her sleep through the night. Rhyss was already lightly snoring.

Beyan moved closer to me and threw a twig into the fire, although it was still burning brightly from Farrah's magic. It sparked and crackled, becoming charred within seconds. The ash from the burned twig wafted into the air, reminding me of the fight with the bandit again.

To distract myself, I said, "I believe, before all the excitement, we were discussing something. Why you wanted to find Joichan."

"Oh, yes," Beyan said. He threw another twig into the fire pit, staring at the dancing flames as if they held the answers to all of my questions. Or, perhaps, his. "Let's see. Where do I begin."

Chapter Nineteen

BEYAN'S STORY RIGHTLY began with Kye, around the time Beyan was born. As Kye had told me, their family had a strong legacy of dragon seeking, going back five generations or more. Because of this, by the time Kye started his career, their family was firmly established as the premier seekers in their field, and were very wealthy as a result. It was a big legacy to live up to, but every seeker in their line had proven themselves up to the task.

When Joichan (supposedly) imprisoned my mother, Kye was in Orchwell. His wife had just given birth to a baby boy and Kye was looking forward to taking some time off to spend time with his growing family. In the nearby kingdom of Calia, the king (or, my grandfather) was desperately seeking knights, princes, or other nobles who were willing to face the dragon and save Princess Melandria.

Over the next two years, while the Calian king threw whoever-was-willing at the dragon, Kye stayed close to Orchwell and his family, taking small, local commissions and proudly watching Beyan grow.

And then the knight Hendon rescued the princess and drove Joichan from the kingdom and everyone was supposed to live happily ever after.

Except that it didn't work out that way.

Three more years passed. The knight and the princess were married shortly after she was rescued, and had a baby girl (me). The king of Calia died peacefully, happy that his beloved daughter was safe and the kingdom's future was secure. Sir

Hendon and Princess Melandria became the new king and queen of Calia, and the baby princess (well, I) was a chubby toddler, getting into all sorts of mischief.

It was around this time that Kye received an interesting visitor, a man who claimed to represent King Hendon of Calia. Kye, the famed dragon seeker of Orchwell, was being summoned to an audience with the king. Kye saddled his horse and rode back with the Calian ambassador, where he met with King Hendon — in private.

Things were, for the most part, going well in Calia. The king and queen were beloved of their people, the kingdom was relatively peaceful, and everyone loved the little princess.

But as the princess grew, King Hendon had noticed something strange about her. Random, unexplained things happened in her presence. She'd be crying fiercely but suddenly quiet down. When her parents looked in on her she was playing with a new doll, but they could have sworn her hands were empty. Or, another odd event: The princess would refuse to eat her dinner, no matter how much her nursemaid would try to cajole her. The nursemaid would turn away for a second, and when she turned back, the princess was happily eating her meal — which had changed from watery porridge to a sweet custard.

And, finally, the most disturbing thing of all: King Hendon swore that the young princess's eyes gleamed with a golden metallic sheen. But when he looked again, all he would see staring back at him were the innocent, big dark brown eyes of the princess.

The king hadn't spoken of his concerns to his queen. But he wondered if, during her imprisonment, the dragon Joichan had somehow enchanted Melandria so all her children would be cursed. He refused to have any more children by her if they were all going to suffer from this same oddness.

King Hendon spun a story about wanting to send envoys to seek an audience with the dragon Joichan, who was widely known in the Gifted Lands as a being of wisdom with a deep understanding of humanity. The king hoped that the dragon could give insight on an important matter related to the future of Calia, one that had stumped all of the king's advisers. It was close enough to the truth, but King Hendon omitted one important detail: Because he thought Joichan had tainted his queen with a curse, he wanted revenge. And he was determined to use Kye to get it, even if it meant Kye's ruin.

A seeker's job is to lead someone to something, or to find something or someone. But such an amazing gift has a dark side to it as well. The seeker's ability was never meant to be used for violence; to do so would be a perversion of their innate ability. If their ability was used for harm against the person or creature being sought, the darkness of the deed could possibly rebound and hurt the seeker as well. The seeker could go insane. Or worse. Only a conscienceless monster would request a seeker's services for violent purposes. The majority of Kye's commissions were from scholars who wanted to study dragons, or people who sought the creatures' wisdom and secrets. Any dragon hunters were promptly turned away.

Kye felt something was off about this commission — King Hendon seemed a little too eager, his eyes shining with a touch of mania as he talked. Kye also did not like the look of the four men that the king insisted would accompany Kye on the journey. The king said they were just ordinary Calian citizens who were good in a fight, but Kye could tell from the way they carried themselves that they were trained Calian soldiers, downplaying their skills for some reason.

The king offered Kye enough money that Kye could have easily retired immediately after the search and supported his family comfortably for the rest of his days.

And one does not say no to a king, especially a king like Hendon.

So Kye accepted the commission. He rode back to Orchwell, prepared for the trip, gathered his team, and said goodbye to his family. No one was worried — this was Kye of Orchwell, was it not? The greatest dragon seeker of five generations. He had never failed a commission.

Besides the four disguised Calian soldiers, Kye's group consisted of three trusted, loyal men and women that often accompanied him on his seeking journeys. It wasn't unusual for the patron or the patron's ambassador to travel with the seeker, but the Calian soldiers made Kye and his team uneasy.

After nine days of traveling, the dragon's lair appeared in the distance. Kye breathed a silent sigh of relief. Soon his part in this odd, off-putting quest would be over.

They reached the cave, expecting to find a dragon. Instead, there was a young man right outside the cave, checking some snares nearby. He stood up as the group approached, calm but wary.

"Hello, gentlemen, ladies," the man said. "What business brings you here today?"

"We could ask you the same thing," one of the soldiers-in-disguise snarled. "What fool tries to hunt near a dragon's cave? There'd be no game for miles. And you'd end up being the dragon's meal, instead."

"And a good day to you too," the man answered politely, as if the guard hadn't insulted him. He pushed his honey-brown hair from his face. "So then, you are here to find Joichan? Do you seek his wisdom, or his head?"

"His wisdom, of course," Kye said immediately. One of the Calian men snorted rudely. Kye turned to him, wary. "That *is* why King Hendon sent you, isn't it?"

The young man, hearing the king's name, stiffened. "You are here on behalf of King Hendon of Calia?"

"What does it matter to you, stranger?" the soldier asked.

Impatiently, a second soldier pointed his blade at the strange young man. "We don't have time for this. Either leave and let us be about our business, or we'll kill you where you stand."

The young man's demeanor changed. It was a subtle shift: from polite fellow traveler to… something else. Something menacing. A force to fear. He remained motionless, eyes locked with the soldier who had him at sword point. Yet even though it was the soldier who had the advantage, something about the changed young man made the soldier's sword waver.

The whole group tensed, silent and watchful.

"If you're here to kill the dragon, I'd reconsider. He's not one to be trifled with." The young man's eyes flashed. His deep brown eyes suddenly glinted gold, bright and hot as fire. Years later, Kye would remember this moment and question if what he saw was true, or if it was just the adrenaline playing tricks on his eyes.

"Thanks for the advice." The first soldier's tone changed from sarcastic to threatening. "Now leave of your own accord, or we'll help you leave this world permanently."

"I'll go," said the young man quietly. "But remember my warning, and know that anything that befalls you is on your heads alone."

He turned and walked away, disappearing beyond the cave.

The second soldier sheathed his sword, muttering, "He's lucky I didn't run him through."

The first soldier turned to Kye, motioning toward the cave. "The dragon must be in there. You're the seeker. Go in first and secure him. Then we'll come in and finish the job."

"Secure him?" Kye looked from his team to the Calian soldiers. "Finish the job? What do you mean?"

The soldier laughed, an unpleasant sound. "Stupid man. We're to bring back the beast's head for the king. He can stuff it and mount it on the wall behind the throne, or make a cape out of the dragon's hide and wear it around the castle, for all I care."

"No! You can't kill the dragon!"

"Those are our orders. And there will be no payment for you unless you bring back proof of the dragon's death to the king."

"This is not what we agreed to!"

Before anyone could blink, the first soldier grabbed one of the women in Kye's group and held a knife to her throat. "If you won't help us take down the dragon, then your usefulness to us is at its end."

Kye and his group moved to save their friend, but suddenly found themselves staring at the points of several swords. They were quickly disarmed. Kye's friends were secured to a tree outside the cave where they wouldn't get in the way. One soldier was left behind to guard them.

Kye, held at sword point, would accompany the rest of the soldiers into the cave to help them locate and kill the dragon. If Kye betrayed them in any way, his friends' lives would be forfeit.

The soldiers, with Kye in tow, moved toward the entrance of Joichan's lair. But before they could step into the coolness of the cave, a great shadow blotted out the sun overhead. The wind stirred up leaves and dust around them; the ground quaked and nearly jolted the men off their feet. As quickly as the commotion had started, it ended abruptly, leaving a deafening silence in its wake. As one, the soldiers fearfully turned to see the cause of the disturbance.

Joichan had come.

Chapter Twenty

THE SOLDIERS STOOD shaking in the long shadow cast by the massive dragon. At least five times bigger than the tallest man among them, the massive dragon tilted his golden head back and roared, deafening the trembling humans before him as he breathed a long slash of fire into the sky. Sunlight skipped off the edges of his scales, making him glow with a blinding brightness.

One of the soldiers, sweat pouring down his brow from the heat, thrust Kye's weapon at him, indicating frantically that Kye was to help the soldiers take down the dragon. Kye barely caught it in hands slick with his own nervous perspiration. He darted quick looks between the dragon, the soldiers, and his friends.

Swords and shields at the ready, the soldiers held their ground, if a bit unsteadily. There was no longer any pretense about who they were — some of King Hendon's finest and fiercest soldiers. But while they were hardened fighters, very few are prepared to fight a full-grown dragon in its prime.

Joichan roared again, as if in warning. He turned his metallic eyes, as golden as his hide, on the soldiers, waiting. Toying with his prey.

While the soldiers and the dragon silently sized each other up, Kye surreptitiously edged his way toward his friends.

Still the silence. Still the waiting. Then, letting out a yell, one of the soldiers charged.

Joichan bared his teeth as the rest of the group joined the fray. The soldier guarding Kye's friends ran to help his comrades.

While their attention was on the dragon, Kye ran to the tree and cut one of his friends loose. Together, they frantically worked on freeing the rest of their team.

The battle between humans and dragon continued. While Joichan was powerful and cunning, four trained fighters were able to hold their own against him. Blood had been spilled on both sides: a claw graze on one man, a cut on Joichan's hide. But both sides were evenly matched, making it a battle of attrition, not of strength.

Kye paused for a brief moment to survey the scene. His eyes met the dragon's golden ones; even though Joichan was frightening in his magnificence, Kye's fear melted away. Perhaps the dragon had hypnotized him? He couldn't be sure.

Another of Kye's friends broke free of her bonds, drawing the dragon's attention. Joichan snorted, somewhat confused as he glanced between the soldiers and Kye's team tied to the tree. One of the soldiers followed Joichan's eyes to spot Kye by the tree, where he had finished cutting the ropes of the last captive. The soldier let out a yell and ran toward the tree.

"Come back!" his fellow soldier shouted after him. "We need to take care of the dragon first!"

"And let these ones stab us in the back while we're distracted? I'll take care of them quickly enough!" Having reached the tree, the man raised his sword to strike.

Kye barely had enough time to raise his weapon to block the soldier's attack. The soldier was relentless, continuing the onslaught as Kye desperately tried to defend himself.

One of Kye's friends had found his weapon and jumped in, hoping to sneak in a strike. But his blow was easily deflected. The soldier ran Kye's friend through with his sword and returned to attacking Kye without missing a beat.

With only three soldiers focused on the dragon, the contest shifted. Joichan was gaining ground and inflicting more injuries on the soldiers, who were yelling for their comrade to come back and help them.

Hearing his friend scream as he fell under the soldier's blade, a horrified Kye looked his way. Kye's arm faltered a bit. He looked back to see his opponent raise his sword for a killing blow.

Then Joichan stepped forward and batted his mighty claw between the two men. Kye felt himself sail through the air, his back hitting the tree, the air rushing out of his body with a *whoosh*. He tried to get up, but everything hurt too much. Before he blacked out, he felt a rush of heat and heard, one last time, Joichan's fearsome roar.

BEYAN'S FATHER WOKE up in a hostel, as a kindly middle-aged woman was changing the dressing on his leg. Her clinical, dispassionate manner — and her plain, serviceable black-and-white uniform — marked her as one who had taken religious vows.

"You're finally awake," she commented when she saw his open eyes.

"Where am I?" He tried to sit up, turning his head to look around. An intense headache instantly blossomed in his skull, and he sank back down, groaning.

"You're in the Monastery of the Silver Rose." The nun finished her ministrations on Kye's leg, and handed him a steaming cup of tea that smelled strongly like feverfew. "Drink this for your head. I wouldn't try to move too much, if I were you." She threw the dirty bandages in a basket by the bed. "You were roughed up something fierce when you came here. I daresay it will be at least a week or two before you can even *think* about moving about."

"What happened?" Kye asked.

While the nun didn't know what had happened after Kye lost consciousness, she did know that his friends had brought him to the monastery. He eventually convinced her he was strong enough for them to visit, and then he was able to piece together the strange and sorry event between the band of travelers and the dragon.

The fight between King Hendon's men and the dragon Joichan ended soon after Kye had lost consciousness. The soldiers had been burned by Joichan's flame; Kye wondered why the dragon hadn't just breathed fire on everyone immediately and killed them all right away. The fight finished, the dragon had shot straight up, into the air, and had flown away.

Of the original four in Kye's group, one comrade had fallen during the fight, and one — Kye himself — was injured. Kye had hit his head against the tree when Joichan had swept him aside. His leg had landed underneath him, twisting at an unnatural angle. The leg would heal, but would forever be deformed and unusable.

As she had predicted, a little over a week passed before the nun declared Kye well enough to travel. He and his friends made their slow, sad way back home. His companions stayed in Orchwell, but Kye continued on to Calia, determined to collect payment on this commission and put the whole sorry affair behind him.

As he relayed his tale to King Hendon, Kye was met with a thoughtful silence from the impenetrable monarch. Even when Kye mentioned that all of the king's soldiers had perished, there was no reaction from the king. When Kye finished his story, the king's silence stretched out so long that Kye's ears rang from the lack of sound.

Then: "What of the dragon?"

"Joichan still lives, Your Majesty," Kye said. "My companions and I are not fighters, nor do we ever harm those that we are commissioned to seek."

The king locked eyes with Kye. Kye held still, afraid to move, to breathe, to blink. The king looked up at his guards and said, almost lazily, "Throw him out."

The guards moved toward Kye and grabbed his arms. "Wait!" Kye shouted. "What about payment? I was promised — "

"*You* were promised? You *broke* your promise, to me," said the king.

"I did not!" Kye said. "I led your men to Joichan, as I said I would."

"I wanted Joichan's head, but you failed to deliver."

"That wasn't what you told me the task truly was!"

The silence following Kye's outburst lay heavily on the room. The king's icy glare pinned Kye where he stood in the grip of the guards.

"Are you saying I lied?" King Hendon's voice was too calm, too even.

"N—no, sire. I just — "

"Four men dead, and you couldn't even give me what I wanted," the king said. "I should have you killed, but your paltry life is hardly compensation for my men."

Kye held his breath, sure his life was now forfeit.

The king waved his hand as if Kye were an annoying gnat. Easily swatted away. Easily crushed. "But I'm feeling kind today. It could have been the dungeon for you, but instead, I'm just going to banish you from my kingdom. If you ever set foot in Calia again, you will be killed immediately. Farewell."

The guards forcefully turned Kye around and began to march him out of the throne room. The doors shut behind him with a sickening finality. Kye was escorted to the gates of Calia with a stern reminder of the king's decree. Despondent, he returned home to his family.

"EVEN THOUGH I WAS A child, I knew something was wrong the minute my father stepped through the door," Beyan said. "And it was like our fortunes changed overnight. Bad luck followed us wherever we went."

Without the money from King Hendon's commission, Kye was unable to pay his team, but he insisted on it anyway. Out of his personal fortune, he gave them their wages, plus an additional stipend to make up for the trouble the group had encountered. He also made sure to compensate the family of his fallen friend.

Word of the Joichan campaign spread, fueled by a vengeful King Hendon. Jobs became scarce. Of the ones that were offered, completing them became an arduous task, since Kye's injured leg hindered him from traveling easily. The family's fortune started to dwindle, and Beyan's mother became ill. They spent all they could — more than they could afford — for medicine to help her, but her condition steadily worsened.

As the next dragon seeker, all of the family's hopes rested on Beyan. Despite his youth, Kye began taking his son with him on jobs, relying on Beyan for assistance and training him in the field.

"I loved seeking, I excelled at it," Beyan said. "But I also felt like I was carrying an immense weight around all the time. There was so much pressure on me to restore the family name. Find the dragon, complete the commission, get the money. Help my mother get the medicine she needed or help my father with some seeking-related task he could no longer do. I grew to hate my abilities, even as I started getting more prominent in my position."

The sky was beginning to lighten; we'd been up for hours talking. Soon Rhyss and Farrah would be up and we'd have to break camp and continue on. But I didn't feel tired, just riveted by Beyan's story.

I lightly touched his shoulder. "I'm sorry," I said. Beyan smiled sadly in response.

"Sometimes I just feel consumed by hate," he said. "I hate that my father is a shell of who he once was. I hate feeling guilty over wishing things were different. I hate King Hendon for ruining my family with his evil and impossible task, for putting my father in such a horrible position and then punishing my family for the failure of his men."

"Do you hate Joichan?" I asked. "I know he injured your father, but it seems to me he actually saved your father's life, by getting him out of the way before he roasted those soldiers."

"He could have done it in a less brutal manner," Beyan said. "But a feral beast isn't capable of rational thought."

I held my tongue, not wanting to give away my secret accidentally in defense of Joichan.

Beyan gazed into the fire, thinking. Finally: "Yes. Yes, I hate Joichan too. He's the reason this all started in the first place. If he hadn't attacked Calia... if my father hadn't had to go find him... if he hadn't swept my father aside with his claw.... Then everything would be different. *I'd* be different.

"I understand that, even after all this time, King Hendon still is offering a sizable bounty for proof that the dragon has been destroyed. I despise the king, true. But I would happily bring Joichan's head to him, on a silver platter and with ribbons tied to the dragon's horns, if it meant my family's fortunes would be restored. And that's what I intend to do."

Chapter Twenty-One

BEYAN FINISHED HIS tale just as the sun peeked over the horizon. It was still too dark in the growing dawn for Beyan to see the horrified expression on my face. Not that he was looking at me. He was still staring into the dying embers of the fire, lost in the memories of his childhood.

While his story rightly saddened and revulsed me, I was also strangely drawn to his passion. He was willing to risk his sanity, his future, and even his life if it meant he could help his father and possibly restore his family to its former glory.

My mother had sent me to Beyan's father for help, unaware of the misfortune that had befallen Kye and his family. I now had to rely on Beyan to help me find my father. And yet, Beyan wanted to *kill* my father. What should I do?

A lone traveler would be an easy target for bandits on the road. The events of the night could occur again, and without the help of my companions I knew I wouldn't survive a similar encounter. So, I would stay with the group. For now. Maybe once we got closer to Annlyn I could strike off on my own to find Joichan. Surely it would be easy enough to find a giant dragon in the area.

As I mulled it over, I found I was reluctantly embracing the idea of breaking away from my group. Aside from the safety of traveling with them, I also genuinely liked them. Rhyss with his sarcastic comments and happy-go-lucky nature. Compassionate Farrah, who had become an invaluable teacher. And Beyan....

I pushed the thought away as one of our sleeping companions stirred and opened her eyes. Farrah sat up slowly, still in a drowsy haze, and saw us sitting by the now-cold fire. "Why didn't you two wake me?" she asked with a yawn. "Did either of you get any sleep at all?"

"We're fine," Beyan dodged the question. Farrah looked at me quizzically. I shrugged.

"What's the plan for today?" Farrah asked. "We're getting close to Joichan's cave, aren't we?"

"I believe so," Beyan said. "It's probably within a day's ride from here, but we've been on the road for so long, I think it would be best if we went to Annlyn and refreshed our supplies." Annlyn, as the southernmost of the Gifted Lands, had always seemed so mysterious and exotic to me. The citizens of Annlyn were rumored to be a people of intuition. Not fortune tellers, exactly, and definitely not charlatans. But they were very wise, and able to see things about you that you didn't know about yourself. Since the kingdoms of Calia and Annlyn were so distant from each other, we rarely had visitors from there. Beyan's announcement filled me with anticipation; I would finally get to see this famed land for myself.

Soon after, Rhyss woke up and we quickly broke camp and set off. We didn't have to go far. A short ride later, our little group had arrived in Annlyn. We dismounted and left our horses at a stable just inside the gates, making sure to grab our packs for our walk around the kingdom's capital city.

The first thing I noticed about it was how serene and calming it was. Cool gray, white, and black stone lined the streets, climbed up the buildings, and set off the tinkling fountains that flowed practically everywhere. Marveling at all the water I saw, I realized we were standing in a literal oasis in the hot and steamy south. It seemed like all of Annlyn was out enjoying the day; we were surrounded by crowds of people in the streets, on errands or visiting with each other.

The second thing I noticed were the Calian riders.

Even though they weren't arrayed as the ones I had seen a few weeks past, opting for plain saddles instead of official Calian trappings, I knew who they were the minute I spotted them. Carefully picking their way through the crowds, they were watching the passersby a little too closely. I shrunk into myself, wishing I had thought to wear my headscarf, hoping they would overlook me.

Rhyss was oblivious as always, but Beyan and Farrah both noticed my apprehension and gave me funny looks. Farrah opened her mouth, about to say something, but Beyan spoke first. "My father said that usually there's a market in the city center. We can probably find most of the the things we need there."

"What *do* we need?" Farrah asked. "Besides food."

"I need to get my knife repaired," Rhyss said. Farrah smirked. Rhyss's knife handle had broken from the blade a few nights ago while he was skinning a rabbit for dinner. The incident had caused endless teasing from Farrah, who thought it was hilarious that of all the reasons for Rhyss's weapon to break, it was for something so innocuous.

"Or, you could just buy a new one altogether," Farrah said. "That knife was ancient. I'm surprised it hasn't broken earlier."

"We'll see," Rhyss said. "It may be old, but it's my favorite."

"The blade is rusty," Farrah pointed out. "And — "

"Let's head to the market, then." Beyan interrupted them before they could start bickering. Without waiting for a response, he strode away, forcing us to hurry after him to keep up.

As we walked through the city, I noticed a third thing: there were animals everywhere. A dog or two here, or even a goat or cow. I supposed that made sense. People would have pets, or have farms.

But then I spotted other animals. A baby elephant, wobbly on its chubby legs. A tiger, sleek and majestic. On the other side of the street, a flash of twisted white antlers caught my eye. I saw an elk walking sedately alongside a gray wolf.

What was going on here?

I rubbed my eyes, thinking they were playing tricks on me. But when I looked again, I still saw all the animals — many who definitely weren't native to this area — all around me.

"Hey," I said, grabbing Beyan's sleeve to slow him down. I motioned to Rhyss and Farrah to come closer and lowered my voice. "Do you see that?"

"See what?" Beyan asked, looking around.

Surreptitiously, I nodded my head in the direction of the elk and the wolf, who were just to our left. "Over there." As one, all three of them looked over to where I had indicated. "Don't be so obvious!" I hissed.

Farrah shook her head. "I don't get it," she said. "What are we trying to see?"

"You don't see them? Any of them?" I asked. "There are animals everywhere."

"So? We're in a city," Rhyss pointed out. "There are bound to be stray dogs and cats and such running around."

"Not dogs and cats," I said. "Wolves and elephants and elk and tigers and none of them are scared of each other."

Beyan surveyed the city again, more carefully this time. "I'm still not seeing anything unusual," he finally said.

"You feeling okay?" Farrah asked me. "I know you didn't get much sleep last night. Maybe it's just exhaustion?"

I didn't think that was it, but I didn't want to argue further, or my friends would think I was crazy. So I just nodded and let Beyan continue leading our group to the market. Walking faster, I peeked up ahead and saw the elk and the wolf still walking together a few feet ahead of us. The two animals stopped moving. Suddenly, the wolf winked out, and in its place was a man.

I gasped. My friends nearby didn't react, but somehow the man heard me, even though there were distance and people between us. He glanced over at me, and I was struck by how much he resembled the wolf: shaggy pale hair and skin, and a lean, muscular body. Our eyes locked, and remained so as my group drew level with the man and his elk companion. The man studied me then smiled, walking away with the elk following.

My mind reeled with everything I had just witnessed. My companions kept walking, completely oblivious.

We reached the city center. The market was even more crowded than the streets had been. Stalls stretched as far as I could see in all directions. We could easily spend a day here and still not see everything the market had to offer. After being on the road for so long, I was drawn to the hustle and bustle of civilization and wanted to immerse myself in it.

The others must have been feeling the same way because Beyan said, "It will take us a few hours to get our errands done.

Why don't we just take our time here and stay in Annlyn for the night? We can get a good night's sleep, and it doesn't make sense to seek out Joichan in the dark, anyway."

Rhyss, Farrah, and I nodded in agreement. Farrah and Beyan decided to split up the list of needed supplies to cover more ground. I offered to help purchase supplies, but Beyan waved me away.

"Go enjoy the market," he said. "Let's all meet back here right before sunset; we can eat together and discuss our plans for tomorrow."

That decided, we went our separate ways. Rhyss went off to find a cutler. Beyan and Farrah disappeared in opposite directions. That left me, standing in the market square, taking it all in. Finally, I picked a direction and started walking.

For a while, I was lost in the scents and the colors and the noise. I didn't have the pack space for frivolous purchases, but I still marveled over the sparkling jewelry and carved trinkets. Perhaps I should buy a gift for Joichan for our first meeting? But I had no idea what a dragon could possibly want, especially from a human market.

After a while, I started to sense that I was being followed. It was just this odd prickly sensation I felt, like something wasn't quite right around me. I turned, but didn't see anyone. Maybe Farrah was right. Maybe I was just exhausted.

The row of stalls I was perusing ended up ahead, into a narrow alley that connected my part of the market with another. I turned the corner into the alley and stopped. The wolf man from earlier blocked my way.

Chapter Twenty-Two

THE WOLF-TURNED-MAN was tall, taller than I had thought from a distance. He pushed his shaggy hair out of his blue eyes. It was a light, light blond, so pale it was nearly white. But the white hair wasn't due to age; he looked to be in his early thirties.

"Hello," he said. He held both hands in front of him, palms up in a gesture of peace, and nodded his head toward me. I backed up, ready to run back the way I had come.

"Don't be afraid," the man said. His voice was gruff. He seemed reserved, yet alert, ready to spring into action if need be.

"What do you want?" I asked.

"I saw you earlier, watching me," he said. "You seemed very aware of what was going on in Annlyn. I found you... intriguing."

"Intriguing? How?"

He studied my wary face. "Come," he said, motioning down the alley.

I stayed put. "No, thank you."

"You've nothing to fear from me," he repeated. "We'll stay in the marketplace, in public. I'd just like to talk to you." When I didn't respond, he added, "I'll go ahead and meet you at the end of the alley, where the market stalls start again." He pointed ahead, the way I had originally intended to go.

"Why should I?" I said.

"Because I don't think you understand exactly what you were seeing," the man told me. "I can help you with that." He started to walk away, toward the continuing market.

I watched him leave, debating. My curiosity won out over my fear and I followed after him.

The long-haired man was waiting for me at a market stall not far from the alley exit. When he saw me, he smiled. "I'm glad you didn't leave," he said.

"I thought about it," I admitted. He laughed, a kind of wheezy barking sound.

We slowly started making our way through the market, stopping at various booths to look at the items for sale.

"What's your name?" he asked me. "I'm Pazho."

"Allayne."

"Allayne," he repeated. "That's not an Annlyn name, is it."

He looked at me closely. "I daresay Allayne is not your real name, either." He said it matter-of-factly, already knowing the answer.

How did this man know?

"No, I'm from Calia, in the north." I sidestepped his second observation.

"I traveled there once, years ago." Pazho studied me, if possible, even more intently than before. "It's all right. You may keep your secrets, Allayne. From Calia. Fascinating."

"What's so fascinating about that?" I asked, a bit snappishly.

We stopped at a booth that displayed simple gold jewelry. The pendants sold here reminded me of the necklace I wore hidden under my dress, but none of them were moonstone.

Pazho picked up one and held it to the light. The warm, honey-colored gem sparkled as it twisted in his hand. Oddly, I could feel a magical hum emanating from the piece.

"Do you know much about Annlyn?" Pazho asked.

"No. I've never traveled too far from my home country."

Pazho held the pendant to his eye level, the amber color of the gemstone catching some similar honey glimmer in his eyes. I felt an answering heat in my own eyes. He blinked, and the glow in his eyes was gone, replaced by the normal blue. He put the necklace down and we continued on our way. Involuntarily, I turned to look behind me at the amber pendant, now tucked among other pieces of jewelry on the merchant's table.

"Every one of the realms in the Gifted Lands is known for a special ability," he began. "We tell the world that ours is for crafting jewelry. But it's only a partial truth. Annlyn is a kingdom of shapeshifters. From infancy, we are able to turn into one kind of animal. As we grow, so does the animal. We share many of the traits and temperament of our other self."

So I hadn't been crazy! I really had seen various creatures walking the city streets.

"Why was I able to see you and other people in your animal forms, and my friends couldn't?" I asked.

"The kingdom has a layer of magic surrounding it that keeps our animal forms from being detected by outsiders," Pazho said. "Otherwise, we would never be able to shift freely. This way, visitors can enter, and trade can continue. But those of Annlyn can see each other in their shifted forms."

"But I'm not from Annlyn," I reminded him.

"Yes, it's very curious," Pazho said. "Which makes me think that you are a shapeshifter yourself."

Chapter Twenty-Three

STRUCK BY PAZHO'S WORDS, I stopped and considered it. Then I laughed. Me? A shapeshifter? I had never done that in my life; there was no reason, as an adult, I would suddenly have that ability.

I glanced over at Pazho. He looked sincere. And serious. My laughter ceased.

"What makes you so sure?" I asked him.

We resumed walking. "I've made the study of the Gifted Lands my life's work," he said. "I find the different facets of each kingdom, and the fact that we're all able to live together mostly in harmony, quite interesting. Of course, Annlyn being my home country, I know the most about it. Being able to change forms is a magical ability, one you are born with, not taught. One shapeshifter can easily spot another. Like calls to like."

"My friend Farrah is half Fae, half human. She has innate magic, like you. But she didn't see anything."

"While those of Faerie do possess magic naturally, very few of them can change their form. I would suspect your friend Farrah comes from a Faery who wasn't able to shift, and her human blood would dilute the magic further."

"I've never done it before," I said.

"Just because you haven't tried it doesn't mean you can't do it," Pazho pointed out. "I'm sure, with the right teacher or training, you'd learn how. Sometimes, in times of stress or excitement, your abilities may trigger without your knowledge or control, especially if you are still learning how to tap into your power."

I paused, thinking of the incidents on the road with the Calian soldiers and with Prince Anders at the inn. And the bandits. Pazho smiled at my sudden thoughtfulness.

"I could be wrong," he said. "But I don't think so. As I said, like calls to like."

We had reached another part of the market. Up ahead, I saw Beyan walking around, laden with new supplies for our group. I started walking faster, hoping to catch up to him. As if he knew I was following, Beyan turned and saw me. Our eyes met across the crowded market, and he nodded at me and started making his way toward me. Waving back in acknowledgment, I was just about to call his name when a tall shadow fell between us.

A horse nickered a few feet in front of me. Astride it was one of the Calian plain-clothes soldiers.

I abruptly checked my pace and instantly shrank back into the shadows. My new friend Pazho, who had been trying to keep up with me, nearly plowed into my back. He instantly caught my apprehension, but didn't say anything. Instead, his eyes narrowed as he observed me, then the lone rider.

Fortunately, the man was looking the opposite way and didn't notice me. But he did catch sight of Beyan, whose clothing and general look marked him as a foreigner to Annlyn. And when the soldier had cut off Beyan's path, Beyan had almost been trampled and had to rapidly juggle his purchases before he dropped something.

Beyan scowled. The rider didn't apologize. "You there." He addressed Beyan imperiously in a voice that carried across the marketplace. "You're not from here, are you?"

"What's it to you?" Beyan responded warily.

"I am looking for someone," the rider said, ignoring Beyan's tone. "A woman, nineteen years old, dark hair and eyes. Perhaps you've seen her on your travels? She's from Calia, like me, so if you talk to her we should sound similar."

"Why are you looking for this woman? What has she done?" Beyan asked. Their voices weren't particularly loud, yet somehow I was attuned to every word they exchanged.

"She is wanted in Calia, as she has stolen something from King Hendon. A gold necklace, with a milky white stone hanging from the chain. I have orders to bring her, and the item she has taken, back to the king as soon as she can be found."

The rider looked at Beyan, assessing. Temptingly, he added, "There is a very handsome reward for the person who knows her whereabouts."

Across the distance, Beyan's eyes locked on mine. I held my breath, afraid that he would give me away.

But then Beyan's gaze softened and his eyes continued to sweep the marketplace. He was so fast, most people would not have caught his momentary pause. I relaxed, only a little, hoping that Beyan's actions had drawn the rider's attention from where I was standing just a few feet away.

"I've met no one by that description, sir," Beyan told the rider. His tone was perfect: just the right touch of firmness and humility. The soldier inclined his head toward Beyan and turned his horse's head toward another part of the market.

"I must continue my search," the soldier said. "But if you see or hear of anything... remember the reward." He kicked his horse into motion, and they trotted away.

Once the soldier was out of sight, I stepped out of the shadows as Beyan walked over to me.

"What was that about?" he asked. "Why are there Calian soldiers looking for you?"

"It's hard to explain. But I didn't steal anything. The necklace was given to me by one who had the right to give it. If anything, King Hendon is the thief. I was told he stole it from its rightful owner, and it is my duty to bring it back."

"Who is the true owner?"

What could I say that wasn't an outright lie? I hated keeping secrets from the ones I counted as friends.

"A man, who lives somewhere in this area," I finally said. It wasn't the complete truth, but it was close enough.

Beyan opened his mouth to question me further, but I cut him off.

"Thank you," I said. "For not giving me away. For... a lot of things. Thank you."

Beyan shut his mouth, obviously changing his mind about what he was going to say. "We don't betray our own," he grinned at me. I smiled back.

Pazho stepped forward. Glancing from me to Beyan, he greeted Beyan with the same hands-out-palms-up gesture he had given me. "Hello, traveler. I am Pazho. You are a friend to this young woman?"

Beyan repeated Pazho's gesture. "My name is Beyan. Yes."

"I met Pazho in the marketplace after we all split up," I explained. "He's been explaining the history of the kingdom of Annlyn to me."

"That sounds fascinating," Beyan said sincerely. "I've only been in Annlyn once, when I was a child. I don't know much about the kingdom, and never had a chance to learn."

"We are such a remote kingdom that we tend to remain a mystery to the rest of the Gifted Lands," Pazho said. "Which, honestly, is the way we like it. But you and your friend Allayne seem to have an interesting story of your own, one which I would enjoy learning."

Beyan hesitated. "I don't think — "

"Are there more of you? Where are you staying?"

"We haven't secured rooms yet for the night," I said. "I don't think so, anyway?" Beyan shook his head, confirming my guess. "There's four of us total."

"Oh, then you must stay at the Red Antler Inn," Pazho said. "It is run by my mate, Denaan, and has the best food in all of Annlyn. You shall stay for free, in exchange for satisfying my curiosity."

"Thank you," I said.

"That's extremely generous of you," Beyan said. "But may I have a moment with my friend?"

"Of course," Pazho said. He pinned Beyan with a suddenly serious look. "I know you are wary, as is wise. But you have nothing to fear from me. I know what you seek, and I know how to help you." He walked away from us and into the marketplace, looking over some of the wares on display.

After he left, Beyan turned on me. "Did you tell him about why we're here?"

"No. He never asked me about our purpose, and I didn't bring it up. He's been explaining the magic of Annlyn to me. It's fascinating; I've learned a lot in just the short time we've been talking."

"Do you trust him?"

I studied Pazho, who was happily chatting with a merchant about some fruit. "Yes," I said simply. "Do you?"

Beyan looked at me, then over at Pazho, then back to me. He nodded slowly. "There's something odd about him," he mused. I bit my lip, trying not to blurt out Pazho's secret. I would leave that up to Pazho to disclose, if he wanted to. "But in spite of that — yes. He seems all right."

"And it's very nice of him to offer us a place to stay for the night," I said.

"It is," Beyan agreed. "Although after last night, we can definitely afford it."

"Save the money for the return trip home," I said. "Do something crazy, like hiring all of us griffins for the return trip. We'd be home in no time."

Beyan smiled. "I'll stick to the horses, thank you. I don't think flying would be for me."

"How would you know unless you've tried it?"

"A fair point. We'll see. But speaking of mounts — we'll have to stable our horses here for a day or two longer while we search for Joichan. Horses don't like dragons much. Although we might need to buy another horse or mule to bring home any treasure we might find."

I refrained from saying I would be worried about purchasing a horse in *this* market. I couldn't be sure the horse was actually a horse and not a human who could shift.

We walked over to Pazho, who smiled at us in greeting. "Well, then?"

"We appreciate your kind offer," Beyan said. "And we'd be happy to stay at your inn."

"My mate's," Pazho corrected. "And we're happy to have you. Come, let me take you to the Red Antler."

"We should probably go meet the others first," I said. "The light's already fading; I hope we're not too late meeting them."

"Where are you supposed to find them?" Pazho asked me.

"Just outside the city center, where the marketplace begins."

"Perfect. That's right where the Red Antler is. We'll gather your friends and all head to the inn for a meal."

As we headed out of the market, Beyan asked Pazho, "Red Antler? Where did that name come from?"

Pazho chuckled. "Denaan fancies himself a fierce warrior. Antlers dipped in blood, dominating over enemies, that sort of thing."

Beyan looked confused, but with a flash of understanding I caught Pazho's meaning. I had seen the wolf Pazho walking with an imposing elk earlier. That elk must be the form Pazho's mate Denaan was able to shift into.

As if he knew my thoughts, Pazho winked at me, giving me confirmation that my guess was correct.

Farrah and Rhyss were at the edge of the market, sitting on a bench. Farrah was reading a book, while Rhyss was lovingly polishing his newly repaired knife. As we approached, we could hear Farrah saying, "If you don't stop playing with that thing, you'll cut yourself, and I'll have to patch you up. And I'm not in the mood."

"But they did such a great job with the repair," Rhyss replied. "It's so nice to have it back, beautiful and whole."

"Rhyss, if you don't put that thing away, I'm going to take it from you."

"Farrah, I won't cut myself, I promise."

"Hey, you two." Beyan cut off their growing argument. "How was the market?"

Rhyss started in surprise and then yelped. Shaking his hand, he stared at the blood blossoming from the nick on his finger. The cut was clean, but deep. Farrah sighed and snapped her book shut in annoyance.

"I won't say 'I told you so,'" she said.

"You just did," Rhyss pointed out.

"Do you want me to heal this, or not?"

She held out her hand, and Rhyss meekly put his hand in hers. Frowning, she studied his finger.

"When you're done, we want to introduce you to someone," Beyan said mildly.

Farrah looked up from Rhyss's hand. The blood was gone. The wound was already closed, with a faint line to show where the cut had been. "All set," she announced. "That scar should fade in time. It wouldn't have even happened if someone hadn't interrupted me." She glared pointedly at Beyan.

"Someone's getting hungry," Rhyss said.

"Someone's already there," Farrah said.

"We'll eat soon," I promised. "Our new friend here has graciously offered us a place to stay for the night, and we'll eat there. Farrah, Rhyss, this is Pazho."

The three of them exchanged greetings, and then Pazho led the way to the Red Antler Inn. True to his word, the place was only a few feet away. As we entered, our eyes adjusting to the dim interior, a deep voice yelled, "Watch out!"

Something heavy and solid whizzed by my head.

Chapter Twenty-Four

THE OBJECT FLEW THROUGH the air, hit the wall, and then clanged to the ground, where it shattered into several sharp pieces.

Incredulous, I eyed the item. It had formerly been a mug, and if the colors and pattern were any indication, an expensive one.

Pazho called out, "Denaan, I've told you not to do that when the inn is open!"

A stocky man wearing a stained apron came into the room. "No one was in here. Well, not until you came in."

"If this is a bad time..." Beyan started.

"Nonsense, it's a great time," Denaan said. "When I'm frustrated, it really helps relieve the tension."

I could tell Beyan was trying to find a judicious way to get us out of here. I started to giggle. Farrah joined in. Rhyss tried to suppress a smirk.

Pazho shook his head. "This is Denaan's idea of testing for quality. He figures, if the dishes can be thrown around and still hold up, then they're worthy of being used at his inn."

"Of course," Denaan agreed. "I don't want to have to buy new dinnerware just because a few rowdy drunks decided to have a tussle."

"Elk logic," Pazho said, implying those were two words that didn't belong together.

"Sorry about that, though," Denaan said. "Didn't know you were coming. If I had, I'd have asked if you wanted to join in."

"Maybe after dinner," I said. Farrah and Rhyss nodded in agreement. Beyan rolled his eyes.

"Don't encourage him," Pazho said to us. "And please forgive my neglectful manners. This is my mate, Denaan. Denaan, meet Allayne, Beyan, Farrah, and Rhyss. They'll be staying here tonight."

"Splendid, splendid," Denaan said, wiping his hands on his apron and enthusiastically shaking each of our hands in turn. "There's room enough for all of you, so you can each have a room to yourselves if you like. Any horses?" Beyan shook his head no. "That's easy enough, then. Just go ahead and go on upstairs, you can pick out your rooms. Dinner starts in an hour."

"I'll see you all in an hour," Pazho told us, turning to go.

"Wait," I said. "You don't have to leave. I'd be happy to stay and talk with you while we wait for dinner."

"I'd rather you have a chance to rest," Pazho said. "I plan on us having a long conversation later this evening. It won't take me long to go home and come back. Denaan and I live right next door."

With that, he left. Denaan went back into the kitchen, where we could hear him giving orders to as yet unseen staff. The rest of us trooped upstairs to pick out our rooms for the night.

AFTER A MUCH-NEEDED nap, I went downstairs, following the savory scent of cooked vegetables and spices. My friends were already seated, with Pazho, at one of the long tables in a back corner of the room. The room was quickly filling up with customers waiting for one of Denaan's meals.

As I joined the group, Farrah smiled up at me. "Finally!" she said. "I know you needed your sleep, but I'm starving! You don't know how hard it was waiting for you to get down here."

My eyes caught the wide array of dishes on the table. All were unbreakable, no doubt, and all were piled high with food. "I didn't mean to keep you waiting. Let's eat."

"Can you believe it, they don't serve a single meat dish!" Rhyss said as I sat down next to him. "I hope you guys aren't too hungry. I'll have to eat twice as much to get my fill."

Farrah smirked at Rhyss from across the table. "You'd eat twice as much as any of us no matter *what* was being served."

Pretty soon, our table was filled with the sounds of eating, drinking, and laughter. Pazho kept the conversation light. Denaan would come by every so often to say hello, but as the night wore on he stayed in the kitchen while a boy and a girl, both about twelve, ran around delivering plates and cups and clearing the tables. Pazho told us that they were twins, the children of Denaan's sister. "They're hummingbirds, that's why they're so fast."

"They're *like* birds, you mean?" Farrah questioned.

"Yes, exactly."

We finished eating. Denaan's nephew quickly scooped up our plates while his sister carefully poured more mead into our cups. Pazho leaned back, satisfied.

"My mate really is the finest cook in the kingdom. He's a huge bleeding heart, even if he does act prickly sometimes. It's the antlers." He said this last directly to me, tapping at his head like he was patting horns on the top. I smiled.

"I'd like to know what all this alluding to animals is about," Beyan said, ever the plain speaker.

"A secret for a secret," Pazho said. "What brings all of you to Annlyn?"

The table fell silent. Farrah and Rhyss exchanged glances, but left it to Beyan, as the group's leader, to speak up. If he so chose.

"We seek the dragon Joichan," Beyan said.

"I thought as much," Pazho said. "But it's good of you to say it so I could be sure."

"You said you could help us. I take it that others have tried to find him?"

"You are not the first to seek out Joichan, no. There have been countless others before you. Very few are successful."

"What do we need to do? We have gold we could offer him. We — "

"Why are you looking for him?"

If I had been alone with Pazho, I probably would have told him the truth. But with the others sitting there, I couldn't disclose the complete reason for my search.

"I was tasked by Queen Melandria of Calia to find Joichan," I said.

Pazho studied me. I sensed he knew I was holding something back, but he didn't pry further. "Your intentions are honorable," he stated.

"Allayne asked me to help her find Joichan," Beyan said. "I am a dragon seeker. Farrah and Rhyss are part of my team when we are on the hunt."

Pazho turned his assessing gaze on Beyan. "Hunt is an accurate word. I would advise you against it. It's not too late to change your mind." Beyan shifted under the weight of Pazho's stare. "Seek wisdom, not vengeance. You will get what you want that way."

"That's the help you offer?" Beyan stood, angry. Farrah touched his arm, but he shook her off.

"My advice is free, but if you choose not to heed it, you could pay a heavy price for years to come," Pazho said calmly.

"Come on, Beyan," Rhyss said. "You know he's right."

Slowly, Beyan sat down.

"Now you know why we're here," Farrah said. "It's your turn now."

"A secret for a secret," Pazho reiterated, nodding. "What I tell you is not widely known beyond Annlyn, and I will tell you now that in the rest of the Gifted Lands, this is viewed as just a rumor, and rarely believed. But my mate and I, and the other citizens of this kingdom, are shapeshifters. We each have an animal form that we can become at will."

Farrah and Rhyss stared at Pazho, openmouthed. Even Beyan was intrigued, although still a little upset.

Farrah regained her voice first. "Wow," she breathed. "Not even the Fae can do that, at least not any of the ones I know. Certainly not anyone in my immediate family. What animal are you?"

"A grey wolf," Pazho told her. "Denaan is an elk."

"Elk logic," Farrah said. Pazho grinned. She turned to me. "Were those the animals you kept seeing when we first entered Annlyn?"

"Yes," I replied.

"But why were you able to see them, and we couldn't?"

"There is a spell on the town masking us from outsiders," Pazho said. "But I believe your friend saw through our illusion because she is one of us."

Now my friends were gaping at *me*. "First you set people on fire, now you can turn into an animal?" Rhyss said. "That's incredible. How can I learn how to do that?"

"You're a shapeshifter?" Beyan said simultaneously.

Farrah overlapped with, "What do *you* turn into, Allayne?"

And while she was talking, Pazho asked, "You set people on fire?"

"Stop, all of you!" I said. Everyone stopped talking.

Denaan came by our table en route to the kitchen, his arms full of dirty dishes. "Dessert, anyone?"

Chapter Twenty-Five

THE TALK AT THE TABLE stopped long enough for us to eagerly devour a heaping plate of honeyed crispel, which Pazho proudly informed us was a specialty of Dennan's. After I told my friends, repeatedly, that I didn't know much about my supposed abilities, they shifted their questions to Pazho. We were all eager to learn more about this mysterious land of shapeshifters.

Pazho repeated much of the things he had told me on our earlier walk in the market. My mind began to wander, since none of the information was new to me. But then the conversation turned in a direction that caused my attention to snap back immediately.

"I saw the most beautiful jewelry in the market," Farrah said. "I wanted to purchase one of the pieces, a bracelet of lapis lazuli, but the merchant refused to sell it to me. He kept saying it was not meant for me, and tried to entice me with other options instead."

"That's odd," Rhyss commented. "Money is money; you'd think he'd be happy for a sale, no matter who was buying or what they wanted."

"He wasn't refusing to sell to you for the reasons you may be assuming," Pazho said.

"But I thought Annlyn was famed for its jewelry," Farrah said.

"Although after everything you've just told us, I don't know if I should believe that anymore," Beyan said.

"We are master craftsmen, it's true," Pazho said. "But the reason we've become such is that our creations are linked to our abilities."

Pazho held up his right hand. On his index finger, a lone ruby set into a silver band caught the glow from nearby lights and winked at us.

"It's exquisite," Farrah breathed.

"Thank you. It's also a part of me, as much as my wolf form is. I rarely take it off. It… hurts too much to be without it for any length of time." Pazho absently rubbed the ruby with his thumb.

"A soulstone." There was no question in Beyan's voice.

"Yes. They are created here in Annlyn."

"So, everything in the market…?"

"Not necessarily. Sometimes a gem is just a gem. But soulstones are rare finds, made even more powerful when infused with our magic. We receive them at birth, and they help us shift until we reach a certain age. Up until that point, transforming into our animal selves can be painful, both physically and mentally. Our soulstones protect us against that potential harm. Of course, the more we use them, the more our soulstones become part of us."

Thinking of the necklace now safely hidden again under my dress, and of King Hendon's theft of my father Joichan's soulstone, I asked, "But what happens if you *did* lose your soulstone? Or if it was destroyed? Are you unable to change forms? Does it cause you to weaken, or die?"

"It depends," Pazho said. "Only the very young would die without their soulstones, because they haven't yet mastered their abilities. Anyone in their prime and in good health should be fine without it. But the longer one is separated from it, the weaker their powers become. If it's never returned, or destroyed, then the person who is linked to that stone would eventually become their animal form completely, with no memory of their human self. And no way to change back."

My blood chilled. My father had been without his stone for at least twenty years, possibly more. My mother hadn't told me how long it had been in Hendon's possession before her abduction, only that the king had stolen it.

"Are you all right?" Farrah asked me. "You look a little... unsettled."

"I think I had one crispel too many," I lied. "If all of you will excuse me... I think I'll retire for the night."

My friends murmured their goodnights and wishes that I'd feel better. Pazho said, "I'll see you in the morning, then. Dennan and I couldn't possibly send you on your way without a good breakfast."

I smiled at him weakly and made my way to my room. Once safely inside with a quick locking spell on the door, I sat down on the bed and took off my necklace. The moonstone seemed to glow in my palm as I rubbed the jewel, reassuring myself that it was still there. What would I find when we finally found my father?

The delicate piece of jewelry held no answers. Sighing, I refastened it back around my neck and crawled under the covers. Soon, I was deep asleep, my hand resting lightly on the pendant in a poor attempt to hide it.

Chapter Twenty-Six

BREAKFAST THE NEXT morning was a surprisingly lively affair. As we were the only guests at Dennan's inn, he sat and ate with us. Pazho joined us later than we expected, looking rumpled and grumpy.

"Wolves are nocturnal," Pazho said as he slid onto the bench next to Rhyss.

"You mean, wolves are lazy," Dennan corrected cheerfully, piling food on Pazho's plate.

"You're one to talk," Pazho countered, rolling his eyes. The rest of us just kept eating, trying not to laugh. Sarcasm seemed to be the way Pazho and Dennan communicated best with each other.

After our meal, we gathered our things and said goodbye to our hosts.

"Thank you for putting us up for the night, and for the food," Beyan said. "Are you sure you won't take any coin at all, at least for the two meals?"

Dennan shook his head. "Just tell other travelers you meet about my inn."

"Choose wisely, choose well." Pazho leveled a serious look at Beyan.

Beyan gave him a tight-lipped smile. "Thanks to both of you, again."

We turned to go. Pazho pulled me aside as the rest of my group started walking away. He pulled something from his pocket. I gasped, recognizing the amber pendant hanging from the delicate gold chain as the necklace from the marketplace yesterday.

"For you," Pazho said, pressing it into my hand.

"I couldn't possibly accept this," I protested, even as my fingers curled around the piece of jewelry.

"You already have." He closed my fingers decisively around the pendant and pushed my hand gently toward me. "Think of it as a souvenir of your time in Annlyn. And maybe something else, besides. You're a long way from home; amber is thought to protect a traveler on their journey. It's the stone of fortitude, as well. Call on it for courage in the days and hours to come."

I gave Pazho a sharp look, marveling again at how he could have ascertained so much in just two short days of knowing me.

"Thank you." I impulsively gave him a hug, slipping the necklace into my pocket. I hoisted my pack up so it sat comfortably on my back, and then hurried after my friends. They hadn't gone far, and I found them quickly. We joined a small group of people leaving through the just-opened city gates.

"You should have tried harder to give our hosts money," I chided Beyan as we walked. "They were so generous, and I hate the idea that they lost money on us by being so kind."

Beyan laughed. "I figured they wouldn't accept payment. So I gave a bag of coins to Dennan's niece last night while he was busy and told her to hide it in the kitchen. He'll find it sometime today, I'm sure. There was enough to cover our rooms and our meals, and a little bit extra."

I laughed as well, imagining Dennan's and Pazho's faces when they discovered the money.

I had wondered how exactly we would find Joichan once we were in the south, but Beyan led our group decisively west of

Annlyn. I thought perhaps that he had been to Joichan's cave before, but when I said that aloud, Beyan shook his head.

"The hardest part of seeking is knowing which way to start the journey," he said. "It's not enough to tell me to find a certain dragon. My connection with such creatures depends on being in their general area, and having some sort of link to them. The stronger the link, the easier it is to seek."

"I haven't given you anything of Joichan's, though," I said, neglecting to mention that I and my necklace might very well have been the link he needed. "How are you so certain this is the right way to go?"

"Because of my father," he said simply. Of course. Kye's history with the dragon, and his connection to his son, would be the strongest link of all.

A few hours later, our early morning energy had faded a bit under the midday sun's blazing heat.

"I wish horses weren't so easily spooked," Rhyss complained, shifting his bag on his shoulders as he walked. "It would be nice to not have to carry so much."

"Maybe if you hadn't purchased so much, you wouldn't have to carry so much," Farrah pointed out unsympathetically.

"All of it is necessary," Rhyss said. "And as a gentleman, I couldn't allow you or Allayne to be overloaded as we journey."

Farrah snorted. "Just admit you didn't want anyone else to carry the food." Her stomach grumbled loudly. "Speaking of food..."

Beyan glanced up, assessing the position of the sun in the sky. "I think we can stop for a break."

We gratefully stopped, unpacking the food Rhyss carried and sharing a quick meal between us. Rhyss, Farrah, and I were glad for the rest, but Beyan seemed agitated and anxious. He bolted his food down and then paced around nervously until Farrah told him, "Go scout ahead, if you're that skittish."

Beyan obliged and was soon out of eyesight, disappearing into a stand of trees.

"He's always like this when we get closer to our target," Farrah explained. "Something to do with his seeker skills."

"He once described it like a waterfall, but in reverse," Rhyss said. "You know how you can hear the water rushing, but faintly, when you're nearby? And then as you approach it gets louder and louder until you're at the waterfall itself? Beyan gets that sensation when seeking, but instead of the feeling getting louder, it starts loud, and only goes soft once he's found the dragon he's been trying to find."

"That doesn't sound pleasant," I said.

"It's not," Farrah said. "He used to get terrible headaches because of it when he was younger. Through training and experience he's learned to dampen the sensation, but once we're near the dragon's area, he can't stop it."

"Seeking always sounded like such a glamorous gift, but from the way you describe it, I don't think I would want that burden," I said.

"I agree," Farrah said. Rhyss just nodded as he polished off the last of his meal.

Beyan came back, moving quickly but quietly. "Come on, you lot of lazybones! We're here."

Chapter Twenty-Seven

AFTER QUICKLY CLEANING up the remains of our lunch, we followed an impatient Beyan. The dragon's cave, it turned out, wasn't exactly "here" — it was still a good mile or so from where we had taken our rest. Beyan had discovered the cave, but had not seen any sign of Joichan. He had then hurried back to get us.

As we neared the cave, I wondered what, if anything, was the plan. I hadn't thought much beyond finding and talking to Joichan. But I couldn't do that in front of the others, and I somehow doubted my companions would be fine just leaving me alone with an ancient dragon. One that had a fearsome reputation.

One that Beyan would not leave alive.

Beyan halted our group, motioning us to silence. In the distance, we could see Joichan's cave, alongside a steadily flowing river in a clearing surrounded by the trees where we were now hiding. Although Beyan had seen no one when he had scouted earlier, this time there was now a man kneeling by the water. He seemed to be checking some traps in the river. Sunlight glinted off his golden hair.

Remembering Beyan's story about the strange man that his father Kye had encountered at the cave, my breath caught. Knowing that the dragon was a shapeshifter, and seeing this man at Joichan's cave... could I be looking at my father?

Beyan glared at me, putting a finger to his lips to indicate I needed to be quiet. I nodded, shifting my weight. Dry leaves crunched underfoot as I did so, and the man at the river froze and looked around. Rhyss and Farrah added their glares to Beyan's. Sheepishly, I shrugged my shoulders at them in silent apology.

As one, we looked back to the riverbank. The man had disappeared.

Beyan pursed his lips in frustration. For a while longer, we stayed there motionless, waiting for the man to come back or the dragon to appear. But nothing happened.

Beyan motioned for us to follow him and moved out of the trees, back toward the direction we had come from originally.

Once we were out of the trees on the other side, I put a hand on Beyan's arm, stopping him in place. Even though I was sure we were out of earshot of the mysterious man, I kept my voice low. "I'm sorry, Beyan. I didn't mean to give us away."

"It's all right," Beyan said, although we both knew he didn't mean it. "The dragon wasn't there anyway. Strange, because I had been so sure."

Hoping Beyan wouldn't come to the eventual correct conclusion about the strange person at the dragon's cave, I tried to distract him. "Well, you've done your job. You brought me to where Joichan lives. I guess... you could all go home now?"

Beyan, Farrah, and Rhyss all gave me matching incredulous looks. "Are you crazy?" Beyan said. "We couldn't just leave you here, by yourself. An unarmed girl? We're not heartless mercenaries."

I bristled. "I'm not an 'unarmed girl,' as you well know from our bandit visitors the other night. I can defend myself."

"Even so," Beyan argued. "We wouldn't head back north without you."

"Fine, then. Why don't you go back to Dennan's inn and wait for me there?"

"No. The dragon is dangerous. You need us here to help you, just in case."

"I don't think your intention is to help."

Beyan, to his credit, didn't argue with that statement. Instead, he said, "What are your intentions? You never told me that, not when you first asked for my father's help, and not any time during our travels."

"I don't think that really matters. Do you ask all of your commissions why they're looking for the dragons they hope to find?"

"No, but since we came all this way without payment, I think we're owed at least that."

Our argument was cut short by Farrah's unsteady voice. "Uh... you two..."

A large shadow briefly blocked the sun overhead. The wind picked up, blowing leaves and dust around us. A heavy thud shook the earth as a magnificent gilded dragon landed just behind us.

Massive amber eyes regarded us. The dragon's mouth opened.

Chapter Twenty-Eight

BEYAN, RHYSS, AND FARRAH instinctively ducked to either side, anticipating an oncoming wave of fire. I remained where I stood, frozen in place.

But instead of incinerating us, the dragon spoke.

"I understand you're looking for me." His thundering, deep voice rumbled through my body.

"How... how did you know that?" Instinctively, I moved closer to the dragon, mesmerized by his liquid eyes.

"Allayne." Beyan's warning — and his hand on my arm — stopped me.

"You have a seeker among you," Joichan said. "And, dragons have excellent hearing."

I nodded. I seemed to have trouble forming coherent thoughts. No one else spoke for a few moments. We just stood there, humans and dragon, staring at each other.

"Well?" Joichan broke the stalemate. "State your business, or be on your way."

Without thinking, my hand went to my neck and tugged the necklace out from under my collar. The moonstone gleamed, catching Joichan's eye. Curiosity aroused, he turned his full attention on me.

And then reared back, screaming in pain.

Beyan's dagger was lodged in Joichan's side, sticking out under one of his golden scales. Blood dripped from the creature, pooling on the grass underneath him.

I had been so focused on the dragon that I hadn't noticed Beyan had moved from my side. While I had unwittingly distracted Joichan, Beyan had taken advantage of the moment to strike.

Now Beyan had his sword drawn, ready to finish the job.

"Beyan, no!" I spun, reaching out to grab his sword hilt. Beyan easily avoided my hand, swinging the sword away from me so he wouldn't accidentally cut me.

"Allayne, move away."

"Beyan, this is insane. You don't want to do this." I looked to Rhyss and Farrah for help. They didn't draw their weapons, but they didn't try to stop their friend either. I turned back to Beyan, trying to appeal to his sense of logic. "This will break your mind. Don't go down this path."

With his free hand, he pointed toward Farrah and Rhyss. "Go join the others."

"Beyan! Stop and think for a second. Kye needs you."

Beyan paused. For a moment, he looked uncertain, and I hoped I had gotten through to him. Then his face hardened. "Some things are worth the sacrifice."

"No. You don't mean that." I stayed firmly in place.

Keeping his eyes on the dragon, Beyan called over his shoulder to his team. "You two, quit standing around and get her out of the way."

Reluctantly, Rhyss and Farrah moved toward me. Panicked, I held out my hand at them, blowing them back with the force of my unexpected spell. Stunned, we shared equal looks of horror, but they continued to advance on me. I waved my hand, gluing them to the ground so they couldn't move.

Beyan growled and raised his hand — to grab me or attack me, I wasn't sure. I sidestepped, narrowly missing his swipe. But while I was safe, this meant that I was no longer standing between him and Joichan.

Beyan raised his sword, ready to thrust it into the dragon's heart.

I shouted and pointed.

The hilt of Beyan's sword turned a dull red. Cursing, he threw the hot metal down to the ground, shaking his hand. The skin on his right hand was beginning to blister from the slight burn.

Beyan drew another dagger from his side with his good hand and charged the dragon.

I yelled again, motioning at Beyan. He blew backwards, forced back by my magical wind spell.

The natural wind began to swirl as Joichan launched into the air. He hovered over us, then grabbed me in his claws. We began to gain altitude.

"No!" Beyan threw his dagger skyward, but thankfully, it missed both the dragon and me. As we flew away, Beyan's screams echoed in my head and burrowed into my heart.

"I trusted you, Allayne! *I trusted you.*"

Chapter Twenty-Nine

WE FLEW HIGHER AND higher, speeding away from my friends. A mountain loomed up ahead, and Joichan made a beeline for what looked to be a gray, unforgiving rock face. He didn't slow as we approached. I screamed, the wind whipping away the sound. I turned my face away, squeezing my eyes shut as I braced myself for the inevitable hit of flesh against stone....

And suddenly the air felt much, much cooler than it had moments before. Joichan had come to a complete stop, setting me gently on a hard rock surface. I opened my eyes, scrambling to stand up.

We were in a cave, dimly lit from the outside of the mountain. Joichan was just in front of me, his wings tucked behind him. He solemnly regarded me with his big golden eyes.

I whipped around to look behind me. I could see treetops, the bright sun, and the blue sky. Turning back to the dragon, I asked, "Where are we?" I knew we had flown a good distance from my group. And to the best of my knowledge, we were nowhere near his cave by the river.

"You are in my true home. Come." Joichan disappeared into the darkness.

I followed the dragon, hoping I wouldn't trip or get lost. The walls of the cave seemed to glow, illuminating each step I took farther in. I found the dragon near the back, curled up against a wall, his breathing shallow. The glow from his scales was gone, replaced by a dull tarnish. The knife was still embedded in his skin, and he lay awkwardly, trying to avoid further discomfort.

"Let me help you," I said, although I wasn't entirely sure what I could do.

"Are you able to heal?"

"Uh... no."

"Then there's not much you can do."

Feeling foolish, I unclasped the moonstone necklace and held it out to the creature. "Would this do anything?"

He held out a claw. I placed the necklace in it, marveling at how small the piece of jewelry looked against his huge talon.

"Yes. Yes, it does." Sounding stronger already, he motioned to the opposite wall. "There's cloth and some medicinal salve stored in a chest over there. After you get it, we'll work on removing this dagger."

I hurried over to where he had indicated, locating the chest and the items Joichan wanted easily. I dropped my bag next to the chest, where it would be out of the way. When I came back, Joichan had already shifted to a position where I could reach the dagger. Carefully, I dislodged the weapon, wincing when Joichan groaned in pain. As quickly as I could, I smeared some salve on the wound and bound his side, hoping the blood flow would stanch soon.

My ministrations done, I stepped back. "What now?"

"Now, I sleep."

WHILE JOICHAN SLUMBERED, I attempted to contact Taryn. But even though I sent out a calling spell several times, she did not respond, nor did I feel any bounced back magic. It was like Taryn didn't even exist. It worried me. However, there wasn't much I could do, except get back home as quickly as possible to find out what was going on.

I felt bad poking around a stranger's home, but Joichan was deep asleep and I was bored. I walked around the cave, noting the human-sized furnishings in one section. Finding some books piled on the floor, I flipped through them, finally deciding on one that looked interesting.

I was about a third of the way through the book when a deep voice said, "That one was always one of my favorites."

I looked up. The dragon still lay in his corner, looking much better. The internal radiance was back, like a small sun lighting up the cave.

"It's entertaining so far." I put the book down, stood up, and walked over to Joichan. "How are you feeling?"

"See for yourself."

Cautiously, I pulled back the bandages. The wound had already closed over. Gaping, I looked at the dragon.

"Thank you for returning this to me." He held up the necklace carefully in his claw. "This made my recovery much faster."

"How — ?"

"Do you know how soulstones work?" When I nodded, he continued, "Part of my magic is stored in here, from my link to it and all the times I've used it in the past. I tapped into that magic to help me heal."

There were so many questions I had, so many things I wanted to say. Of course, my brain stopped on the most inane of these. "I have got to get one of those."

He laughed. "You had one of those. You had mine. Most people would never give up such a treasure. Why did you?"

I took a deep breath, fearful and hopeful all at once. What would he say when I told him?

"I had to," I said. "It was yours. And you're my father."

Chapter Thirty

FOR A VERY LONG MOMENT we just stared at each other. In the depths of his mesmerizing golden eyes, I could see my image, dimly. It felt like not only was he seeing me, but he was seeing in me and through me.

"How...?" Joichan's voice trailed off.

"Queen Melandria of Calia is my mother," I said.

"Melandria." The dragon seemed to grow bigger and brighter. "How I've missed her. She's never far from my thoughts, even after all these years."

"Twenty, at least." I chuckled. The dragon joined in, a snort of smoke curling from his nostrils.

"Forgive me..."

"Jennica. My name is Jennica."

"Your friend called you by a different name."

"Yes. I couldn't give my companions my real name. It's not safe for me to use right now."

Joichan nodded gravely in understanding. "Forgive me, Jennica. I find this all quite hard to believe."

"I know. It was a shock to me too." Remembering something, I gasped. "Wait. Let me show you something."

I hurried to my pack, rummaging around until my hand closed on a packet of paper buried at the bottom. Returning to Joichan, I held out my mother's letter to him. "Here. My mother — Queen Melandria — wrote this."

Joichan gingerly took the papers from my outstretched hand. Belatedly, I thought perhaps maybe I should have waited until he was back in human form. But no, the dragon before me was avidly reading the pages, holding them with a single delicate claw.

When he finished, Joichan turned his great amber eyes on me. There was a watery sheen to them, and I realized that the great dragon was about to cry.

"My daughter," he breathed. "I am truly sorry. Had I known you existed, I would have returned to Calia a long time ago to find you."

"Mother made sure to hide the truth from everyone," I reassured him. "She was worried what the king — her husband Hendon, not her late father — would do if he found out I wasn't his child. Although we think he suspects it anyway."

Joichan's countenance darkened at the mention of Hendon. "So, that thief is now the ruler of Calia. And married to Melandria."

"Yes. I'm sorry."

"I should have gone back, even without my soulstone. Hendon was able to use my magic against me, but I would have figured out something. Or died in the attempt. But it would have been better than leaving Melandria alone with that man."

I didn't know what to say, so I just kept silent. His anger spent, Joichan fell silent in his own brown study. His tail twitched, keeping time with his thoughts, and kicked up some dust in the cave. I sneezed. Joichan blinked, remembering that I was there with him.

"No use in regretting the past," he said. "You're here now, that's what matters. Speaking of which..."

The creature in front of me shimmered, and the air in the cave grew thick and opaque. I looked around blindly, but no amount of blinking or straining would let me see anything.

When the air cleared, there was a man standing in front of me.

He was tall, at least a foot taller than me. He looked like fire in human form, from his golden brown skin to his dark honey hair, which changed from light brown to red to gold, depending on how the light from the cave walls caught it. He was dressed in a homespun shirt and trousers, and I idly wondered how he included the clothes in his transformation, since the dragon hadn't been wearing anything.

The man held his arms open, and I stepped into my father's embrace.

Even though I had only known Joichan for a few hours at most, hugging him felt like the most natural thing in the world. Hendon was not a warm person, and he had certainly never treated me like a father would his daughter. But something about Joichan spoke to my heart. The missing pieces I had always felt, if not outright acknowledged, suddenly fell into place.

Joichan held me out at arm's length. In turn, I was able to get a good look at the human side of my father. There were streaks of gray at his temples, something I hadn't noticed from a distance. He smiled, crinkles reaching his eyes as they flashed gold, then back to a more human brown. The moonstone pendant hung from his neck, half hidden under the collar of his shirt.

"You look just like her," he said.

"Mostly," I said. "Apparently I have your eyes."

His smile grew broader. "Yes, I can see that."

He walked over to a cupboard in the human-sized area of the cave and pulled down two porcelain cups. "Tea?"

"Yes. Thank you."

"Have a seat." Joichan gestured toward a small table, and I sat down, watching him putter around. He snapped his fingers, and steam suddenly spouted from the teapot on his counter. He added some leaves to each of the cups, poured boiling water into them, and brought everything over on a silver tray. The crisp smell of mint wafted toward me. Joichan gave me a cup of tea, then took the other and settled back in his seat.

"We have a lot of catching up to do," he said. "Tell me about yourself, your mother, your life in Calia."

"Wow, where should I start?" I quipped. "Let's see... well, after you left, Mother married Sir Hendon. Grandfather passed away when I was very young; I don't remember much about him, but I think he took a lot of the kingdom's happiness with him when he died."

"Does Hendon treat you and Melandria well? Does he at least rule the kingdom well?"

"He's done decently by Calia, I guess. I haven't heard of any major grumblings against him, just the usual 'taxes are too high' or 'things could be better' kind of thing. I don't think he and Mother are truly in love, the way the stories about them say, but they have an understanding of sorts."

Joichan looked away at that. I knew he was remembering my mother, and wishing he could rewrite history. "And you? Is he a good father to you?"

I laughed, but it was a bitter, forlorn sound. "He tolerates me, I think. He's mostly left me alone, until now. Now..." I sucked in a breath, remembering why I was here in the first place.

"Now?" Joichan prompted me.

"The king promised me in marriage to Prince Anders of Rothschan. Not only do I find the man hateful, but Mother said that Hendon wants to use the marriage alliance as a way to conquer the rest of the Gifted Lands. That's why she sent me south, to find you, and gave me your necklace. She stole it back from Hendon and told me to keep it from him."

Joichan growled angrily, an echo of the fierce dragon he was capable of becoming. "There's more, isn't there?"

"There is, but I don't know what to make of it," I admitted. "I left immediately after the betrothal. Somehow Hendon found out I was gone, even though we tried to hide it under the guise of my being sequestered for the traditional Calian wedding preparation month. But Prince Anders doesn't know — he went back to Rothschan to prepare for the wedding and bring his family back. And on the road we ran into other nobles who were headed to Calia for the wedding. Hendon is searching for me; we saw Calian soldiers on the road and in Annlyn who were asking around about me. But Hendon hasn't called off the wedding, or postponed it, or anything."

Joichan's rumbling grew louder, and I half-expected him to breathe fire, even though he was in human form. "Whatever he's planning, it can't be good. For Calia, or for you and your mother. When is the wedding?"

"I'm not sure. Time seemed to blur when we were traveling down here. I think it took us about a little over a week to reach Annlyn, so... in another two weeks or so?"

"We have a little bit of time, then." Joichan touched his side gingerly, pressing against the newly closed wound. "Which is good, because I'll need the time to finish healing."

"I thought — "

"That I was already healed? Mostly. But magic can't do everything. Time and rest will do the job better than magic could; magic just speeds things up a bit."

"Speaking of magic..." I told my father about my lady-in-waiting Taryn back home, how she had helped me escape, and how she had been keeping me informed on what was happening back in Calia. "While you were resting, I tried to contact her. But I can't get a hold of her. I'm not sure if it's something I'm doing wrong? But every other time I've used that spell I've been able to get in touch with her, easily."

Joichan frowned. "I do have some anti-magic spells on my home, but those spells are to stop intruders or to block visitors from harming me, physically or magically. You should be able to contact your friend within these walls with no issue."

"Your home? But isn't the other cave your home?"

He laughed. "I suppose it is, although I hardly ever sleep there. It's more of a decoy than anything else."

"Since I wasn't able to contact Taryn here in the cave, then maybe it *is* my magic?"

"I doubt it. But let's go outside to get clear of my protective spells, just in case. You can try your spell again."

We set our now empty tea cups down on the table, and went to the cave entrance. From our vantage point, we could see the tops of trees as the setting sun painted the sky with pinks and oranges. I looked down and instantly regretted it. The rocky mountain face and the jagged treetops promised a treacherous fall and painful demise for anyone who fell off the ledge.

"It's better not to look," Joichan said mildly.

"Now you tell me."

"We should be clear of all magic on the cave now." Joichan gestured at me. "Go on, try your spell."

With practiced ease, I ran through the words and motions of the spell, concentrating on Taryn's face in my mind. I made the final gesture, but my friend didn't appear. I held on to the spell for a few moments longer, but released it when it became apparent I couldn't get in touch with her. Worried, I looked at my father.

He shook his head. "Your spell was flawless. Every part of your execution was perfect. It wasn't your magic, Jennica."

"Then what's wrong? If I did it right, then Taryn should have felt and answered my call. What do you think I should do?"

"I think you — and I — should get back to Calia as soon as we can."

Chapter Thirty-One

ALTHOUGH WE BOTH WOULD have left that night, we also knew it wasn't a wise idea. Not when Joichan needed to rest to get back to his full strength. And not when I needed to learn more about myself as a shapeshifter.

After I had returned Joichan's necklace, I had felt a little bereft. I mentioned this to Joichan, and my father explained that, as the bearer and his child, I had begun to bond with the moonstone, even though it was linked to him. It was sympathetic magic, as the stone could feel the blood link between kin. Further strengthening the bond was the fact that one day I would inherit his soulstone and could merge it with mine.

One thing that concerned me was that I was much older than most beginning shapeshifters. Not only did I need to learn how to change forms, but I wouldn't have a soulstone to aid me.

With the sun gone, it was cold both in and outside the cave. I jammed my hands into my pockets as we walked back inside, looking forward to settling in for the night. My right hand brushed against a small hard object, and I pulled out the necklace that Pazho had given me. The amber caught the dull glow from the cave walls, glimmering faintly in my hand.

"What's that?" Joichan asked.

"It was a gift from a friend in Annlyn," I said.

Joichan snapped his fingers, and the cave walls grew brighter. He stopped, reaching out to touch the necklace. I stopped too, watching him. My father nodded, satisfied.

"Your friend is very astute. This will do nicely."

"What do you mean?"

Joichan smiled. "This will make a perfect soulstone for you." He began walking again, leaving me gaping until I closed my mouth and hurried after him.

But working magic would have to wait until the morning. Both of us were exhausted from the day's events. Joichan pointed out a small bedroom tucked away in the back of the cave just off the human-sized area. The room was fairly spartan, only boasting a neatly-made bed and a nightstand.

"But where are you going to sleep?" I asked.

Joichan left the bedroom, going back into the main cavern. I followed. He changed back into his dragon form and curled up in the corner he had occupied earlier in the day. "There's only one bed, which you can have. Besides, oftentimes I prefer my animal self, especially since I live alone. It's easier and more comfortable for me to sleep, and I can defend myself easier."

"If you're sure... thank you."

"Of course," my father said. "Now, I suggest you get some sleep. We have a busy day ahead of us tomorrow."

"BUSY" DIDN'T EVEN BEGIN to describe it. Although Joichan still needed to rest, he insisted on tutoring me in the basics of shapeshifting. Fortunately, my Calian training in magic and my on-the-road lessons with Farrah had given me a good foundation for Joichan's teaching, as well as the confidence to execute it.

Because a lot of changing one's form, I learned, required confidence and focus. That's why the fledgling shapeshifters of

Annlyn used soulstones, because it helped them in both areas. But even with my magical experience, my first shapeshifting experience was both exhilarating and scary.

We woke up early, hoping that the sleepy quiet of morning would keep us safe from prying eyes. We stepped outside of the cave, where Joichan, still in human form, waved a hand. A magical barrier went up, barring access to the entrance. To casual lookers, it would have seemed there was no cave at all, since the magic also created the illusion of a sheer rock face on the mountainside. I now understood what had happened when I first came here.

"Clever," I complimented my father.

"Thank you." His voice grew deeper as his form changed from human to dragon.

Dragon Joichan carried me on his back into the forest below the mountain, where the surrounding trees hid us in a small glade from any errant observers who might be in the area. Once we landed, my father changed back into human form, to give me more room to try my transformation.

Magic — at least the way I had learned it in Calia, or when I was practicing on the road with Farrah — usually required memorizing spells, and combining those spells with hand gestures, movements, charms, or potions to acquire the desired effect. But shapeshifting was different. It was a magical transformation, to be sure, but it was also something else. My father had explained the theory in depth to me the night before. It was as simple as changing one's outfit or hairstyle. However, it required a bit of finesse to make sure the transformation worked. After all, changing your hairstyle didn't help if you didn't know how to properly dress hair in the first place.

Under Joichan's watchful eye, I stood in the center of the glade, closed my eyes, and sent my awareness deep within. I was acutely aware of my bones, my blood, my breath. My magical senses took note of where and how my body was knit together; my mind imagined my spine lengthening, my arms and legs growing bigger and heavier, my olive-toned skin hardening and turning into reptilian scales. Nails turned into claws; my nose changed into a golden snout. Breathing in, I was assaulted by my suddenly super-sensitive sense of smell. My hearing had gotten sharper as well. I could smell the rabbit that was currently burrowing into its den several miles away. Deep in the forest, I heard the footsteps of a hunter who was moving near-soundlessly as he tracked his prey. Marveling at my new awareness, I opened my eyes to take it all in.

My eyes met the tops of the trees. A bird flying by at my eye-level squawked in alarm at me and clumsily changed its course mid-flight. I laughed, a rumbly sound several octaves lower than my normal pitch. From somewhere near my feet, I heard an answering laugh, and looked down to see Joichan staring up at me with an enormous grin on his face.

"Very good, Jennica! An amazing first attempt!" He clapped his hands in delight.

I tried clapping my hands too, laughing even harder at myself when I realized how stupid my clumsy claws must look. I laughed so hard that I accidentally snorted fire, just barely setting a treetop aflame. My laughter turned into a coughing fit, and my magical concentration broke. Soon I was back on ground level with my father, lying on the grass trying to get my breath back.

"Jennica! Are you okay?" Helping me sit up, Father grabbed a waterskin out of the bag I had brought with me. He handed it to me and I took a deep drink before answering.

"Yes, I'm... fine," I panted once I had my breath back. "That...didn't... last long, did it?"

"No, but for your first attempt, it was wonderful!" Father raved. "With more practice, you'll be able to maintain and control your form easily."

"That's... good.... to know. I can't... wait." A small, weak cough escaped me. "That... took more out of me... than I expected."

I tried to stand up, but wobbled on my feet and fell to my knees, feeling ready to throw up. Taking in my pale face and still heavy breathing, Father stood up. "You'll master this in no time. But, for now, I think you need to rest. Let's get you home."

He stepped back and changed into his dragon form. I was too weak to climb onto his back, so he gently picked me up in his claws and flew back to the mountain cave.

Chapter Thirty-Two

THE NEXT FEW DAYS PASSED in a blur of activity as we prepared to head back to Calia. I practiced shifting into my dragon form as much as I could, although the process still took a lot out of me.

During my first few barely successful attempts, I would only just be able to change into my dragon form — a much smaller version of my father's majestic figure. My transformation wouldn't last long; I could barely sustain it for about a quarter of an hour before my body would involuntarily revert back to my human form. And changing back left me even more winded: out of breath, curled into myself, with a massive headache.

Which is why the other big undertaking my father insisted we do before we left was to create a soulstone for me. Being able to channel my magical energy through it would ease the transition, as well as help me maintain my creature self longer. When I asked my father why I wasn't able to hold my dragon shape, Joichan explained that the mental control needed for shifting required time and practice. It took most Annlyn children a year or two to master that power, and I was trying to perfect that skill in a few days.

So, I needed a soulstone. The amber pendant that Pazho had gifted me provided the perfect conduit for magic.

I drew out the necklace with its clear dark yellow jewel. Joichan took it from me and placed in on the table between us.

"How does this work?" I asked.

My father, lost in studying the amber stone, absently replied, "I'll need your blood."

"Excuse me?" Horrified, I reached out to grab the necklace back, then stopped myself. Instead, I drummed my fingers on the table, full of nervous energy.

Joichan broke off from his intense scrutiny of the pendant. "Don't worry, I don't need a lot. And dragons heal fast. It comes from being an innately magical being, you know."

I didn't know, and the reassurance didn't make me feel much better. I hastily removed my hand from the table, as if my father had suggested that cutting off a few digits was necessary for the soulstone spell.

Joichan laughed. "It's not as bad as it sounds. I suppose because most shapeshifters are so young when they go through this, no one remembers the pain. But you'll be fine."

The hardest part — according to my father — was finding a stone that was suitable for spell casting. Not all gemstones were able to hold magic; sometimes a rock was just a rock. But my father could sense the aura of enchantment around my amber pendant, and deemed it a worthy blank slate waiting to be linked to the right owner.

My father took a sharp knife, heated the blade in the fire, and set it aside on top of a clean cloth that was lying on the table. While we waited for the knife to cool, he gathered other items from around the cave. A smooth ceramic bowl. A candle, slightly used from the look of it. Some small pieces of fabric for bandages. Various dried herbs in smoky glass jars. A pitcher of water. The table was rather crowded by the time my father found the last thing he wanted and sat back down at the table with me.

Joichan had me open the jars and pour out a scoop of each herb into their corresponding jar lid. While I did that, he poured water into the bowl and touched a fingertip to the the water's surface. It instantly boiled and steam wafted up. Impressed, I raised an eyebrow at my father. Joichan grinned. "One of the other advantages of being an innately magical being."

"One whose specialty is fire?"

"There is that, yes."

Joichan threw herbs into the bubbling water, in varying measurements. The water turned greenish, with a somewhat sweet smell I couldn't identify. I breathed deeply. It wasn't unpleasant, but it was definitely potent.

Joichan held out his hand expectantly. "May I see your hand?"

With trepidation, I placed my hand, palm up, in his. With his free hand, my father picked up the now-cool knife. Holding my hand steady, he made a quick cut across my palm. It barely stung; my brain only registered that he had cut me when I saw the red bloom of blood on my hand.

Joichan put the knife aside and pressed against the wound, making the blood flow faster. He turned my hand upside down so the blood dripped from my wound into the bowl of water below. The water turned muddy-colored. The metallic scent of my blood mingled with the herbal aroma, and I turned my face away, trying to not breathe in too deeply.

My father put the necklace, amber first, into the bowl. When the last gold glint had slid beneath the surface, he said, "*Junctus*. May the two become one. *Fiat*."

There was a flash, and the sickly smell grew stronger, then completely disappeared. As did the water in the bowl. All that was left was my necklace and a few soggy herbs at the bottom.

"Did it work?" I breathed.

"Let's check, shall we?"

My father quickly bound my cut with one of the bandages lying nearby and released my hand. He lit the candle and waited until there was a nice, steady flame. Then, picking up the necklace, he held the amber up to the light and studied it intensely.

"Well?" I tried to hide my impatience.

"See for yourself." My father waved for me to come closer. I leaned in until I was practically touching the pendant with my nose. I studied the gemstone, but didn't see anything. I looked at my father, who just shook his head at me and nodded back at the jewelry he was patiently holding over the flame. I looked again.

There — I could see something. At first I thought it was my reflection, but it couldn't be. The image of myself in the amber was too clear for that. It was more like my likeness had been caught inside the amber. And I felt it pulling me in, crying out for me. My father willingly dropped the necklace into my outstretched hand. Once my fingers touched it, I felt much better. Complete.

"May I?" My father took the necklace from me and clasped it around my neck. He beamed. "Perfect. It suits you, daughter of dragons."

Chapter Thirty-Three

I SPENT THE NEXT DAY practicing my magic and shapeshifting skills, aided by my new soulstone, while Joichan rested in the back of the cave. With the stone, I was able to change forms faster and maintain my dragon self longer.

After several hours of intense spell casting, I sat down next to my father for a much-needed break.

"Even with my new soulstone, it's much harder work than I thought," I said.

"You're doing well, considering other shifters have been practicing since they were children, and you're trying to cram a lifetime of learning into just a few days," Father said. I basked in the glow of his praise, something I had rarely gotten from my false father, Hendon.

Which reminded me...

"Father, something has been bothering me."

"Yes, Jennica?"

"How did Hendon get a hold of your soulstone? And how was he able to use it against you?"

In dragon form, Joichan arched his back, stretching. "I was a fool, overly trusting. Hendon sought me out, claiming he hoped to learn from my dragon wisdom. I allowed him to stay with me for several days, in which he learned much about Annlyn and dragon magic — and my soulstone. Including how to create one, and how to tap into the magic of an existing one. Soulstones, while primarily used by shapeshifters, can aid other users of magic. It's just that the secret of how to create one is very well protected by us shapeshifters. My only consolation is that he never learned I was able to change into a human too, as I didn't shift at all when he was staying with me.

"One night, he drugged me and stole my necklace while I slept. I woke up and my stone was gone, with no way of tracking him. I could only surmise that he must have cast or carried some kind of spell to disguise himself and obliterate his tracks. I spent several months hunting him down, finally locating him somewhere near Calia. So I settled down there to wait for him, hoping his greed would cause him to be foolish."

"Greed? What do you mean?"

Joichan pointed at my amber pendant. "A soulstone is linked to only one person upon its creation. It gains its power through the constant usage and link it has with its person. A symbiotic loop, if you will. If someone else were to use it, they would eventually deplete its magic, since they are not 'keyed in' to the soulstone. My stone would have run out of power and then Hendon would either need to create his own or replenish mine."

"But Hendon's not a shapeshifter. How could he create a soulstone?"

"Ah, that's the trick, isn't it? As I recall, he's from Rothschan. They're about as magically dry as you can get — not only does that kingdom have no magical abilities, they pass down teachings about how evil it is, so they have generations of mental defenses built up against it. It would take a lot of magical power for someone like him. An immense amount of power. And it's dangerous; it could backfire on him and cause him to go insane. Or even kill him. It's incredibly risky, but if he could do it successfully then he would have a source of magical power to tap into. It would eventually run out though, since, again, he has no innate magic. He'd have to find a way to replenish it somehow."

BY THE END OF THE DAY I had just about mastered conscious control of my changing, even if I wasn't able to stay a dragon for more than half a day.

My father declared his pride in my progress, and with the next breath, announced that he was completely well and we would leave in the morning for Calia. I was glad to get going; I still couldn't connect with Taryn. But I was also worried about what we'd face back home — and facing Hendon.

We didn't prepare any provisions for the trip. Since we'd be flying to Calia in our dragon forms, we would hunt for food along the way. But my father didn't think it would be necessary, as he said the trip would take just under a day. I hoped I would be able to keep up. I hadn't had a chance to practice flying, since just changing into a dragon had been such an ordeal for me.

In the morning, before we left, I prepared an extremely large breakfast. Bemused, my father grabbed a single roll and sat down, eyeing me as I wolfed down my food.

"Flying on an overly full stomach can slow you down," he cautioned. "Not to mention give you stomach cramps."

I piled a second helping onto my plate. "I just don't want to hinder our journey by having to stop."

"Hunting on the go is not a problem. It's quite easy, actually, and a skill you should learn."

I shuddered. "No, thank you."

My father laughed. "When you're in dragon form, the instincts take over. You don't even notice the raw meat."

I tried not to gag. "I'd prefer not to have to hunt at all."

"It's inevitable. Dragons, even small ones, eat at least five times as much as any human. How are you going to make up that food deficit if you won't hunt?"

"I'll eat trees or bushes or something. If we find a nice apple orchard..."

My father snorted. "A vegetarian dragon. Imagine that."

I stopped eating as a thought suddenly hit me. "When you hunt... you don't hunt anywhere near Annlyn, do you?"

Joichan shook his head. "Shapeshifters don't taste very good. It's the confusion between which form you're eating. Human? Or animal?"

The food I had just swallowed threatened to come up. I pushed my plate away, my appetite gone. "Oh."

My father laughed. "I'm just kidding. I'm a shapeshifter myself; I don't hunt my own."

I nodded, but it was some time before I was ready to finish my breakfast.

After we cleaned up the morning meal, we got ready to leave for Calia. On the ledge, I looked over the steep slope going downward. There wasn't enough space for us both to transform, much less for me to get up to speed for flying. "Uh... Father? How are we going to do this?"

"We jump."

"You can't be serious." We would plummet to our deaths within moments.

"I am. Now, jump." With that, Joichan took his own advice and leapt off the ledge. I screamed, but I wasn't sure if it was because of Joichan's plunge or because suddenly there was an immense golden dragon flapping its mighty wings in front of me. The dragon didn't say anything, but I could just see the exasperated amusement in his eyes. *What are you waiting for?*

Okay, here I go, I thought. *I hope he can fly fast enough to catch me before I hit the ground.*

I closed my eyes and stepped off the cliff.

I may have screamed again. I'm not sure; the air was rushing by me so fast that any sound from my throat got ripped away. I opened my eyes, expecting to see my father flying right next to me.

Instead, he was still hovering in the same place I had last seen him in.

And the ground was coming up way too fast.

I closed my eyes, trying to slow my anxious breathing so I could concentrate. In. Out. In. Out. My nerves calmed somewhat, enough for the hasty training of the last week or so to take over.

My awareness turned into myself, pushing out any intrusions from the outside world. My magic settled deep within me, filling every part of me and heightening my sensation of my self. My body tingled with the latent power within me. When I was ready, I *pulled*.

There's no better way I can describe it. It felt like I was tugging my human skin over my head, revealing my dragon form underneath. My nose elongated into a snout, smoke trailing from my nostrils. My body grew larger, skin becoming thicker with shining golden scales, new muscles rippling. Wings unfurled from my back, and I was aloft.

I glided a little unsteadily back to my father, who had been watching, unmoving, as I went through my shift. Was he laughing at me? There was a smile in his eyes, something I never thought that was possible for a dragon.

"Good job." Joichan's rumbly voice held a tremor. He was definitely laughing at me. We started our flight northward to Calia.

"You just stayed there. Would you have flown after me if I couldn't have changed in time?" I asked.

"Of course," he said. "But I knew I didn't need to."

Chapter Thirty-Four

WE HEADED STRAIGHT for Calia, with a few stops for rest and food. The dragon's body was much stronger than my normal form, but as I was unused to being a dragon for any length of time, I tired faster than Joichan did. Also, I was still learning to fly — some of it was instinctual, which helped, but I definitely needed more practice.

My father was highly amused when I insisted we cook the game we hunted. Even though I was resting in my dragon form, the human side of me couldn't stomach the idea of eating raw meat. Joichan obliged, and kindly turned away to eat his share, one of the cows we had taken from an open field. I was pretty sure I could still hear it mooing, although my father assured me he had killed it first before consuming it.

As we flew I asked my father about his solitary life. In general, dragons didn't enjoy living near civilization. But if you were a dragon who could also become a human, wouldn't you want to live near other people?

"Not necessarily," Father said. "Dragons are, by nature, very reserved creatures. In my case, my dragon nature won out over my human side."

When he was eighteen, my father said, he moved to the nearby cave where my friends and I had first encountered him. But with constant interruptions from dragon seekers (or worse, dragon hunters), he moved to his second cave in the mountains, occasionally using the first one as a base to visit his foster family or his few friends in Annlyn.

And Father lit up when I mentioned meeting Pazho. "He's a good man; he just accepts things as they are and never imposes his viewpoint on them. He's one of the few people who never treated me like I was cursed."

"He's the one who gave me my soulstone," I said.

"I'm not surprised. Pazho is one of the wisest people I've ever known. He has an uncanny ability to clearly see to the heart of things — or people."

We were gliding through the air, our huge shadows skimming the ground below us. Admiring the fast-moving countryside, I looked up and ahead — and flew straight into a cloud. Suddenly I was being attacked by hundreds of little wispy feathers made of cold air. I began sneezing uncontrollably, bits of flame snorting from my nostrils.

Father laughed. "That's why you should pay attention to where you're flying."

"Easy for you to — *a-choo!* — say," I said, my voice thick. "*A-choo!* I need to rest."

Spotting an empty field, I winged toward it, my father still laughing heartily as he followed me.

Despite our frequent stops, we still made good time to Calia. The sun was dipping low in the sky when we saw the towers and crenellations of the kingdom's castle. We landed several miles away from the kingdom's gates. It was partly out of a desire to stay hidden. Dragons weren't common in Calia, and it would have raised an alarm if we were spotted so close to the kingdom. But also, we *couldn't* get any closer.

Surrounding Calia for miles around were bunches of tents and makeshift camps. Twilight was just giving way to nighttime, and the random fires that flared up illuminated our way. We kept to the shadows, but most of the campsites were too busy to pay attention to two nondescript people walking through.

We passed by one tent, an imposing emerald-green affair that could have easily housed me and my former traveling companions and had room to spare. I fleetingly wondered what became of them after Joichan had taken me away. Most likely they had returned to Orchwell. Perhaps they were already on a new seeking mission. My heart twisted, and I wished I could have had a chance to explain things, or at least say goodbye.

A tall male servant returned to the campsite holding an empty chamber pot. A stout woman sitting by the fire, roasting a rabbit on a spit, looked up as he approached.

"His Grace has kept you hopping tonight." She turned the rabbit slightly.

"I'll be glad when this wedding is over and we can go home to Shonn," the man said. "Bad enough it took so long to come this far west. We can't even get a room in the city, everything's so full. Camping makes His Grace irritable and then he takes it out on us. And we still have the journey home, too."

The woman clicked her tongue in warning. "Don't say that too loud. You never know who's listening."

"He's not here," the man assured her. "He's at the castle, for some dinner party King Hendon is throwing for all the nobles prior to the wedding. Don't expect him back until late. If he can even stumble his way back after drinking all night."

The woman turned the spit again, this time with enthusiasm. "Perfect. More for us."

The man laughed and disappeared into the deep green tent, presumably to put the chamber pot away before joining his companion for dinner. Joichan and I continued on.

On the outskirts of the campgrounds, I saw two familiar figures hunched around a fire. I gave a little cry of recognition and moved toward them, even as my father tried to grab my sleeve to hold me back. Two faces turned toward me: Farrah and Rhyss.

"Allayne!" Farrah jumped up, about to embrace me, but Rhyss stood up warily.

Now that I was face to face with my former traveling companions, I wasn't sure what to say. "Uh. Hi, Farrah. Rhyss. Um. How have you been?"

"Well enough," Farrah said. "You?"

"Same." There was an uncomfortably long silence. I looked around their campsite. "Where's Beyan?"

At that moment I heard footsteps approaching the camp. Beyan stepped out of the darkness and into the firelight. He stopped short when he saw me. "Allayne."

"Beyan. It's good to see you again."

He stepped closer to Farrah and Rhyss, forming a human wall that quite clearly kept me out. "I don't know that I can say the same."

"I know you're angry at me for what happened at the dragon's cave." I looked at each of them in turn. "I'm sorry you felt like I betrayed you. I couldn't let you kill him."

Farrah and Rhyss shifted uneasily. I knew that they had been against Beyan killing Joichan — indeed, any dragon — as it would have corrupted the mission and Beyan's soul. But he was also their leader and their friend, and they were duty bound to support him and his decisions.

"Why not?" Beyan's voice was bitter. "You knew what it meant to me."

I looked back uncertainly, to where my father was waiting in the shadows. He stepped forward, nodding slightly. Now that I had his unspoken permission to share our secret, I felt better. With more confidence, I turned back to my friends, who were staring open-mouthed at Joichan.

"That's ... that's the man from the cave!" Rhyss said.

"Yes. This is Joichan," I said. I turned to Beyan, who stiffened but didn't move. "I know you wanted to kill him because you wanted to avenge your father. I couldn't let you do that because... Joichan is *my* father. That's why I wanted to find him."

Now all my friends' gaping faces were fixed on me.

"My mother asked me to find him because we need his help. My mother is — "

"Queen Melandria of Calia," Beyan said flatly.

Now it was my turn to gape, at Beyan. "How did you know?"

"When we came here, to Calia, your name was on everyone's lips," Farrah said. "The upcoming wedding of Crown Princess Jennica Allayne Kenetria Denyah of Calia to Prince Anders of Rothschan. When we asked around, the description people gave of the princess matched yours. Simple, really."

"Why did you come to Calia? I figured you would all return to Orchwell, since you had technically fulfilled your task."

Suddenly no one in the group would meet my eyes. Was it embarrassment? Beyan said, "We wanted to find you, and thought you would eventually make your way back home."

"We've been camping here for a few days, enough time to ask questions," Farrah added. "That's how we discovered you were the princess."

I was amazed that my luck in hiding my identity had lasted so long. "If you knew that I was the princess, then didn't you wonder why I was on the road headed south instead of here in Calia preparing for my wedding?"

"Once we figured it out, we did discuss it among ourselves," Farrah admitted. "But nothing we came up with made any sense."

I took a deep breath. "I do not want the marriage, but King Hendon is pushing for it for reasons unknown. My mother fears that the king is using the wedding as a way to take over all of the Gifted Lands. She sent me to find my real father, Joichan, to help us stop the wedding. Which is why I asked for your help to find Joichan. I'm sorry I didn't tell you sooner."

Another long silence met my words. Blood pounded in my ears. Now that I was no longer keeping secrets from my friends, I hoped that they wouldn't reject me, but I knew I had no right to ask that of them.

I suddenly felt arms around me, and looked up into Farrah's sympathetic face. "All is forgiven."

Suddenly embarrassed, she pulled away. "I meant to say, Your Highness, it doesn't matter that you lied to us. Uh, I mean...... Oh, dear. Was it okay that I hugged you?"

I smiled. "Of course. I'm glad you've forgiven me. And... I'm so used to not being called 'Your Highness' now that it seems odd to hear you say it."

Farrah laughed as I pulled her back into a warm embrace. Behind her, Rhyss grinned, the tension gone from his face. I hugged him next. When I let Rhyss go, I turned to Beyan. His expression was more enigmatic, but he smiled at me. Our embrace was brief, yet somehow felt full of unspoken thoughts. Next to me, I felt the tension in my father ease.

Beyan gestured toward the fire. "Feel free to stay awhile. I'm sure we have a lot of things to talk about." His glance lingered on Joichan.

"I wish we could," I said. "We need to get inside the castle. If we can come back, we will."

"Please do." Beyan looked like he wanted to say something more, but Joichan touched my shoulder, indicating we should leave.

As we turned to go, Beyan called out to us. "Allayne... I mean, Your Highness. Princess Jennica. Before you go..."

He pressed something into my hand. I looked at the simple little ring in the center of my palm. I slipped it onto my littlest finger, grateful to have it back. "Thank you," I said. Beyan nodded at us and stepped back.

Joichan and I continued on our way. We had reached a rare quiet spot in the midst of the campsites when my father stopped me. "Can you get ahold of your friend? If she's available, she can help us get into the castle."

I doubted Taryn would answer my call, since we had been unable to connect the last several times I had tried her. But there was no harm in trying again, and my father was right — it would be near impossible to gain entrance into the castle without assistance. And I certainly didn't want to alert the guards, or worse, King Hendon, to the fact that I was back.

I quickly sketched the gestures and spoke the words for the calling spell. I held my fingers out, not expecting anything to happen. So I was taken by surprise when Taryn's face appeared almost immediately.

"Taryn! I can't believe it! I tried to get in touch before, but — "

"Princess! I'm sorry I wasn't able to respond before, and I don't have much time now. It's all gone so very, very bad here. I'm being watched as well."

"But what — "

"I don't have much time, and there's too much to tell you." Taryn glanced over her shoulder at something I couldn't see. As much as I wanted details, I could sense her fear.

"Then I'll be brief. Taryn, we're back in Calia, just outside the gates. We need help getting back into the castle."

"We?"

Joichan shook his head at me, warning me not to give away his secret just yet. "I'll explain when I see you. But for now — can you help us?"

"Yes, of course! I'll mark the path through the tunnels, just in case you need to use them without me around. But I'll meet you outside the castle, where the secret door is. You remember the location?"

I nodded. "We should be there shortly."

"Good. I'll see you soon."

Taryn's face disappeared as the magic faded.

Joichan and I made our way to the castle wall without incident. Even though there were so many visitors camped outside the castle — and presumably, overflowing the nearby town — the guards didn't challenge any who passed by them. I guessed they were probably used to it by now. The servants we had overheard talking had seemed to imply that the days and weeks leading up the wedding celebration were full of around-the-clock revelry.

We loitered by the hidden door, trying to blend into the deep shadows and not attract attention. We waited. And waited. And kept waiting.

Joichan's quiet voice in my ear startled me. "She definitely should have been here by now. Do you think something happened to your friend?"

I worried about that too, but hearing him say it out loud made it now seem like a real possibility.

"What should we do?" I whispered.

"I suppose we'll need to find another way in." He sounded doubtful.

I nodded absentmindedly. There was something small fluttering in the breeze, caught in the wall right around eye level. I stepped closer, reaching out to grab it. It was a hair ribbon, pale in the moonlight.

I reached out again, my hands brushing against the smooth unbroken stone... until suddenly it wasn't unbroken anymore. My father and I looked at each other. I grabbed the lip of the hidden door and pulled it open a little wider.

"I think Taryn was here." I indicated the ribbon in my fist. "I don't know what's happened, but I don't think we should wait any longer. She said she'd mark the passageway, so we should be okay."

My father followed me into the cool, dank tunnel. He tugged the door shut behind him, making the darkness in the passage complete. "*Illumine*," I said, and light flared above us.

True to her word, Taryn had marked the way we should go. At each turn a ribbon pointed the way, indicating the path she had taken. It made me wonder if the ribbon I had found at the hidden door had been left on purpose or not. When we found Taryn, I would ask.

It didn't take us long to reach the end of the marked path and find the door leading back into the castle. Since I wasn't sure where Taryn's path had taken us, I indicated to my father that we should be quiet, and snuffed out the magical light. Slowly, carefully, I pushed open the door and peeked out.

A hand reached out to pull the door open wider. Standing on the other side was my mother; we had made our way back to her chambers. When she saw me she immediately pulled me into her arms and held me tight.

"Jennica! I'm so glad you're back, and you're safe! I worried so much."

I hugged my mother tight, never wanting to let her go. She pulled back, looking me over. Then her eyes went to the person who had walked in after me, and was standing just behind me. She gasped.

"Joichan?"

Chapter Thirty-Five

MY MOTHER AND MY FATHER stared at each other. I stared at them, staring at each other.

Then suddenly they were in each other's arms. "Joichan! It is you!" My mother was laughing and crying at the same time.

"Melandria. It's been far, far too long." Joichan's voice was thick, as if he was also fighting back tears.

I looked away, feeling like I was intruding on a private moment.

"Melandria, I'm sorry," Joichan said. "I should have returned sooner. I should have — "

My mother cleared her throat and stepped out of Joichan's embrace. Her bearing changed, and we were suddenly seeing Melandria the queen, not Melandria the woman.

"It doesn't matter anymore, Joichan." Her voice was gentle but steady. "We have a beautiful daughter — " she smiled at me " — and you've come back when I needed you the most. I... We... The kingdom... need your help to stop... my husband."

Joichan nodded. There was a definite change between them, a wall of propriety and obligation that neither dared cross. My heart ached at how fate had treated them both.

"I am at your service, Queen Melandria." Joichan made a little half bow, using the formality to put more physical distance between them.

I spoke up, hoping to ease the awkwardness in the air. "Mother, what's going on? Are you well? Taryn said you were under house arrest. And that our wedding deception had been discovered. And she was supposed to meet us to lead us here, but — "

My mother laughed softly and sat down, indicating that we should do the same. I closed the entrance to the secret passage, and then sat down next to her. My father took the chair across from us.

"I know you have a lot of questions," she said. "As do I." She pointedly looked between my father and me. "But let me tell you what's happened while you've been gone."

As Taryn had told me, King Hendon had grown suspicious of the queen and placed her under house arrest. When my disappearance was discovered, the king had questioned my mother intensely, for several hours.

"He tortured you?" I asked in horror. Joichan stirred restlessly, looking ready to strangle the king with his bare hands.

"Not physically," my mother said. "He knows he can't lay a hand on me and get away with it, especially with the wedding day being so close. People would see something was wrong and question it. He may be the king, but he only holds the title because *I* inherited the kingdom."

"What did he do, then?"

"He used magic to force my mind, and my mouth, open against my will." My mother looked down at her clasped hands, which were so tense her knuckles were white. "I held out as long as I could, but he's too strong now."

"Now? What do you mean? I thought he hated magic."

"He does, outwardly. But he's not above using magical items or people to gain what he wants. And somehow, over the years, he's acquired some magical skill of his own. I didn't realize... I've failed you, Jennica. Us. Because I should have been paying attention. I didn't know what he's become. I worry that we may be too late to stop him."

I shook my head, still not quite understanding. Hendon was a spell caster in his own right? If this was true, then he had fooled us all. And how had this happened?

My father took off his moonstone necklace and held it in his hand, studying the stone and scowling ferociously. "I think I have an idea of how this occurred," he said, and I realized I must have asked my questions aloud.

He held the necklace toward us, as if we could see what he saw in its creamy depths. "When a soulstone is created, it contains the essence of the person it is linked to." He indicated my amber necklace. "As you saw when we created yours, Jennica. And as you use your soulstone, it will gain more and more of your power, which is shared freely between you and the jewel as you use it. It is, quite literally, an extension of you. You can do without it, of course, as I did all these years. But it will always be a part of you."

He rubbed his thumb over the moonstone. "When Hendon stole my gem, he was able to tap into it and use my power to drive me away. He couldn't defeat me with it, because how could I defeat myself? But he definitely used it to cripple me and drive me away. I often wondered how he was able to do it, but when we did Jennica's ceremony I figured it out.

"I think somehow Hendon blood-linked to my soulstone, which should be impossible, but somehow he did it. And by linking to it, he was able to draw on its power, and also learn how to use magic — whatever spells I had cast using my soulstone. And as I am a long-lived dragon, and was rather ambitious in my youth learning magic... he would have been able to learn a lot."

"Hendon wears a lot of jewelry, but I've never seen him wearing the moonstone necklace. And it's been *years.* I don't think he's tapped into your necklace in all that time." I looked to Mother for confirmation, who shook her head as if to say, *I don't know.*

"He wouldn't have to," Joichan said. "When you gave it back to me to help me heal, I noticed there was hardly any power left. There was just enough to tap into to close my wound, and that was it. As I've been using my necklace these past few days, it's been replenishing the magical supply, but I think Hendon siphoned my essence from the necklace. Either he used it all, or — more likely, I would guess, if he's grown as powerful as Melandria has said — he's stored it in something."

This was so disturbing, neither my mother nor I commented on the fact that Joichan had used the queen's name so familiarly.

"That makes sense," my mother said. "How will we find it? And once we find it, what do we do?"

"If he's able to perform such powerful magic, then my guess is that it's something he's carrying on his person," Joichan said. "So he's able to tap into it at will. Once we identify it, we need to take it from him. And destroy it."

Chapter Thirty-Six

IT WOULDN'T BE EASY to discover. The king reveled in his powerful station, and loved showing off his wealth and position. Besides his wedding band, he often wore a lot of jewelry — several rings, a few necklaces, wrists full of bracelets. I had never sensed anything magical emanating from any of them, but then again, I hadn't known what to look for.

My mother quickly summed up the rest of her story. King Hendon was enraged to find out I was gone, but had decided to go ahead with the "wedding" anyway. We had thought to use the pre-wedding isolation tradition to our advantage, but now he was using it to his. Citing Calian custom, the princess didn't need to appear at any of the state functions and pre-wedding celebrations leading up to the event. So my disappearance wasn't widely known, except to the king and queen. And Taryn.

My mother said, "She waits on me regularly, so we can plan and discuss. When Hendon discovered you were missing, he changed the servants' schedules so only Taryn was allowed to 'attend' you until the wedding. I'm unsure if he knew that Taryn was involved in your disappearance, but he threatened her with her family's safety to keep her silent. I know she's being watched as well, but to my knowledge she is still able to move about freely."

I showed my mother the ribbon I had found in the castle wall's hidden door. My mother gasped. "I gave her the ribbons to hang in the passageway, but this is Taryn's own hair ribbon. It's her favorite; she said it was a gift from her brother. So if you found this... and she wasn't at your appointed meeting place... darling, I hope it is nothing, but I fear that it might mean something has befallen her."

I started to shake, overcome with sobs that I tried desperately to hold back. Mother held me, stroking my hair. My father stood up and started pacing.

"So we need to find your friend," he said. "And we need to stop this wedding."

My mother and I both looked at Joichan. He answered our unasked question. "I find it suspicious that Hendon is still moving forward with the wedding, even though he doesn't have Jennica in hand, and has no guarantee that he will. There's something more here than just saving face with Rothschan. If he wanted to do that, he wouldn't have invited all the other five kingdoms to come here. It doesn't make sense."

"Find Taryn. Stop the wedding. Stop Hendon. How are we going to do all of that?" I hated how thin and scared my voice sounded.

"First things first," Joichan said. "We can't stay here." He looked longingly at my mother. "As much as I'd like to." She looked away. "Nowhere in the castle will be safe for us, and we can't risk your mother's safety."

"We can stay with my friends outside the city."

My father nodded slowly. "Yes, that could work. We'll head there now, and figure out what our next steps should be. Perhaps your friends would be willing to help us."

"You should go now, then," my mother said. "Hendon is hosting a feast for all the visiting nobles, and while I'm sure there may be some who will continue the festivities late into the night, most of them will be leaving soon."

I hugged my mother fiercely, fighting tears for the second time that evening. Our meeting was much too brief, but I was glad to know she was safe.

My father and I made our way through the secret passage and back outside the castle. Although there was less activity on the grounds than earlier, we were still able to get back to the campgrounds without incident.

Beyan, Farrah, and Rhyss were where we had left them, sitting by the fire. Beyan looked concerned. Farrah had a scowl on her face. Rhyss was eyeing them both, as if he was unsure if it was safe to say or do anything. When we approached, Beyan jumped up. "You made it back!"

I shifted uneasily. "Yes. Um. Would it be too much of an imposition if we joined you for the night? It's not safe for us in the castle."

"Of course. We still have your bedroll. And I'm sure we can cobble something together for... um..." Beyan refused to look at Joichan.

My father held his hands out toward Beyan in a gesture of peace. "Come. Take a walk with me, young man. I think we have a lot of things to talk about."

To all of our surprise, Beyan actually obeyed. The two men left the campsite and disappeared into the night.

While they were gone, Farrah, Ryhss, and I caught up with each other while we ate a late supper. Finally I was able to learn what had happened after we all got separated.

When Joichan had flown off with me, the group hadn't lingered in the area. My behavior — or, betrayal — had made it clear that a rescue attempt would not have been welcome. Instead, they immediately headed north. Beyan's new mission was to come to Calia, to demand an audience with Queen Melandria to find out what had been the real purpose of our trip.

"He encouraged us to return to Orchwell." Farrah looked at Rhyss, who seemed uncharacteristically somber. "But it didn't seem like a good idea to leave him alone. In all of the years I've known him... I've never seen him so... I don't know. So single-minded. Heaven help anyone who got in his way."

"With the upcoming wedding, I can't imagine he'd be able to see the queen. Even during regular times it would be hard enough. What did he plan to do with the information, if he could get it?" I said. What could Beyan possibly be thinking? Farrah's and Rhyss's blank faces told me they didn't know, either.

Farrah shrugged. "Some sort of catharsis for him? We don't really know, and he wouldn't tell us."

"Was he able to see her?" If my mother had met Beyan, I was sure she would have mentioned it to me.

Farrah and Rhyss exchanged glances. "He was at the castle earlier today. I... we... it's probably best if you talk to him about it."

I nodded, wondering why my friends were being so cagey. I supposed they were still trying to suss me out, to see if I was truly trustworthy. It hurt, but I couldn't blame them.

We cleaned up and then prepared the campsite for the night. With all the constant activity around us, Farrah and Rhyss said a watch wasn't necessary, but I offered to stay up to wait for Joichan and Beyan.

By the time the two men returned, my eyelids were growing heavy and I had to jerk myself awake several times. But as tired as I was, I could tell something had changed between them. What had they talked about? They were much more at ease in each other's company. Not quite friends, but no longer enemies either.

My father curled up near the fire, eschewing the bedroll Beyan offered him. "One of the advantages of being able to change into an animal is that you adapt easier to your environment." Well, now I knew how much Joichan had shared about his history. What had he shared of mine? "I may not be able to shift my body, but I can shift my mindset, and it will simply feel like I'm sleeping in my dragon form."

"I wish it was that easy for me," Beyan said. "Even after years of traveling, I still have trouble sleeping when I'm on the road."

"I do too," I agreed, but my jaw-cracking yawn belied my words.

Joichan laughed and settled in to sleep, as did Beyan and I. Soon my father's light snoring joined Farrah's and Rhyss's gentle breathing. I yawned again, trying to get comfortable on the hard ground.

"Allayne? I mean, Your Highness?" Beyan whispered.

"Just Jennica is fine." I yawned again "Yes?"

"I... I'm glad you're back." His fingers reached out, barely brushing mine.

"I'm glad you and the others aren't mad at me anymore. I haven't had many friends in my life. Political acquaintances, yes, but not true friends. It killed me to think that you and Farrah and Rhyss would think poorly of me."

"It wasn't Farrah and Rhyss so much as it was me. I was the one who was the angriest. I had a good talk with your... father. He explained a lot of things to me: what he is, what really happened when he was in Calia. What happened when he met my father. I... I understand things better now."

"Do you still want revenge for your father?" My exhaustion was beginning to outweigh my discomfort, but I fought it, wanting to hear Beyan's answer.

"Yes. But not against Joichan. The one who should pay is King Hendon. I was looking at the wrong person — dragon? — all along."

"We have something in common, now." I laughed softly. Then, in a more serious tone: "Help me, Beyan. Help me stop the king. My mother says he's grown incredibly powerful. We'll need all the allies we can get."

"Of course... Jennica. Whatever help you need, I'll be there. And I know the others feel the same."

"Good." I yawned.

We fell silent for a long moment. Beyan's fingers curled more tightly around mine. The last thing I heard before I gave in to sleep was him murmuring my name. "Jennica..."

Chapter Thirty-Seven

I WOKE UP A LITTLE chilly and disoriented. The cold was from my arms being outside my bedroll. And the confusion was from a very vivid dream about Beyan. I blushed at the memory. Had he been holding my hand when we fell asleep? I turned to face him — and then was really confused. He wasn't there.

I sat up and surveyed our campsite. Farrah and Rhyss were just waking up as well. My father and Beyan were missing.

"Where is everyone?" I asked.

"Your father just left a few minutes ago. He went to get water for us," Rhyss said. As I recalled, there was a river about two miles away.

"Where's Beyan? Did he go with Joichan?"

"I don't think so, I think he was already gone," Farrah said. "We don't know where he went."

"Hopefully he comes back soon," I said.

With uncanny timing, Beyan appeared at the campsite. He was breathing heavily and there was a sheen of sweat on his forehead. He quickly surveyed our group. "Where's Joichan?"

"He's headed to the river," Farrah said. "Where have you been?"

Beyan ignored her and started grabbing whatever he could from the campsite, hastily packing things haphazardly. "Come on, we have to get moving."

Farrah, Rhyss, and I didn't move. "What's going on?" Rhyss asked.

"I'll explain later, but for now, we have to *go*," Beyan said.

"What about Joichan?" Farrah said.

"We'll find him later. Come *on*, we don't have much time."

His unceasing urgency finally galvanized us into action. We jumped out of our bedrolls and started packing, but it was too late. Heavy footsteps made us look up. Several of King Hendon's soldiers marched into our campsite.

Two of the soldiers instantly targeted me, grabbing my arms and forcing me away from the others. My friends tried to come to my aid, but found themselves facing the sharp ends of the soldiers' swords. One of the men stepped forward. I recognized him as Kestos, the Captain of the Guard.

"Kestos! What are you and your men doing? I demand you let me go, right now!" I tried to dig in my heels, but the two men holding me easily lifted me as if I weighed no more than a feather. With the guards holding my arms, I was unable to cast any spells. Not that I would have wanted to; I would never have wanted to do anything, magical or otherwise, against my own people.

Kestos looked at me sadly. "I have to follow orders, Your Highness. Otherwise, there will be *consequences*."

He turned to Beyan, who was glaring at the men holding me. "His Majesty, King Hendon of Calia, thanks you for your help, young man."

Farrah gasped. Rhyss's eyes grew wide. Beyan turned his glare on Kestos.

"For your service." Kestos threw a small, dull brown pouch at Beyan's feet. The clink it made as it landed promised a hefty reward.

"You can keep your filthy money," Beyan spat out. He made a move, like he was going to pick up the pouch and throw it, but the soldier who held him at sword point moved in closer. Beyan stepped back.

My guards started to haul me toward the castle. The people at the other campsites looked away as we passed; no one wanted to get involved in whatever issue had occurred. My vision was blurring; tears were flowing down my face, unchecked. Through my watery eyes I saw Beyan, Rhyss, and Farrah get smaller and smaller as they helplessly watched me get taken away.

Chapter Thirty-Eight

MY TEARS HAD STOPPED somewhere after we had entered the castle, but once the soldiers dragged me down to the dungeons, they threatened to start again.

I could see through my watery haze that I wasn't the only one down here. Each cell we passed had at least one or two occupants, sometimes more. Young and old, male and female. Some of the prisoners were mumbling to themselves, while others sat or lay on the ground and stared at the walls. I was shocked to recognize one or two nobles in the cells; I had been informed, months ago, that they had left for their country estates and would be gone for a while. And yet, here they were in the palace dungeons. With me.

One boy started screaming as we passed. I longed to put my hands to my ears to drown out the noise, but since two soldiers had a firm grip on my arms, I didn't try. Instead, I stared at him as we passed, overcome by some morbid fascination. The screaming boy was in the same cell as a young girl who was staring sightlessly out into the corridor. They had similar features. In fact, they were twins. The girl was —

"Sava?" I gasped, and stopped walking to get a better look. It *was* her, the blueberry-loving kitchen maid that Taryn and I had discussed oh-so-long ago.

"Sava, are you okay? Why are you in here?" I spoke a little louder, trying to drown out her screaming brother and get her attention. Sava didn't respond when I called her name. She just kept staring, dead-eyed, at something beyond me.

One of the soldiers holding my arm shook me a little, tightening his grip. "Keep moving."

Reluctantly, I started walking again. We passed two more cells before the guards unlocked a door and shoved me into a cell. My tears started falling in earnest.

Sniffling, I blinked rapidly, trying to stop the tears and adjust to the dim light coming from a small, barred window near the ceiling.

I stared despondently at the magic-blocking band one of the soldiers had clamped around my wrist before shoving me into the cell. The dark metal bracelet glared back at me, as if daring me to try my abilities. I tried to cast a calling spell; my magic sputtered and recoiled back on me, shocking my hand and causing my heart to beat erratically. I sat down hard, breathless and scared. It was a good thing I hadn't tried a bigger or more complex spell. Who knows what the repercussions might have been? But it also meant I would not be able to contact Joichan or anyone else through my magic.

I heard rustling somewhere to my left. I gasped and lifted my skirts. Rats?

"Jennica? Is that you?"

My eyes had adjusted enough to see a shadowy figure on the floor. A slim woman with tangled blond curls, whose voice sounded like...

"Taryn?"

She barreled into me, giving me an enormous hug. "I'm so glad you're okay!" She stiffened and stepped back, eyes downcast. "I mean... forgive me, Your Highness, for being so familiar."

I reached out and pulled her back into an embrace. "Taryn, you ninny. Titles don't matter down here. Especially not between friends. I'm so glad to see you safe."

My face was wet again, but I was laughing. Taryn was laughing and crying as well. For several minutes, we let it all out, the tension and hysteria and relief and uncertainty. When we had finally controlled ourselves, Taryn sat down on the stone floor and patted the area next to her. Gingerly, I joined her, gathering my skirts around me and keeping a lookout for rats, roaches, and other vermin.

"I guess you could say I'm safe, in a manner of speaking." Taryn ran her fingers through her hair, which was a dusty mess from sleeping on the floor. "The guards took me while I was waiting for you. I had just closed the secret door when they came for me. I hope they didn't find the passage."

"Not to my knowledge. We did find your ribbon, though." I handed back the bit of blue cloth that I still carried in my dress pocket.

Taryn took it back gratefully and tied it around her hair. "It must have gotten caught in the door. Thank you for bringing it back to me."

"Of course. I'm just happy to find you again. What happened after the guards took you?"

"They brought me before the king. He questioned me about you, how long you had been gone, where you went and why. He seemed to know a lot about your leaving already; it felt like he just wanted me to fill in some of the missing pieces."

"Mother said he used magic on her to force her to give him information."

"I didn't know the king could do magic. I thought he didn't *like* magic."

"He doesn't. Which makes me wonder how he is able to do any magic in the first place, let alone become so powerful. It takes a certain amount of skill and power to force information out of someone without breaking their mind. Did he do that to you?"

"No. He didn't use magic on me." Taryn paused, looking confused as if trying to recall something just beyond her memory's reach. "At least, I don't think so. Maybe he felt, as a lowly servant, I wasn't worth it. And I don't think I added too much to his knowledge; once he started having me watched, I made sure you and I weren't in contact as much. I'm sorry for that, but often it just didn't feel safe to answer your summons."

"I understand. So then what happened?"

Taryn massaged her temples, as if her head hurt. "I... I'm not sure. He questioned me, then the next thing I remember is being in this cell. But when the guards took me, it was nighttime. When I was in here, it was noon. Or maybe early afternoon, from the slant of the sun. I didn't fall asleep; if anything I was exhausted, as if I had been up all night. But I can't recall what happened between meeting the king and coming in here. I've tried and tried to remember, and every time my head aches and I draw a blank."

She squeezed her eyes shut against the pain, digging the heels of her hands into her head. I reached out and touched her shoulder. "It's okay, Taryn. Don't push yourself to remember if it hurts too much."

Taryn relaxed, but only a little. "It frightens me, not knowing."

I wished I could reassure my friend, but we both knew there was nothing I could say or do that wouldn't ring false. Instead I changed the subject, hoping Taryn might have information.

"Did you know Sava is in here? And her brother as well? They're a few cells down from us."

"I didn't know that," Taryn said. "I tried talking to whoever is locked up next door, but they seem to have lost their mind."

"That seems to be true for everyone in here." I told Taryn what I had seen in the other cells.

"I don't know what's going on," Taryn said. "But it sounds an awful lot like all those people they keep finding in the town."

"Whatever Hendon's doing, I'm going to find out. And I'm going to stop him," I declared.

Taryn didn't say anything. I think we both knew that my bravado was just my way of trying to make us feel better. So we just sat in silence, leaning against each other more for human connection than for support.

TIME PASSED IN A SLOW, mind-numbing crawl. How many hours had passed since the guards had thrown me in here? It was hard to tell.

Taryn didn't have any more news, so I told her mine — finding my father, developing my shapeshifting abilities. When I mentioned I could change into a dragon, Taryn perked up, wondering if I could transform and then break us out of the cell.

I perked up as well, looking around our prison with renewed interest. After a thorough investigation, I shook my head sadly.

"I don't think it would be wise," I said. "I'm not as big as my father when I transform, but a dragon is still way bigger than any human. I could transform and break the walls. Or I could transform and be too big for this space, cramped and unable to move or do anything useful."

Taryn blew out her breath, disappointed. "I suppose you're right; now's not the time to experiment. But maybe as a last resort...?"

"I'll definitely keep it in mind."

I finished filling Taryn in on the rest of my story. "And then Beyan, that *liar*, brought back a bunch of soldiers to our camp! We didn't stand a chance. They grabbed me and took me away, and that's how I ended up here."

Taryn clicked her tongue in sympathy. "I can't tell if you're more upset over being captured or over leaving Beyan behind."

"*Excuse* me?"

"Okay, fine. Beyan — *and the others* — behind."

"I could care less what happens to that two-timing seeker! I *trusted* him."

"And *he* trusted *you*, and look what happened. His charge taken by a dragon, his mission in ruins... I think if you two didn't care so much it wouldn't have mattered so much."

"He only cared about killing my father!" I said indignantly. Taryn just raised an eyebrow at me. "Well, it's true!"

She shook her head, trying to hide her smile. But I could hear it in her voice. "Of course, Princess. Whatever you say."

I wanted to keep arguing, but I wasn't even sure what we were arguing about. Plus, I knew I wouldn't be able to win the argument. Not when Taryn was in *that* mood.

It put *me* into a mood. And why was I so flustered about this, anyway?

We fell into a companionable silence. Eventually I dozed off, since there wasn't much else to do.

In my half-hazy state, I heard the heavy tread of boots in the hallway. I instantly came awake. Looking out into the dim torch-lit hallway, I could see two long shadows on the ground. The footsteps stopped right outside our door, and then metal grated on metal as a key turned in the lock.

Taryn and I jumped to our feet, trying to press into the wall.

The cell door swung in and a guard appeared, stepping to the side to allow someone in. The newcomer sniffed in disdain as he looked around our dirty prison, making a pretense of trying to keep his pristine robe from dragging in the dirt. His all-white tunic and breeches were already dusty from the trek down into the dungeons. I had a fleeting, idle moment of sympathy for the servants who would have to clean such an outfit.

Taryn's fingers dug into my arm as the man turned to appraise us. Contempt dripped from his expression even as the jewels dripping from his body dazzled in the dim light.

It was King Hendon.

Chapter Thirty-Nine

"HELLO, FATHER!" I PASTED the sweetest smile I could muster on my face, desperately turning on the charm. "Thank goodness you've come to straighten out this misunderstanding. Please don't punish these men too severely."

Turning my fake smile on the guard, I expected to see some sort of relieved or scared reaction from him. But instead, there was... nothing. His eyes were completely blank; he wasn't registering anything that was happening before him. I covered my confusion as I looked back at the king.

Who did not look at all happy to see me.

"Drop the act," King Hendon hissed. "We both know you're not my daughter."

My heart sank. I had assumed he only knew about my journey to find Joichan. Now I knew: he knew *everything*.

"Dragon spawn." Hendon practically spat the words at me. "Had I known how faithless your mother was, I would have had her killed long ago."

My eyes narrowed. Since he knew the truth, there was no point in pretending anymore. "Don't flatter yourself. She could never have been faithless to you. You never had her heart to begin with."

The king stiffened, and I realized with surprise I had hit a nerve. "Who needs a silly queen's love when you can have a whole kingdom?"

He came nearer. Taryn shrank behind me. I wanted to back away, too, but didn't want to show any fear.

Hendon stopped just in front of me. He was so close I could have spit in his face. Or wrapped my slim hands around his neck. I subtly shifted, readying myself to take action.

"Don't even think about it." Hendon toyed with the dark red jewel at his throat. It glowed unnaturally, too bright for the small amount of light in our cell. Its crimson beam fell across Taryn's eyes.

Suddenly, her fearful fingers on my arm changed to a heavy clamp, effectively holding me in place. Surprised, I tried to pull free, which only made her hold me harder. "Taryn? What are you doing?"

She didn't answer me.

"Taryn? Taryn!"

But her eyes had the same blank expression as the guard who was blocking the open door.

I eyed Hendon's ruby pendant. A soulstone. He caught my glance and, with a smug smile, displayed it proudly. "You know what this is, then? Such a handy thing. I don't know how I ever ruled this cursed kingdom without it."

"Where did you get that?" I gasped.

"I made it, of course. Using my original soulstone, a lovely little piece of moonstone, to provide the magic to infuse in this one. I had nearly finished transferring all of its dragon magic into my beautiful ruby charm when it was unfortunately stolen from me."

"Your soulstone? The one *you* stole from the dragon, you mean."

He waved his hand, brushing away my accusation. "Mere semantics. The dumb beast didn't deserve to have power like this at his fingertips."

Seeing Hendon with a soulstone of his own made me sick. And curious. "So you were able to create one. But why? I thought you hated magic. And you're not a shapeshifter. Are you?"

"Alas, no, I am not," Hendon said. "If I was, it might have made things much easier. And magic is abhorrent... too many people have it, but refuse to actually use it to its fullest potential. There are so many things you could do if you had all that knowledge and power. But instead, we teach our children about magic and then place restrictions on its use. Better for them not to have it all."

"So what do you propose?" I asked somewhat sarcastically. "That no one has any magic at all?"

"I doubt it will even be missed."

"Magical ability is innate. You can't just strip people of their inborn abilities. They'll lose their minds — at best. If you don't outright kill them."

"I'll admit that my first experiments had... less than favorable results. But I was able to get what I needed out of it." He stroked his ruby soulstone possessively. "From there, I was able to find more, ah, volunteers to help me. Some unfortunately didn't make it out of the tests with their wits intact. If they made it out at all."

With a gasp, I realized what he meant by *experiments*. "The people that kept turning up in the town alley... Sava and her brother."

"The magic of twins." Hendon licked his lips as if he was tasting an especially delectable dessert. "Especially potent."

"All these other people in the cells...?" My vision swam as I turned away, trying not to be sick.

King Hendon shrugged, unconcerned. "The pursuit of knowledge is rarely easy or neat. But failure is an unfortunate necessity."

"Experimenting with people's *lives* is not a *necessity*."

"Don't worry, Princess." My honorific sounded like a curse word coming from his mouth. "I've had plenty of time to perfect the process." Hendon's manic smile was chilling to behold. "Would you like to see?"

"Not really, no." I tried for defiant, but the nervous crack in my voice gave me away.

"You don't really have a choice, my dear."

Hendon reached out and tipped my chin toward him so I was forced to meet his gaze. I struggled against Taryn's hold. Hendon waved in her direction, and her grip grew even tighter around my arms.

"Just think, tomorrow is your wedding day. Aren't you excited? I understand every young woman dreams of what her wedding day will be like."

"I doubt Prince Anders wants to get married inside a jail cell," I said.

"Of course you won't get married in *here*." Hendon absentmindedly palmed his necklace with his free hand. "I'll release you, just in time for your wedding, if you promise to be on your best behavior. And I'll make sure you keep your promise."

The red jewel at his throat pulsed and gleamed; the unnatural light was reflected in his eyes, tinging his eyes crimson. Mesmerized, I couldn't look away from the light, although every part of my being was screaming that I should.

Hendon murmured a spell under his breath. I could feel the magic forming around me, heavy and expectant. I didn't know a counterspell, but I knew with all my being I did *not* want Hendon's spell to reach me.

At my throat, safely hidden under the bodice of my dress, my amber soulstone started to warm.

Hendon finished his spell. Whatever the spell was, its tendrils were trying to sink into my mind and body, but finding no purchase.

I didn't know what to do. Should I pretend his spell worked? But without knowing what he was trying to do, I didn't think I would be very convincing.

I hesitated too long. And, unfortunately, Hendon was smarter than that. He could tell immediately that, whatever his spell was supposed to accomplish, it hadn't worked.

He snarled at me. "How are you resisting? This spell has never failed."

His ruby grew brighter, looking like a bright stain of blood at the king's throat. It pulsed faster, as if in response to his anger. He gripped the necklace so hard his knuckles turned white.

My amber pendant grew hot, as if in response to Hendon's soulstone. Surprisingly, the heat from my necklace didn't burn me. I was afraid its reaction might cause Hendon to notice it despite its concealment, but he was concentrating too hard on his spell for anything else to catch his attention.

He repeated his spell over and over. His voice, already loud, continued to rise in volume. But still his spell didn't affect me.

The more Hendon chanted, the hotter my necklace burned. Somehow, it was protecting me from Hendon's magic.

Hendon broke off mid-incantation, his hand jerking away from my face so fast I involuntary flinched, afraid he'd strike me. But he didn't. Instead, he studied me with those calculating eyes. His face was mottled and he was practically panting, like he'd just been running or fighting.

"No matter," he said. "There's always an alternate path to achieving one's goals. I *will* get what I want, in the end. This is just a little detour."

He snapped his fingers, and Taryn released me and walked out the door, still in her spell trance. I started after her, but the guard blocked me.

Hendon left the cell. The guard followed, pulling the door shut with a decisive thud. I ran to the door and peered out through the bars, watching helplessly as the king placed a possessive hand on Taryn's unresisting arm.

The king turned to me. "I don't know how you resisted me, but don't think it will last for long, Princess. It will be quite a pleasure to figure out how you did it, and dismantle your defenses. I do so enjoy learning new things." He patted Taryn's arm and gestured down the hallway. "After you, my dear."

They walked away from my cell and out of my line of sight. Hendon's sickly sweet laughter echoed down the hallway, taunting me as it faded away.

Chapter Forty

MORE TIME PASSED IN an excruciatingly slow daze. Boredom and anxiety warred for supremacy in my mind. Eventually I dozed, exhaustion setting in after the adrenaline had worn off. When I woke up, the light from above had seeped away. The only illumination in my cell came from the flickering torches in the hallway.

Thanks to my afternoon nap, I was now wide awake during a time when most of the palace had gone to sleep. The torchlight didn't penetrate very far into my cell, and I jumped at every little shadow. Was that a rat? I gathered my skirts around me and pulled my legs tight to my chest, trying to take up as little space as possible.

I heard more soft skittering, but it seemed to be coming from outside my cell rather than from inside. I shrank down even further. Was Hendon coming back?

In the hallway, I heard a soft, low voice. "Princess Jennica?"

"Beyan!" I flew to the door, sticking my hand out the bars into the hallway. I waved my hand around, hoping it would catch his attention. "In here!"

Beyan's face appeared on the other side of the grille. "Jennica! Are you unharmed?"

"Yes!"

"Good. Don't worry, I'll get you out right away."

I stepped back from the door, expecting Beyan to break it down, or maybe pick the lock or something. Instead, I heard a key turn in the lock and Beyan opened the door, squinting into the gloom. He held a key ring with several keys clanking together on it.

"Beyan, how did you — "

"Come on, let's get going. I can tell you as we go."

"Wait." I held out my arm, showing Beyan the magic-blocking band around my wrist. "Can you get this thing off me?"

Beyan squinted at the key ring in his hand. He quickly tried two keys in the band's lock before finding the right one. It fell to the ground.

"What is that thing?" Beyan asked.

"A band the guards put on prisoners to keep them from using magic." I kicked it as hard as I could, sending the hateful thing into the farthest recesses of the cell. With that accomplished, I hurried out of the cell. Beyan carefully closed and locked the door behind me, then led the way down the hallway.

I wanted to free the other prisoners, but it would have been hard to help them quickly in the state they were in. I silently promised myself that after this was all over, they would have their freedom — and justice.

"Farrah put a sleep spell on the guard to get the keys," Beyan said. "It doesn't last long; we need to get back there and make sure to return the keys to him before he wakes up."

I nodded and we quickened our pace. But, I was still curious. "You came back for me."

"Did you think we wouldn't?"

"I... wasn't sure... *you* would. I thought —"

"That I sold you out?" Beyan spared a moment to shoot a remorseful look at me. "I'll be honest with you. I nearly did. When I was unable to meet with the queen, I thought to offer information to King Hendon. I tried to get an audience with him, which is where I was when you came to our campsite the other night. Farrah and Rhyss didn't know, they thought I was trying to see the queen again. If I had told them, I know they would have tried to talk me out of it, and they would have been right. But I was so upset, I couldn't think straight. And then you showed up.... and I realized I had made a terrible mistake. I went back to the castle this morning hoping to undo the damage, but it was too late. Hendon sent his soldiers after me, hoping I would lead them to you. Which, like an idiot, I did, even though I thought I had led them astray. I'm so sorry, Jennica."

"What changed your mind?"

"Seeing you again... hearing your side of the story. Meeting your father. I've jumped to a lot of conclusions on a lot of things. It was just... easier that way. Easier to find something to fight against instead of something to fight for." He reached back and grabbed my hand.

"Well, to be fair, I did thwart your life mission of killing the dragon."

"You did. But I got you captured by the evil king. So I think we're even." We smiled at each other.

After navigating a series of hallways and a set of stairs, we reached Farrah and Rhyss, who were standing vigil by the guard Farrah had cast a spell on. Rhyss was keeping watch on the hallway while Farrah focused on the guard, ready to throw another spell at him if he woke up.

When Farrah saw us, her face broke into a relieved smile. She hurried forward and grabbed the keys from Beyan's outstretched hand. Behind her, the guard stirred and moaned softly. Farrah's smile quickly turned into a frown as she looked back.

"Drat! I really thought that would last longer. I must be exhausted."

Farrah raised her hands, getting ready to recast her sleep spell. The guard's eyes fluttered open. Eyes widening, he opened his mouth to sound the alarm —

— And slumped over again, unconscious from Rhyss's blow to his cheek.

"I nearly had it." Farrah frowned at Rhyss.

"This was faster." Rhyss shrugged. "Plus, you just said you were exhausted."

"Don't baby me, I hate it when you do that. You know I'm more than capable of — "

Beyan coughed pointedly. "You two can argue about the merits of using brute force instead of subtle spell casting later."

Sticking her tongue out at Rhyss, Farrah planted the keys back in the guard's pocket. Rhyss opened a hidden door in the wall — another one? how had I never noticed any of these before? — and motioned for us to enter.

Beyan turned to me. "Can you create a light? I don't think Farrah is any condition to do so right now." Farrah stuck her tongue out at Beyan.

I nodded to hide my smirk and conjured a light. The bright little ball bobbed in front of me.

"Perfect." Beyan put a finger to his lips. "From here on out, we all have to stay absolutely silent."

He walked through the door into the darkness beyond with me right on his heels. Farrah released her spell, gulping in air, and quickly followed us. Rhyss came last, closing the door firmly behind him.

My spell gave us just enough light to see several feet ahead. Beyan confidently led the way through the secret tunnels, and soon we found ourselves outside the castle. We started toward the campgrounds but didn't head back to our original campsite.

Instead, we went to a small clearing within the trees, hidden from view from the main campground. I was surprised no one else was using it, but figured none of the visiting nobles would want to be away from the never-ending party atmosphere leading up to the wedding.

Joichan was at our new campsite, tending the fire. When he saw us, he immediately jumped to his feet and hugged me. "You made it! I was so worried."

All the tension I had been feeling for the last several hours surfaced in a torrent of tears. My father's shoulder was soaked in a matter of minutes. "Hendon tried to cast a spell of control on me... He took Taryn... The wedding is still happening... I couldn't stop him."

Joichan just held me, silently allowing me to let it all out. Eventually my tears subsided. Through my watery eyes I could see Rhyss and Beyan getting things ready for the night, deliberately avoiding looking our way. Farrah was helping them, but smiled at me sympathetically when she caught me watching.

Joichan led me over to the fire and sat me down. "All right, now that you've calmed down a bit, tell us what happened."

I relayed to the group what had occurred with King Hendon, Taryn, and me. When I was finished, a thought occurred to me. "How did all of you find me, anyway? And how did you know about the secret passageways?"

"I took them to meet your mother," Joichan said. "She showed them the passageways and told them how to find you, and how to get out."

"Them?"

I could have sworn Joichan blushed. "Yes, I... it seemed wise to let them go on without me."

I smirked, but didn't say anything.

Joichan continued, "Your news is distressing, but not unexpected, considering what Melandria told us earlier."

"What should we do now?" I asked.

"*Now*, we get some sleep. We'll be up early tomorrow. After all, we have a wedding to stop."

Chapter Forty-One

IN THE CHILLY PREDAWN hours, we silently and quickly ate a cold breakfast as we prepared for the day ahead. I thought we were going to try to sneak back into the castle, to find Taryn and my mother. But instead, my friends produced various bits of finery to wear. They looked like they were ready for, well, a wedding celebration.

Rhyss struggled with the high collar of his shirt, trying to tease it into a comfortable position. "This is incredibly itchy."

Farrah shook out the wrinkles from her full satin skirt. "I have no sympathy. Try wearing a corset."

I stood in the middle of all the action, staring at my companions in bewilderment. "I thought... aren't we going to try to find Taryn?"

"Of course we are," Farrah said. She shoved something at me, a balled up bunch of pale green fabric. "You'd better hurry up and get changed, so we can get going."

"Get changed?"

"Even though the wedding isn't until this evening, there are pre-ceremony events planned for the entire day," Farrah explained. "Everyone's going to be headed to the castle grounds this morning. We'll blend in better if we look like actual wedding guests."

"But... how — ?"

"We did a little bit of 'shopping' in the castle before we came to rescue you." She indicated the dress in my arms. "Although that is your mother's. She said it doesn't fit her anymore, but should suit you perfectly." Farrah gave me an appraising look. "I suppose you need help dressing?"

I shook my head. "I've actually grown pretty adept at dressing myself. Surprising, I know. What kind of princess am I?"

Farrah laughed, but it sounded more determined than full of mirth. "One who's going to get her kingdom back."

I disappeared into the trees, making sure no one was around. I shook the dress out, admiring the lacework and embroidery on the bodice and skirt. It was definitely fancier than my current outfit, but the style seemed a bit old-fashioned. Certainly I had never seen my mother wear it.

I stepped into the dress, surprised at how well it fit. I laced the front tighter and ran my hands over the skirt, then gathered up my original dress.

Beyan, attired in a navy blue velvet jacket, saw me as I walked back into the camp. "You look absolutely fetching, milady."

Was he being sincere or sarcastic? I smiled. Knowing him, it was a little of both. I held out my hand, and he took it and kissed it, bowing low.

"Look at that, Beyan's finally learned to be a gentleman!" Rhyss teased.

Beyan straightened. "You wound my honor, sir. Therefore, I am forced to challenge you to a duel. Give me a moment." He patted his pockets. "Now, where are those gloves?"

We all laughed. At that moment, Joichan stepped out of the trees, adjusting the sleeves on his golden brown jacket. It not only fit him well, it was very fitting; I couldn't imagine him in anything but his dragon colors. My father finished fiddling with his suit coat and saw me. He stopped still, looking thunderstruck.

"Well? What do you think?" I asked, crossing over to him.

My father finally found his voice. "Oh, Jennica. For a minute there I thought... you look exactly like your mother did, all those years ago. She was wearing that dress when we first met."

My throat suddenly constricted. I didn't know what to say. Even if we were successful and stopped Hendon, it didn't necessarily mean there would be a happy ending for my parents.

My father nodded sadly as if he knew what I was thinking. He took a deep breath, visibly composing himself. In another moment he was himself again: Joichan, the proud dragon shapeshifter, incredibly wise and controlled. "Shall we?"

The five of us joined a group of nobles headed toward the castle. The sun had risen overhead in a cloudless sky, promising a beautiful day for a wedding. Although we had gotten up early, we hadn't beaten the crowds into the castle grounds. There must have been a hundred or more people milling about: leaders of the neighboring kingdoms, their families, other heads of state, lesser visiting nobility, and their servants. Not to mention the Calian nobility, their servants, and the castle servants, tasked with attending all the visitors and preparing for the wedding.

I felt a little twinge of sadness. Although I did not want to marry Prince Anders, it *was* supposed to be my wedding day. Would I ever get to have a real Calian wedding someday? Or would this sham be the closest I would ever come to it?

A guard at the gate called out to the crowd, repeating the same instructions: "All weapons must be left with the castle guards! No exceptions! You will get your weapons back upon leaving the castle."

We turned in our weapons to the guards manning the castle gates, Rhyss hesitating over his prized knife.

"You promise I'll get it back?" He reluctantly handed it over to the waiting guard.

"Of course, sir." The man eyed the old dagger with distaste. "It's a very... fine weapon, sir. I can see why you want it back."

Mollified by the compliment, Rhyss breezed into the courtyard. Farrah rolled her eyes at his retreating back as she gave her sword to the guard and hurried after Rhyss.

We walked along the grounds, taking everything in. The day had barely begun, but the festivities were already well underway. Besides a myriad of entertainment for the visitors, food and drink were flowing freely.

"King Hendon is notoriously tight-fisted." I dodged two children playing tag, who were being chased by their frazzled nursemaid. "But it looks like he's spending more in one day than he does in an entire year. Why go to such expense, especially since the wedding is fake?"

"These people don't know that." Beyan's sweeping arm took in all of the people carousing around us.

"Appearances count," Joichan chimed in. "But more importantly, if everyone's happy and drunk, they won't be looking for anything untoward during the wedding."

By the look of things, I wasn't sure any of the visiting nobles would even be awake for the wedding, let alone somewhat sober.

We found a quiet spot away from the majority of the crowd and stopped to talk.

"So, what's the plan?" Rhyss asked quietly.

Beyan turned to me. "Jennica, I hate for you to go back, but you're the best person to find your friend. I'll go with you in case anything happens."

"As will I," said Joichan.

"Too many of us running around the castle may attract attention," I said. "If it's okay with you, I'd prefer when we get inside that you make sure my mother is safe."

"We'll stay out here, then, and see what we can learn," Rhyss said.

"If we find out anything important, we'll try to find you. Otherwise, we'll see you at the ceremony," Farrah said.

With that settled, we split up. Joichan, Beyan, and I easily strolled inside the palace. We didn't have to worry about getting caught in the hallways; with all the hubbub of servants scurrying to and fro, and random nobles wandering around the Calian palace, we just looked like wedding guests enjoying the festivities.

However, as we headed farther in, there were fewer wedding guests around. We also had to avoid any of the palace guards, as they would recognize me as the princess.

We reached the castle wing that housed the private rooms of the royal family. I was betting that, due to the ongoing celebration, King Hendon would either be celebrating with the other guests or overseeing the final touches for the wedding. But my mother, still under house arrest, would most likely be confined to her room until right before the wedding, when it would be necessary for her to make an appearance.

I also hoped that my mother might have an idea of where the king had taken Taryn.

I knocked, low and urgent, on the door.

"Enter." My mother sounded weary and resigned.

We slipped into my mother's chambers. She stood up immediately, surprised to see us.

"Jennica! Joichan! And..." She broke off, unsure of how to react to Beyan's presence.

Beyan sketched a quick bow. "Beyan, son of Kye of Orchwell, at your service, Your Majesty."

My mother smiled at him, then at me. "I should have guessed who you were, since Jennica was successful in finding her father."

"Mother! The king has Taryn. It happened last night," I said. "We were being held in the same cell; he tried to cast a spell on me, but it didn't work. So he took Taryn instead. She's under the king's control. What do you suppose he wants with her? He said something about 'an alternate path' to getting his way."

My mother looked both troubled and intrigued at my words. "I heard them in the hallway last night. I believe he's locked her in your rooms."

Immediately, I spun around to leave. Mother's voice stopped me. "Wait, Jennica. You were able to resist his spell?"

Turning back, I fished my amber soulstone out from beneath my bodice. "I don't know if *resist* is the right word... I only knew, with every part of my being, that I didn't want him to succeed. The more Hendon tried to hurt me with his spell, the more this... shielded me somehow."

Mother looked at Joichan, a question lighting her eyes. "I'm glad he wasn't able to hurt you with his vile magic. But how?"

Joichan shrugged, but smiled at me proudly. "We don't have time for a more thorough study right now, but... you are a stronger magician than you know, Jennica."

I smiled back, but it faded quickly as I remembered something. "Mother, Father... Hendon has a soulstone of his own. It's a red jewel he wears around his neck."

My mother gasped. "I've seen that necklace. He had it on the day he forced me to talk. Come to think of it... he's been wearing that necklace for some time now."

"So he's been able to tap into that magical ability for a while, and is obviously growing more proficient in it every day," Joichan said.

"But it doesn't explain how he plans to conquer all of the Gifted Lands," I argued. "He can't exactly cast individual spells on each person here. It would take too long and be too noticeable."

Beyan coughed slightly, catching my eye as he nodded toward the door. He was right; we needed to continue our search for Taryn.

I gave my mother and father quick hugs goodbye. Beyan opened the door and we slipped back into the hallway. Looking at him, I could see my question mirrored in his face: *Now what?* He shrugged. We walked toward my suite, which we had passed on the way to my mother's set of rooms, with me leading the way.

Ahead of us, a door opened further down the hallway.

It was the door to *my* rooms. Those of the princess.

And leaving my room was Taryn, dressed in one of my gowns. It was a few inches too short for her, but she didn't seem to notice or care. Which was odd, because Taryn was always conscientious about fashion, whether it was hers or mine.

And why was she wearing my clothes at all?

"Taryn!" I cried out. She looked over at us.

In an undertone, Beyan said incredulously, "Are you two related? She looks just like you!"

"Of course not." Brushing his comment aside, I strode toward Taryn. "I've met her family, and trust me, it's definitely not my own."

"Wait, Jennica — "

As I approached Taryn, I could make out the expression on her face. She did not look happy to see me.

"Taryn?" My happiness at seeing my lady-in-waiting changed to uncertainty.

Something seemed odd about Taryn. Her face seemed fuzzy, like I was viewing her through a veil or a dirty window. Focusing on the layer of magic floating around her, I realized Beyan was right — Taryn looked like an exact copy of me. Instead of her usual blonde curls and bright green eyes, she stared back at me with dark brown eyes, her now-black hair piled high on her head. Even her heart-shaped, fair-skinned face had transformed into my own rounded olive-skinned features. Her true self was an extremely faint shadow underneath the skillfully crafted illusion.

Subtly, I tugged at the magic around her, trying to twitch it off or look for a weakness. It wouldn't budge. My heart sank, knowing that during an event as momentous as a royal wedding, no one with magical ability would be close enough to Taryn to ascertain the illusion, let alone have the time to do anything about it.

No one, except King Hendon.

"Are you lost? Who is this Taryn person you're talking about?" Taryn had never taken such a disdainful, haughty tone with me before.

"Taryn, stop playing. We need to get you out of here."

"I'm not Taryn, whoever she is. I am Her Highness, the Crown Princess of Calia, and you should address me as such."

I stared at Taryn in disbelief. "Taryn, what has Hendon done to you? Don't you remember me at all?" I reached for her, but she recoiled in horror. "Taryn, it's me. *I'm* Princess Jennica."

Taryn blinked. For a brief moment, the arrogance in her eyes disappeared, replaced by confusion and a bit of recognition. "Jennica..."

I breathed a sigh of relief. She remembered me. It was going to be all right.

Taryn opened her mouth and started screaming. "Guards!"

Chapter Forty-Two

BEYAN AND I TURNED and ran down the corridor, leaving Taryn behind us screaming for the guards. It wasn't long before we heard several boots running after us, and a gruff male voice yelling, "Stop!"

We had a good head start, but hampered by our heavy wedding finery, we would soon lose our lead. "Where should we go?" Beyan said.

"I have no idea!"

"It's *your* castle!"

He had a point.

Passing my mother's rooms, we skidded around the corner and kept running.

"Jennica!" Beyan huffed behind me. "We can't just run back to the courtyard. They'll catch us for sure."

To my right were the doors to King Hendon's rooms. There was the large ornate door that opened into the king's bedroom; nearby was the smaller, plain door to the bedroom's antechamber.

The guards' footsteps echoed off the stone floor — they would be upon us soon. Frantically, I flung open the antechamber door, my relief palpable when it opened easily at my touch. Beyan crowded into the room after me, and I shut the door as quietly as I could in my haste, quickly reciting a spell to magically seal the lock.

The spell took hold just in time.

We could hear the guards outside, their voices muffled through the heavy wooden doors.

"Should we check the king's rooms?" one guard asked.

Beyan instinctively reached for his sword, realizing belatedly that, per wedding protocol, he wasn't carrying it. He reached down and pulled out a hidden dagger in his boot.

"You know you were supposed to turn in all your weapons!" I hissed into his ear.

"And aren't you glad I don't always follow orders?" he smirked in a barely audible voice.

The handle of the antechamber door rattled, but held firm.

There was muffled cursing from the guard who was nearest the door. "It's locked. As is the other door."

A second guard, a little further away, snorted. "If you want to break into the king's rooms to search, be my guest. It's your head."

The guard by our room stepped away. "No, you're right. They must have kept running, there's no way they could have gotten through a locked door."

Their footsteps echoed down the hallway as they continued their search. Finally, all was quiet.

Beyan said softly, "Good job on the locking spell."

"Thanks." I exhaled, trying to still my frantically beating heart. "Do you think it's safe to leave now?"

"I think so, but let's wait a little bit. Just to give them time to look around and give up for good. Do you think they got a good look at us?"

"I hope not. But if we could disguise ourselves, that might help."

Turning to the curtained windows, I flung them open, sneezing from the dust that flicked off the curtains as I moved them. "Maybe we can find something in here while we wait."

Sunlight streamed in. Outside, we could see the revelry continuing below. Inside, the light from the window angled across the floor, through an open doorway that led into the king's bedroom.

Following the ray of light, I found myself staring through the doorway, drawn to explore the room beyond. Now that the danger had passed, another feeling had surfaced. Something in King Hendon's room was calling to me. Something magical. Something... kindred.

Beyan was rifling through a chest, examining musty clothes and shaking out a pair of pants. Doubtfully, he held up a linen tunic that had probably been in fashion in my grandfather's day. "If we can't find anything else, I guess this will do." He caught my mesmerized expression. "Uh. Princess?"

I didn't respond as I followed my instincts into Hendon's bedroom. The room was lush and ostentatious — much like its owner. I crossed the room to an ornate chest of jewelry, wondering if perhaps what I was sensing was Hendon's ruby soulstone. But I found nothing unusual. Disappointed, I closed the chest, although I knew that Hendon wasn't stupid enough to leave behind the soulstone he prized so highly.

Beyan appeared in the doorway between the antechamber and the king's bedroom. His search had been successful. There were two short, hooded cloaks in his hands. "Jennica? What's wrong?"

"I don't know," I said, turning around and around, trying to find the source of my discomfort. "There's something here. I don't know what, but it wants me to find it."

Blindly reaching out, I ran my hands along one of the walls of the bedroom. Then another. Then —

"Here. It's here."

Noting the urgency in my voice, Beyan dropped the cloaks by the door and stepped quickly to my side. I continued to run my hands over the wall, frustrated that I couldn't just break through to find out what was hidden inside. Beyan joined me, searching the wall on the opposite end.

My fingers found a very small catch, so minute it seemed like a chink in the stone wall. Flipping the latch, I gasped when a small panel noiselessly slid open to reveal a hidden recessed area.

I hastily called up some light, bringing the magical sphere closer to the wall.

Before us was a myriad of glass vials with cork stoppers, holding various amounts of colored liquid. I drew the light closer to the vials. The liquid in the vials sparked in the glow of my magical light as they changed from blue to green to red to gold. Most vials were labeled, although some were unmarked. Darya. Petan. Sava.

Sava.

Horrified, I stepped back, trying not to retch.

"What is all of that?" Beyan asked, uncomprehending.

I forced myself to speak, although my breath was coming in fast pants as I fought my rising panic. "It's... it's magical essence. The people in the dungeons... he's been experimenting on them, somehow stealing their magical power and taking it for his own."

Beyan breathed a curse as he looked over all the vials. "There's so many."

"All those people... some didn't survive the experiments... the others he locked away. Maybe to take more from them in the future."

Beyan reached a hand out, intending to grab a vial for closer examination, but was stopped short by an invisible magical barrier. At the same time, a spark flew from the invisible wall and Beyan snatched his hand back, shaking it. "Ouch!"

I felt I had seen enough — too much, really — but Beyan pulled my attention back to the hidden cache. "Jennica, there's something else in there."

"There is?" I stepped up to the wall again, joining Beyan where he peered intently inside. He was right: there was something beyond the vials, tucked away in a dark corner. I could just see it if I angled my light correctly. A brightly glowing, blood red jewel, it was a twin to Hendon's soulstone.

Chapter Forty-Three

NOW FESTOONED WITH garlands and flowers for the wedding, the courtyard was packed with the lords and ladies of the Gifted Lands, their voices buzzing in excitement. Part of the excitement was from the all-day party that they had attended; part of it was from being involved in one of the biggest events that was happening in the Gifted Lands in recent history. Not just a royal wedding, but an alliance between two of the Kingdoms! Such a thing had never occurred before.

The wedding was due to start soon. While the benches were all occupied by the visiting nobility, Rhyss and Farrah had managed to get a spot near the front, where they would be able to view both the ceremony and the guests. Prince Anders was at the dais with his parents, the king and queen of Rothschan, seated nearby. My mother was seated on the opposite side, looking apprehensive.

Beyan and I joined our group where they stood. Farrah jumped when we approached. "For a minute, I didn't recognize you!"

Beyan and I both lowered our hoods. Although we had found some dressier items in the king's antechamber, they didn't fit right. And, if I was being honest, I didn't want to leave my mother's dress behind. We had found some lightweight, embroidered cloaks that covered up our outfits without making us look out of place.

"What's with the cloaks?" Rhyss asked us.

"It's a long story we can share later," Beyan said. "More importantly, we have a few things to tell you *now*."

"We found Taryn," I said in a low voice. "She's still enchanted, and she thinks she's me. And she's been spelled to look like me. I think the king intends to use her as the bride, since he couldn't enchant me."

"And we know how the king will steal everyone's magic," Beyan added. "It's — "

Trumpets sounded a fanfare. All heads turned to the doors of the castle. The court musicians began playing a lovely, lilting melody.

King Hendon appeared at the doors, Taryn as "Princess Jennica" on his arm. There was no spark in Taryn's usually lively eyes; Hendon looked positively smug. He led her outside and down the aisle, toward Prince Anders.

Taryn was resplendent in a brilliant white gown delicately embroidered with small red flowers and trimmed with red ribbons. My heart ached just looking at her; part of me wished it really *was* her real wedding day.

But as gorgeous as her wedding dress was, it was her headpiece that stood out. A gauzy white veil flowed down her back from a golden circlet that was nestled in Taryn's hair. The circlet was encrusted with a myriad of tiny sparkling rubies, with one huge, perfect ruby in the center. Just large enough to convey status without being overly ostentatious, the headpiece was the real eye catcher of Taryn's ensemble.

Which was what King Hendon was counting on.

Beyan and I exchanged worried looks, and I looked down at my hands ruefully. Although we had found Taryn's circlet while we were snooping in the king's bedroom, we had been unable to do anything with it or to it. Neither Beyan nor I were able to get past the protective shield protecting the vials and the circlet. My hands were already sporting slight blisters from my attempt to reach into the alcove. I couldn't throw any spells into the recess to try to call the circlet to me or destroy it, either. I was sure that there was some spell or trigger word to release the circlet from its protective shell, but nothing I tried worked. We finally had to abandon our efforts when we heard the musicians warming up outside and realized the ceremony was imminent.

The king kissed his "daughter" on the cheek and moved to the side, sitting down next to the queen. My mother moved away from him, ever so slightly.

"Welcome, all, to the wedding of Prince Anders of Rothschan to Princess Jennica of Calia. Not only will we witness these two becoming united as one in matrimony, we will also bear witness to the union of two great kingdoms joining together as family and political allies." As the priest continued his speech, my group began moving closer to the dais.

From where we now stood, I could see King Hendon's face. At a quick glance, he looked like a doting father watching his only daughter as she embarked on a new life. But watching him closely, I could see his eyes were a little too bright. His attention was completely focused on her ruby crown. His hand wasn't on his heart because he was overcome with emotion; he was surreptitiously touching his necklace, silently mouthing a spell. The circlet seemed to glow, brighter and brighter. I looked out at the sea of guests. All eyes were fixated on Taryn's circlet as it sparkled in the sunlight. Even the priest's words were slurring, as he started to become mesmerized by the jewels.

I was seeing red, but it wasn't just the reflection from Taryn's headpiece. How many people's lives — including my own — had Hendon ruined with his selfishness? And how many more people would get hurt due to his ambition?

We had to stop him *now*, before he completed the spell.

I moved toward him, not sure what I would do, but just wanting to end this, somehow. Beyan reached for my arm to pull me back and just missed me. My slight movement caught the attention of Taryn. Her face flushed, as bright red as the rubies in her crown.

"You!"

Chapter Forty-Four

KING HENDON'S HEAD whipped toward me, his eyes snaring me in their grip. "How convenient! I'd wondered where you'd gone."

He stood, drawing his sword. My mother gasped. "Hendon, no!"

He backhanded her. The smack of his slap echoed loudly. Joichan growled and stepped in front of me, drawing Hendon's focus.

Hendon studied Joichan. "You... you seem familiar."

"Let me help you remember." Joichan transformed, faster than I'd ever seen before. His magnificent golden scales glittered in the sunlight, competing with Taryn's jeweled circlet.

Hendon gripped his necklace and yelled something incoherently, his sword aloft, running at my father to attack. With his control on the crowd weakening, the hypnotizing hold on the wedding guests broke. Someone screamed at the dragon in their midst. Nobles and servants alike scattered. Some hid behind benches or barrels. Others ran into the castle or behind the castle walls. The Queen of Rothschan fainted. Her husband hurriedly tried to revive her, while fearfully eyeing the dragon. Prince Anders ran to check on his mother.

Guards ran to the aid of the king, and of the "princess" who was screaming orders on the dais.

"Arrest those people and kill that dragon! They're ruining my wedding!"

Momentarily stung, I turned to my friends. "Do I really act like that?"

Farrah shrugged as she and Rhyss each drew swords, which had been cleverly hidden in their finery. "Like a spoiled brat? Not really. You're more of a take-action type of princess."

"Yeah, remember the bandits?" Rhyss grinned, turning the length of steel in his hands so it caught the light.

A quick glance at the items in their hands told me that these items weren't my friends' usual weapons; I wondered where Farrah and Rhyss had gotten them since we had all turned over our weapons to the guard at the entrance earlier in the day. Could none of my friends follow a simple edict? Although, as the wedding descended into chaos and we faced an infuriated King Hendon, an ensorcelled Taryn, and several heavily armed and well-trained soldiers, I was very glad that my friends had ignored the rules.

Rhyss tossed a short sword to Beyan, who had pulled his dagger out of his boot to fend off one of the guards.

"Where did you get the swords?" Beyan called to Rhyss, never taking his eyes off his opponent.

It was Rhyss's turn to shrug, even while he was engaged with his own opponent. He called back, "We just found them, you know, laying around."

I rushed to my mother. "Are you all right?"

A blotchy oblong bloom had formed under her left eye. "I'm fine, I'm fine. Take care of Taryn."

I looked around wildly. "Farrah!"

She had knocked out a guard and was stepping back, avoiding his falling body. "What?"

"Come with me!" Together, we dodged the guards, the majority of whom were focused on the dragon.

As we dashed toward Taryn, I asked Farrah, "How long does it take for you to prepare a sleep spell? I don't want to hurt Taryn if I don't have to."

"It's kind of hard on the run, but..." Farrah began reciting the incantation.

If I had any doubts that Taryn was enchanted, watching her at the dais would have cinched it for me. Alternately crying, pouting, and shouting, she was in full spoiled princess mode. If I didn't know better, I would have thought she really was royalty.

"Taryn!" I approached her slowly, hands out.

"You're that imposter from earlier!" She advanced on me. "Why are you trying to ruin my wedding? Do *you* want to marry the prince?"

"Believe me, no. You can have him. Taryn — "

"That is not my name! Guards! *Guards!*" No one came to her aid. They were too busy trying to take down Joichan.

At that moment Prince Anders looked up from his mother and toward us. His eyes widened. "My lord, there's two of you!" His mother woke up, saw us, shrieked, and fainted again.

The Queen of Rothschan's scream pulled Taryn's attention away from me. While Taryn was distracted, I leapt at her, clawing for the circlet around her head. She screamed and grabbed at her headpiece while trying to twist away. She kicked out at me, but I stepped out of the way. I looked up. Her fist was coming right toward my face. I ducked, still trying desperately to get her crown. My hands closed around the circlet, but it was so well-secured that I feared I'd rip out half her hair if I tried to yank it off her head. My goodness, was it glued on?

She wound up again to try to hit me. I twisted, trying to avoid her, but wasn't quick enough. Right before her open palm made impact, she dropped like a stone. The ruby circlet stayed in my hand as she fell, her tangled hair falling around her face.

Curled on her side, Taryn didn't move. Worried, I started to reach down to her when she let out a loud snore.

I straightened up and glanced around. Farrah stepped up, hands outstretched toward Taryn as she silently mouthed her spell.

"Took you long enough!" I clutched the circlet to my chest.

Farrah finished her incantation and tied off her magic. With the spell complete, she stuck her tongue out at me. "You're welcome!"

"How long will your spell hold?"

"About a quarter of an hour. If you need her to stay asleep longer, I'll need to recast the spell."

"That's good enough. Here, help me destroy this thing!" I waved the circlet in the air.

Farrah joined me, throwing random spells at the circlet in an effort to break it. Her magic ripped at the still-attached veil, quickly turning the gauzy fabric into rags. But her spells bounced harmlessly off the circlet. It didn't even look singed.

The torn veil was getting in the way, so I ripped it off and began banging the circlet against a nearby bench. The jewels stayed intact.

"Try melting it!" Farrah shouted.

I reached within, recalling the spell I had used against the bandits who had invaded our camp weeks ago. I had more control now, so I wasn't worried about accidentally roasting Farrah. I concentrated, bringing forth fire and heat into my hands. But even though I called forth my hottest flame, the circlet remained unharmed.

And it was pulsing with a heartbeat of its own. Its magical aura had steadily grown stronger, aided by Hendon's attempt at stealing the essences of all the people at the wedding. Holding the small crown in my hands, I could feel it writhing like a living, breathing creature. I found myself looking between the circlet and King Hendon without knowing why.

Hendon and Joichan were circling each other. Joichan was bleeding from a myriad of cuts; a few guards lay on the ground nearby, but there were still enough men continuing to harry my father. Hendon didn't seem particularly eager to press the attack; I realized his goal was to weaken my father enough so that he could eventually overpower Joichan.

Hendon waved his arms lazily. The jewel at his neck pulsed. The dragon recoiled. The circlet in my hands throbbed as well, cycling from blush to crimson to burgundy.

Two guards had my mother's arms pinned. "Unhand me!" she commanded imperiously. "Did you hear what I said? Release me this instant! I am your queen!"

Upon seeing my mother captured, Joichan growled and lashed out at Hendon. Hendon swiped with his sword, creating a new slash of blood on the dragon's golden hide. Joichan growled again, sounding weaker than before.

"Oh, does this upset you?" Hendon swung his sword from Joichan to my mother. "Surrender, or she dies."

Joichan roared, but the massive beast backed away. Hendon stroked his necklace and began a sonorous incantation, pointing at the dragon. Joichan howled in pain, a terrifying sound that caused all the fighting to cease. Some of the guards fled; others clapped their hands to their ears. Beyan, now opponent-less, started to make his way to the queen. Rhyss engaged a guard who tried to stab Beyan in the back.

But Joichan's cry caused them to have trouble walking; it was as if the air had turned to mud or snow that they were forced to wade through.

The circlet glowed again.

My face flushed, as red hot as Hendon's jewel and the circlet in my hands. I breathed in, and as I exhaled I transformed into my dragon self, faster than I ever had before. While I wasn't as large a creature as my father — maybe about a third of his impressive size — I was still imposing. And unlike Joichan, I was uninjured. For the most part.

Now fully in dragon form, I roared an answer to my father's cry of pain. Hendon whirled around, paling at the sight of a second creature to contend with. Taryn's wedding crown encircled my hand like some odd piece of dragon jewelry.

Screams echoed around the courtyard as those left got a look at me. The loudest and shrillest of all was the Queen of Rothschan, who had apparently revived long enough to see me become a dragon. I had a feeling that after this new shock, she had fainted yet again. *Poor lady. I'm probably not what she had in mind for a daughter-in-law.*

Farrah clapped her hands in delight. "Girl, you gotta show me how to do that!"

Across the courtyard, Rhyss and the guard both broke off from their fight to stare at me, slack-jawed.

Farrah yelled at Rhyss, "Pay attention, you idiot!"

He blinked, almost casually disarming his still-stunned opponent. The guard didn't hesitate, hightailing it out of the courtyard after one last fearful glance at me and my father.

Even with Hendon holding her at sword point, my mother's pride and love for me were evident as she gazed at me, eyes shining with unshed tears.

And Beyan just grinned. Like he had somehow known all along.

"I knew it!" Hendon's angry shout echoed around the courtyard. "I always knew you were some sort of abomination. How your mother could love and shelter such a disgusting creature, I'll never understand."

Snarling, I bared my teeth and advanced on King Hendon, wanting nothing more than to slash at him with my sharp claws. Or better yet, bite his head off. *That* would be most satisfying.

I hadn't taken more than three steps when I felt a sharp prickle reverberate through my skull. It began as little pinpricks that grew in intensity, becoming sharp daggers repeatedly pounding in my head. The pain was so intense, I couldn't move. I could barely breathe.

Before me, Hendon broke off from his spell casting to laugh at my consternation. His momentary lapse gave me a brief moment to catch my breath and steel myself against further magic. I shook my golden head as if I could shake off the remnants of Hendon's spell, and took another step.

And howled in excruciating pain. Hendon's spell washed over me again as he redoubled his efforts. I roared in anger at the sky, and heard an answering, weaker roar —

— And I lifted myself from the pavement, dazed and much smaller than I remembered being. I had shifted back to my human self without conscious thought, perhaps as a defense mechanism against Hendon's spell. The ruby circlet lay next to me in the dusty courtyard.

Looking up, I saw Hendon clutching his arm as he spat out a curse. The thin red line trickling from beneath his fingers told me that Joichan's swipe had solidly connected. But my father, weak from loss of blood and Hendon's offensive magic, wouldn't be able to hold out much longer.

Hendon laughed at me lying on the pavement, just a few feet away from him. "Not only are you an abomination, you're pathetic. Can't even control your own abilities. Don't worry; after I take care of your father, I'll put you out of your misery." He patted his sword menacingly, then focused on his necklace — and Joichan — again.

My head screamed in agony, and my vision wavered. Any movement made me want to throw up.

Without thinking, my right hand crept up to find my amber pendant. As I touched it, it grew warm and glowed bright, the magic inside it flowing through my fingers, up my arm, and into my head.

The pain throbbing behind my eyes eased somewhat. Enough that I could force myself to reach out with my other hand, close my fingers around the wedding crown, and sit up. I needed to stay upright, just for a moment. *Long enough to do this.*

I gripped the jeweled crown and sent my thoughts into it, as deep as I could, quicker than I had ever cast magic before. My soulstone kept the worst of the pain at bay as I concentrated on the crown.

Down, down, down I dove, hoping I would find what I needed before it was too late. And then, just when my magical strength was nearly spent, there it was!

Gripping my soulstone harder, I willed it to join its stored magic to my own ability. I would need every bit of magic I could muster.

I reached through the link that joined the ruby circlet to Hendon's soulstone, and *pulled.*

My magical self flew backward, out of the crown. My actual self sailed through the air, landing in a heap on the cobblestones. The circlet flew through the air with me, shattering on the stones, bits of red stone flying everywhere.

Farrah ran over to me. "Princess Jennica!"

"I'm fine." Actually, my head was splitting, made worse from the extensive use of magic. "Where's my mother? What's happened?"

Farrah helped me to my feet. She pointed. The battle seemed to be finished. The remaining guards had surrendered, their swords at their feet. The few soldiers who were loyal to my mother were gathering them up, aided by Beyan and Rhyss, who had their weapons trained on Hendon's henchmen. Joichan rested on the cobblestones as my mother, unhurt and now freed, fussed over his wounds. Taryn was still sleeping on the dais. Prince Anders and his father fussed over the Rothschan queen, who kept fainting at all the goings-on.

And in the middle of it all was King Hendon, sprawled out on the ground with his hand clutching at his throat, not moving. The setting for his ruby pendant was empty; red fragments littered near his head attested to the broken jewel.

"It's over," Farrah said. "Good news: we've won."

"Oh, great," I said hazily. "That's great. You know, I have the worst headache."

And then I pulled a "Queen of Rothschan" and blacked out.

Chapter Forty-Five

I SLOWLY BLINKED MY eyes open. There was a concerned face hovering above me that looked a lot like Beyan. "Jennica? You're awake!"

"Yes, that's a very astute observation." I tried for sarcasm, but my voice came out weak. Beyan rushed to help me as I struggled to sit up. I realized I was in a comfortable bed, in a well-appointed room — my private rooms, in the castle. "What are you doing in my room?"

"You really don't remember anything?"

I frowned, trying to tease memory forth. The wedding... the fight in the courtyard... King Hendon.

"The king is dead." The words felt funny on my tongue. Even though he wasn't my true father, and we hadn't had the best relationship, and he had tried to manipulate and hurt everyone I loved, I had grown up with him and should still mourn him. Right?

Beyan was oblivious to my private dilemma. "Yes, Hendon is dead. Those loyal to him are in the dungeon, awaiting the queen's judgement. Princess Jennica, whatever you did — you saved us all. We were barely holding our own. You stopped the king."

A perfunctory knock at my chamber door sounded before it opened. A young attendant poked her head in the doorway. "Her Majesty and the Dragon Consort are here to see you, Your Highness."

I blinked. "Dragon Consort? Send them in." I turned back to Beyan. "Did I... did I kill Hendon?"

My mother and father strode into my chamber.

"Not exactly," Joichan said, overhearing my question. "From what I could tell, you destroyed the link between Hendon's soulstone and the headpiece. Hendon was in the middle of an intricate spell when it happened; it recoiled on him and the power between the two items overwhelmed him. You're lucky you didn't get caught in it too, or you might have died as well."

My father's explanation was meant to reassure me, but I still felt vaguely guilty over Hendon's death.

I wanted to clear my head. "Where are Farrah and Rhyss? Did they go back to Orchwell?"

"No, they're still here," Beyan said. "The queen has been kind enough to offer us hospitality for as long as we wish to stay."

"It's the least we could do, for all you've done for the kingdom," my mother said.

"You've been more than generous, Your Majesty," Beyan said.

I looked at Beyan more closely. His everyday clothing had been replaced by something finer. Better fabric, better cut. Even the way he held himself was different than before. In fact, he looked almost like a...

"Lord Beyan and his father, Lord Kye, will be relocating to Calia in the next two weeks, as I understand it," Mother said. "Until they are settled into their new home, they are welcome to stay here at the palace with us for as long as they need to."

"*Lord* Beyan?" I looked from Mother to Beyan incredulously. "What did I miss? And how long have I been out?"

"About four days," Beyan said. "The palace healer said you'd recover, your body just needed time to repair on its own. We were very worried, though."

"Four days!"

"Doing that magic — whatever you did — took a lot out of you."

"No need to be worried, I'm awake now. But maybe I *am* dreaming... what's this about you being a lord?"

Beyan smiled sheepishly. "After... everything that happened in the courtyard... we've had a lot of time to talk. She was aware of what happened between the king and my father, but she didn't know how it had affected my family."

"I fear I have failed Calia greatly," Mother said. "I suspected Hendon was creating havoc, but I didn't know the extent of the damage he caused, both in our kingdom and beyond. Now that you've uncovered the wrongs he's created, I can do my best to right them. Restoring Beyan's family to their former glory was a small step toward that."

"That's wonderful news," I said. "And now you're a *lord*?"

"Yes," Beyan said. He looked, if possible, even more embarrassed. "And my father and I will be living in Calia. After the messenger came back immediately with my father's answer, saying he was happy to come to Calia, Her Majesty sent a group of servants to pack up our belongings and bring my father here. He should be here soon, I believe later on today."

"If he's not too tired, I'd love to see him when arrives," I said.

"Of course, Your Highness."

"Please. Don't you start with the titles, or I swear I'll never talk to you again. Jennica is just fine for me."

Beyan laughed. "I'll call you Jennica if you *don't* call me Lord Beyan. I'm still not used to it. When someone says my name, I keep looking around wondering who they're addressing."

"It's a deal, unless I'm mad at you," I teased. "Then I'm definitely using your title."

Still laughing, Beyan stood up from my bedside and bowed to my parents. "If you'll excuse me, Your Majesty, Joichan. And *Jennica*." He nodded at me, his eyes twinkling. "I should go find Rhyss and Farrah. They'll want to know the princess is awake."

"Wait. Beyan?"

"Yes, Jennica?"

"Where did Rhyss and Farrah get those swords? During the wedding? We had left everything with the guards. Or so I thought, until I saw you still had your dagger."

Beyan shrugged unapologetically. "I know I didn't quite follow the rules... but you have to admit, it came in handy."

"That's true. But it still doesn't explain how Farrah and Rhyss happened to be carrying weapons."

"Apparently we weren't the only ones exploring the castle," Beyan said. "After we split up, Rhyss and Farrah snuck into the Great Hall. They saw a bunch of swords hanging on the walls and thought they might be useful. Rhyss was particularly drawn to the one near the throne; he said he had to climb on the throne to get it down."

I blinked in disbelief. "You mean to tell me that he *stole* the ceremonial Sword of the First King?"

"He gave it back," Mother interjected. I could hear the laugh she was trying to hold back. "But as a reward, we promised to have the royal blacksmith create something similar for him."

"While it *was* a good idea to have it on hand, only Rhyss would do something like that." I laughed too, Beyan joining in.

"I'm sure by now Rhyss has also eaten your food stores into oblivion." Beyan winked at me. "I'll go check."

He left. Mother, Joichan, and I watched him go. A smile tugged at the corner of my mother's mouth. "Not bad. You could do worse."

"Mother?" I wasn't sure if I was asking for her approval or chastising her.

"Trust me, a match born of duty isn't all it's cracked up to be. Better to go with your heart."

"Thanks, Mother. I think."

My mother sat on my bed, cupping my face in her hands. "I can tell Hendon's death weighs on you," she said gently. "But you saved many more lives by your actions. Remember that, when you start to despair."

She embraced me. I rested my head on her shoulder, enjoying the safety I felt in her arms.

My mother pulled back, brushing the hair from my face. "Let us talk of happy things. A lot has happened since you've been asleep. Now that you're awake, we can talk about — "

A light knock on the door interrupted us. "Enter," I called out.

The attendant poked her head in my room again. "Your lady-in-waiting, Taryn, is here to see you, Your Highness."

"Send her in."

Taryn walked into the room, eyes downcast. She curtsied to the queen, then to me. "Your Highness, I came to apologize for my horrible behavior. And to say, I understand if you no longer want me as your lady-in-waiting. I'll pack my things and leave immediately."

She turned to go. "Stop," I said in my most imperious voice. "Come back here."

Taryn approached, wringing her hands.

"Taryn, I accept your apology, but I do *not* accept your departure. Unless... you want to go."

"Oh, no, Your Highness. Never!" She looked up at me, tears in her eyes. "But, Your Highness, how could you ever forgive me?"

"Because you weren't in your right mind, and we both know it. How could I *not* forgive you? And, if I recall, my friend Taryn calls me Jennica. Her friend."

Taryn smiled at me through her tears. I held my arms open to her, and we embraced in a tight hug.

She pulled back, still sniffling. Mother smiled at her. "Taryn, you and your brother have done an immeasurable service to the kingdom of Calia."

"Rufan told me that you sent his family a most generous gift of gold. Thank you, Your Majesty." Perched next to my mother at the edge of my bed, Taryn dipped her head in thanks to the queen.

"You're welcome. And as for you, Taryn — the kingdom could use a sharp mind like yours to guide it. If you're amenable to it, we'd like to start training you for your new position as the Queen's Advisor."

Taryn's jaw dropped. "Your Majesty, that would be incredible. Thank you!"

I smiled, although now *I* wanted to cry. "I'll miss you, Taryn. You're a wonderful lady-in-waiting, and I know you'll be an incredible advisor."

Mother laughed. "Silly. Taryn won't be going anywhere. She'll be *your* advisor, not mine. We're just getting a head start so she'll be ready to go when you become queen."

Now *my* jaw dropped. "But... I thought..."

My mother regarded me with gentle, solemn eyes. "While I love my kingdom, it's time for a new way of thinking, a new take on life. I'll be here to guide you and help you grow into the position, but it's time for love and honor to lead Calia instead of forced duty and tradition." She and Joichan exchanged loving smiles. "And I think it's time I learned how to listen to my own heart."

Taryn stood up from my bedside, curtsying to both my mother and me. "Excuse me, Your Majesty, Your Highness. I have some tasks to attend to before dinner. Thank you, again, Your Majesty. I didn't dare dream it would turn out so well. I — thank you."

"You are extremely welcome, my dear," my mother said. "And Taryn, if I may add one more task to your list..."

"Of course, Your Majesty. How may I assist you?"

"Please find the steward and have him remove the painting by the Great Hall. See if we can't have a celebratory bonfire in the courtyard later today. Crisis averted, narrow save of the kingdom of Calia, and all that. I'm sure it would make great kindling."

The slowly widening smile on my face was reflected on the faces of Taryn, Joichan, and my mother. Fervently, Taryn said, "With pleasure, Your Majesty." She hurried out of the room.

I turned back to my mother. "What were you saying before Taryn came in?"

"Oh, yes. Now that you're well, we can start getting you ready for the wedding."

"The wedding? But, I thought... Do you mean I still have to marry Prince Anders?"

My mother laughed. "No, not unless you want to. The prince and his family snuck off sometime after the fighting ended, during the clean up. They didn't say it outright, but I think the betrothal is off."

"Then whose wedding...?"

My mother stood up and walked back to Joichan, who reached for her hand and held it proudly. "Ours. In a week's time."

I smiled. "Oh, *that* wedding. Yes, I'm definitely looking forward to that wedding. But if you don't mind, I'd like to pick out my own jewelry."

Our laughter echoed through the hallways, a promise of the brighter days to come for the kingdom of Calia.

Epilogue

QUEEN MELANDRIA AND Joichan had a lovely — and small — wedding. My parents hadn't wanted the pomp of a big wedding. Plus, there really weren't any relatives to invite. Mother's immediate family had passed away years ago, and my orphaned father actually didn't know who his family was. He had been left as a baby at a storefront in Annlyn and been adopted by the merchant who nearly tripped over him when opening the shop.

The private event was witnessed by me, Beyan, Farrah, and Rhyss. Lord Kye was also there, looking very at ease in his newfound position. Part of it was from, of course, the restoration of his family name and fortune. And part of it was from the fact that Lord Kye no longer limped or needed a cane.

Bringing Kye to the castle had been a somewhat risky proposition. After all, Kye and Joichan's first and only meeting hadn't gone well. The two men had a long, private discussion — similar to the one Joichan had had with Kye's son Beyan. But when Joichan healed Kye using his dragon magic, that changed the tenor of their relationship from a wary truce to a true friendship.

After the wedding, Kye gifted the queen and new king with a familiar-looking carving of a stately golden dragon. They loved it instantly, exclaiming over the intricate detail and the perfect likeness of our new king (when he was in dragon form). The carving would eventually find a place of honor on a pedestal by the Great Hall. Right below the space where, formerly, a painting of Hendon had hung, depicting him fighting the dragon while Princess Melandria was held captive in its claws. Instead, in the old picture's place, there was a new painting: two golden dragons and Queen Melandria fighting side by side against the evil red-eyed King Hendon in a battle to save the kingdom of Calia. The new painting never failed to make me smile proudly every time I saw it.

Now that I knew my true father, I was determined to find the rest of his family and learn more about our lineage. Even though Joichan hailed from Annlyn, kingdom of shapeshifters, those who could become dragons were rare. Often those who were dragon shapeshifters were considered to come from unlucky or cursed unions.

"I'm glad you never considered me cursed," I told my mother. *Unlike Hendon.* The unspoken thought hung in the air between us, punctuated by the occasional sounds of laughter and the tinkle of a fountain nearby. We were sitting on a low stone bench under the warm, late summer sun. There was a decided chill in the mornings now; fall was on its way.

"I would never have thought that of you, my darling," she reassured me. "If anything, I think it's a boon for the kingdom. A ruler who could take down an invading army single-handedly? Why, think of the money you'd save by not having a standing army! Fewer taxes, too... your subjects will adore you."

I laughed. "Speaking of adoration... I think it's going well with introducing Joichan to the people, don't you?"

We looked over to where Joichan was, crouched low to the ground in the town square. He barely fit, but the children loved it. Some were shy of the great dragon in their midst, but a few of the braver ones were climbing on or over my father like he was a giant horse.

My mother had decided, before the honeymoon, that the best thing to do was to visit the nearby towns and see her subjects face-to-face in a long overdue meeting. Hendon had always insisted on an aloof distance, something that my mother had never agreed with. She also thought a more personal touch was needed to gain the trust and acceptance of the people for her new husband. After all, their first impression of him was of a ferocious, fire-breathing beast.

Although, watching the curious townsfolk and their carefree children, I thought the people of Calia were just fine with a human-turned-dragon for a new king.

In the crowd, I spotted Rufan standing with his sister Taryn and another woman, his wife Patrice. Their two little girls finished weaving a garland of flowers and presented it to Joichan, placing it on his nose as a present. He sneezed, and the majority of the flowers went up in a quick snort of fire. The ashes slid off the dragon's nose as he said to Rufan's children, "Sorry about that."

Instead of shrieking in fear, the two girls giggled. One piped up, "Don't worry, we'll find you more!" And they ran off, in a fit of more giggles. Joichan's eyes sparked in alarm.

An anxious dragon is quite a sight. Mother and I shook our heads, unable to contain our laughter. Joichan heard us and looked at us reproachfully.

A young mother with a baby on her hip rushed after a little boy. The boy clambered on top of Joichan, nearly stepping on my father's eye with his eager little foot.

"Be careful!" the mother called. "Don't play so rough with the dragon!"

Don't play so rough with the dragon. Now that was something I never thought I'd hear. I laughed even harder.

Wiping the tears from my eyes, I finally calmed down enough to say, "I'll miss you both while you're gone. But I know you'll have a wonderful trip."

"We'll miss you too," Mother said. "But you'll have a lot of things to keep you busy while we're gone."

"That's true. Research takes up a surprising amount of time."

"Have you learned anything new?"

"A few things. We've narrowed it down to the southeastern part of the Gifted Lands. We'll start at Annlyn and work our way out east from there. We contacted Pazho and Denaan and they're delighted to have us visit again. The messenger said that while Denaan could barely speak after discovering my true identity, Pazho took my message with surprising calmness. Like he had known all along I was the princess of Calia."

"From what you and your father have said about this Pazho, that makes perfect sense. It's a fine plan. And you'll be in good company. I'm not worried about you." My mother looked out in the distance.

I followed her gaze. Beyan was walking toward us. "Who better to help me find the other members of my dragon family?"

Beyan smiled as he reached us, bowing to the queen. She nodded back in acknowledgement. "Beyan, you'll have to be ready to leave the minute Joichan and I return from our honeymoon. Jennica won't want to wait one second longer to start her search."

He laughed as he sat down next to me. "I know, it's all she talks about. Finding the rest of her family."

I laced my fingers through his as Mother stood up and joined her new husband. Sighing, I smiled as I watched the happy couple, thinking of Taryn, Rhyss, Farrah... and of course, Beyan, sitting right beside me. "In some ways, I already have."

Dear Reader: YOU ARE AWESOME.

Thank you for reading this book.

I HOPE YOU ENJOYED taking this journey into the Gifted Lands as much as I enjoyed creating it.

If you liked this book, please leave a review wherever you like to buy books and learn about new titles.

Don't worry, there will be many more adventures to come. In the meantime, let's be friends!

Instagram: @rachaneelumayno[1]
Twitter: @rachaneelumayno[2]
TikTok: @rachaneelumayno
Sign up for the newsletter on the Website: www.rachanee.net[3]
Join the community on Discord: Kingdom Legacy[4]

---

1. http://www.instagram.com/rachaneelumayno
2. http://www.twitter.com/rachaneelumayno
3. http://www.rachanee.net
4. https://discord.gg/BRXcJJ3c6f

Read on for an exclusive excerpt from the next book in the Kingdom Legacy series

Prologue

IT HAD BEEN FOUR MONTHS of sleepless nights and anxious dreams.

Every night, the dream replayed in my mind in the same way, coming in sharp fragments.

Bowing over the lovely young woman's outstretched hand as I agreed to assist her. Seeing the sunlight halo behind her head as we rode together. Hearing her sweet laughter and hopeful smile, knowing that the world was full of possibility.

And then, as always, the change.

Her tears. Not the restrained, dignified sniffles that would have been expected of someone of her standing, but instead great gulping sobs that racked her thin frame and threatened to break her in two. Just as her heart was breaking.

I had been taught to remain neutral, but it was hard to see the poor young lady react so violently to the news. But what had she honestly expected?

I tried to calm her, to comfort her, even though it wasn't my place nor my business. I held her firmly by the shoulders, speaking in a low, soothing voice as if she were an easily spooked animal.

The wild look in her eyes began to settle. The tears began to slow.

I breathed easier. It would be all right now.

Then, without warning, her hand shot out toward me. I instinctively recoiled, expecting to feel the sting of a slap. Instead, she grabbed the hilt of the dagger sheathed at my belt. In one swift motion, she drew the knife out and plunged it into her heart. Her eyes never left mine as the light faded from them.

I must have screamed, although I never heard any sounds in my recurring nightmare. I just saw myself, my mouth gaping open in shock, her blood everywhere. On my hands, my arms, splashed all over the front of my shirt. Pooling on the floor beneath her crumpled body. Her now sightless eyes, still fixed on me.

And then, the aftermath. The waking nightmare.

Ten days of what had seemed like an endless trial. Because my commission had ended so brutally, I had had to endure ten long days before the Council of Seekers, repeatedly reliving the events that led to the young lady's death. The Council had ultimately decided that the woman had been mentally unstable, that the rigors of travel and the commission had set her over the edge. I was not responsible for her unfortunate death. They would not strip me of my ability.

I would remain a seeker.

Although I was exonerated in the eyes of the public, deep down I disagreed with the ruling.

I had burned the shirt and sold the dagger for a pittance, not wanting to keep either of those items as a reminder of that day. Days passed, dulling the edge of the memories.

But when night came, I was afraid to sleep. I knew that once I did, I would see her eyes. Wild, hopeless, and accusing.

They hadn't taken away my seeker ability, thinking they were granting me some small mercy.

But the real mercy would have been to take away my gift permanently, and with it the chance that I could ever hurt someone again.

Chapter One

LET IT BE KNOWN TO all that I, Kaernan Asthore, really, really hated love.

It wasn't because society expected young men of my age and status to find love silly, unnecessary, or inconvenient. It wasn't even because I saw, all around me and all too frequently, people blissfully happy with their soulmates, their one true loves.

No, I hated love because, in my experience, it usually involved death, or worse. If I was involved, it was definitely *or worse.*

The sound of approaching footsteps pulled me out of my brown study. Their echo against the wooden floor vibrated in my skull, causing my daylong dull headache to spike. I squeezed my eyes shut against the pain as a young woman's lilting laugh floated gently my way.

"There you are." It was the voice of my twin sister, Kaela. I opened my eyes to see her broadly smiling down at me. "I just got home from the Veilan commission — can you believe it took three weeks, but at least we have another happy patron! — and..." She stopped, really getting a good look at me. "Are you all right?"

I started to shake my head, then winced as the headache pulsed again. Kaela sat down next to me, rubbing circles on my back like our mother used to do when we were little to soothe us. "Rough night again?" she said, indicating the circles under my eyes.

I sucked my breath in between my teeth, forcing the word out. "Yeah."

"I'm sorry, Kaernan," she said. "It's been two weeks since the trial, longer still since... well. I'm surprised you still have the nightmares. Have you talked to Father or Mother about it? Maybe we should fetch the doctor."

"No." I hated how weak I sounded, but the restless nights were definitely taking their toll on me. "I don't want to alarm Mother. And Father thinks I should be over it by now. It's easier to just avoid both of them when I can."

"Ah... speaking of avoiding them..."

When Kaela used that tone, it usually meant trouble for me. Warily, I said, "What?"

"I saw Father right when I walked through the door. He sent me to find you. He wants to talk to both of us."

I groaned. "Do we have to? Can't you tell him you couldn't find me?"

"I'm sorry," Kaela said again and sighed heavily, wincing as if she herself were in pain.

It was quite possible she was. As twins, Kaela and I had a sympathetic connection, often sensing each other's feelings and physical presence.

"Come on," Kaela stood, grabbing my hand and turning to go. She stopped short; I hadn't budged from my spot. Turning back, she dropped my hand and sat down next to me on the wooden window ledge.

We sat in silence for a moment.

"You know what happened with Rosemary was not your fault," Kaela said cautiously.

"I can't do this any more, Kay. I know I'm dangerously close to the madness; if I don't use my ability my mind will break. But I can't handle the outcome of my commissions. They often end poorly. I wish there was some way I could just be rid of my 'gift' for good."

My shoulders slumped. I turned away from my sister to face the wall, not wanting her to see the tears that threatened to fall. "You're the one with the proper gift, Kaela. I'm just... an aberration."

Kaela threw her arms around me and pulled me close. "That's not true." It was a well-worn argument from my sister, but after all this time — and all my failures — her argument was showing its wear.

Fading sunlight through the window illuminated a golden tassel that adorned the braided rope tying back the heavy curtains. I reached out, absently flicking the tassel back and forth in my hand. I remembered a time, many years ago, when I played hide-and-seek with Kaela, using these very curtains to shield myself from her view. Not that I was ever successful in hiding from her, thanks to our bond. Life had been so much simpler then. Before Kaela and I had come into our gifts properly.

Kaela gently took the tassel from my hand and tugged me to my feet. This time I let her. "Come on," she said.

I followed, unhappy but unresisting.

KAELA MOVED QUICKLY down the familiar hallways, me on her heels. Our hurried footsteps echoed on the wooden floors, even as the tasteful tapestries and family portraits on the walls blurred past in our haste. Stately and elegant, the Asthore family manor lay near the palace in the kingdom of Orchwell, just on the border of the merchants' district. Our family had a long and storied history of seeking in Orchwell, making us one of the richest and most revered families in the kingdom, second only to the monarchy.

Of course, it helped that even the royalty of Orchwell occasionally sought out the Asthores for their services. Because who didn't want to find their true love?

In the Gifted Lands, Orchwell was known as the Land of Seekers. If you needed to find something, you came to Orchwell, where even the lowliest citizen possessed the ability to locate what you sought. But Orchwellians aren't hunting dogs in human form; depending on a patron's needs, the finder would have to solicit a specific group or family, as certain abilities ran only in certain bloodlines.

One seeker family was renown for its ability to find dragons. Another famous seeker clan had built its reputation upon finding other families' lost fortunes. For a fee, of course. But they were very popular, as so many people were convinced they had a spectacular destiny.

The Asthore family was known for its ability to find a person's true love.

We weren't matchmakers, exactly. Most often, a patron just wanted to find their perfect match, and didn't care about their future beloved's background. But occasionally, a patron had specialized requests — such as needing a good love match who also happened to be a good political alliance — and they would bring those specifications to an Asthore seeker.

The Asthore seeker found the person's perfect match every time.

Each successive Asthore generation, drawing on the wisdom of their predecessors, was more gifted than the last. My sister and I were still refining our abilities, but we had already showed immense promise. Indeed, Kaela was so talented that she was taking on commissions instead of our father, Lord Asthore, even though it would be at least four or five more years before we were considered fully trained seekers who could take over the family business in earnest.

But what made Kaela such a formidable talent was the same reason that I hated the family business.

Stopping in front of a plain wooden door, Kaela knocked, barely waiting for the deep baritone on the other end to say, "Enter," before she pushed the door inward. She sailed into the room confidently, with me reluctantly following behind.

Father stood to greet us. As Kaela moved eagerly into Father's arms, I realized with a start that I was now taller than my father, who had always seems to loom over me. When had that happened?

Sunlight illuminated the gray that feathered Father's temples. The crow's feet at the corner of his eyes deepened when he smiled and embraced his daughter.

Kaela stepped back so Father could greet me. "Look who I found," she chirped.

Neither Father nor I made a move to close the distance between us.

"Good, you found him," Father said warmly to Kaela. He nodded to me. In a voice just a shade colder, he said, "Son."

I nodded back in an equally chilly manner. "Father."

Kaela flopped down on the leather love seat in front of the fireplace. I followed suit with less abandon than my twin sister. Kaela was acutely aware of the tension between Father and me, but she often was at a loss as to how to handle it. While our mother, Lady Asthore, tried to play the peacemaker between the two men in her life, Kaela chose to ignore the issue, hoping that if she pretended all was well, then it would be.

While I appreciated her optimism, I sometimes wished my sister would take a stronger stance in regards to the family dynamic. Father would listen to Kaela, if she truly wished to exert her influence.

Father sat down at his desk, angling his chair so he faced Kaela and me. "Children, another commission has come our way."

Kaela clapped her hands in delight.

Their father smiled indulgently at Kaela, but turned his gaze on me. "This one is for Kaernan."

I couldn't help it; a small groan escaped my lips. Kaela's happiness dimmed a bit as she gave me a sympathetic smile, but Father frowned.

"You're not still upset over what happened with that Rosemary chit, are you?" he asked me.

"I —"

"It honestly couldn't have gone any other way," Father said dismissively. "You did your job. What the client does next is no concern of yours."

"That's a bit callous to say, don't you think, Father?" I said hotly.

"Really, Father, it was a most unfortunate situation —" Kaela said at the same time.

Father slammed his hand down on his desk, hard. The echo of the slap stunned us both into silence.

"When will both of you learn?" he said sharply. "A commission is just that — a commission. We may help people find the one they are fated for, but there is always a choice.

People always have a choice. Our family is proof of that. The sooner you understand that, the happier you will be in your careers as seekers."

Maybe I don't want a career as a seeker. The thought came unbidden to my mind, startling me with its intensity.

The room suddenly went deathly silent.

I looked around, at my sister's horrified stare, at my father's cold and steely gaze. I realized belatedly that I had actually spoken those words out loud.

"You don't really have a choice," Father said. His tone left no room for argument.

"But you just said —" I began.

"In your private affairs, yes," Father said. "But when it comes to seeking — no. No seeker has a choice about accepting their fate. You know that."

"But there must be —"

"You will take this commission, and you will fulfill it to the best of your ability." Father's jaw worked back and forth, and his breathing was heavy, like he was trying to keep himself under tight control.

There was a knock on the door, which was still slightly open. A servant's voice sounded timidly through the small crack. "Milord, there is someone here to see you."

Father stood. "And here is your new patron now, Kaernan."

Acknowledgements

THIS BOOK WOULDN'T have happened without the love, support, and encouragement of many, many people.

Thank you to Tom, Jaime, Michael, and Katie for reading the early drafts, giving amazing notes, and being cool with re-reading the same story multiple times.

Thank you to my Monday night writers group, for reading countless other projects and scripts that helped me build up the confidence to write this novel.

Thank you to my husband, for putting up with my late nights, early mornings, and my incessant talking about the characters like they were real people.

And finally, thank you to Mrs. Menard, my 6th grade English teacher, who pulled me aside during class to talk to me about my creative writing skills. "You can do this, you have a real talent for this." I've carried those words with me across multiple states and over the years. Thank you for believing in and encouraging a shy young dreamer. Those simple words of encouragement helped me find my voice.

About the Author

RACHANEE LUMAYNO IS an actress, voiceover artist, screenwriter, avid gamer and amateur dodgeball player. She grew up in Michigan, where she spent way too much of her free time reading fantasy novels. So when she decided to try her hand at writing a book, it made sense that it would be in her favorite genre. *Heir of Amber and Fire* is her first novel. You can find her online at www.rachanee.net[1] or on Twitter, Tiktok, or Instagram[2] (@rachaneelumayno).

---

1. http://www.rachanee.net

2. http://www.instagram.com/rachaneelumayno

Ingram Content Group UK Ltd.
Milton Keynes UK
UKHW010839280623
424184UK00001B/43